DRAGON FURY

HIGHLAND FANTASY ROMANCE

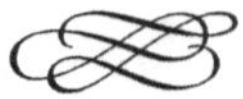

ANN GIMPEL

CONTENTS

DRAGON FURY

A DRAGON LORE SPIN-OFF

Dragon Lore Series, Book Five

Highland Fantasy Romance
By
Ann Gimpel

Tumble off reality's edge into myth, magic, and Selkies.

Aegir, the Selkie king, has a lot on his mind. He and his pod all but raised a young seer, and it damn near kills him to turn the boy over to his father. Especially when the father makes it abundantly clear he plans to erase the lad's memories of his first two years.

Fuming, Aegir retreats to an island in the Orkney chain that holds a gateway to Arcadia, a magical land protecting the source of White Magic. One morning, a strange Selkie catches his eye. Alarmed, he swims out to investigate. Unknown Selkies are bad news. Either spies or rejects from their own pods, they're never welcome.

Raene spends most of her time running a small bakeshop in the Highlands, but she seeks refuge in the sea once a year. She's only just taken her seal form when another Selkie accosts her. It's obvious he wants her to clear out, but she stands her ground. It's either the bravest thing she's ever done, or the stupidest. He might be rude and abrasive, but she has a problem, and he's her best bet to solve it.

Highland Secrets, Book One

    To Love a Highland Dragon, Book Two

    Dragon Maid, Book Three,

    Dragon's Dare, Book Four

    Dragon Fury, Book Five (spinoff from earlier books in the

series)

AUTHOR'S NOTE

Selkies are mythical creatures capable of therianthropy as they shed their seal skins and become human. The best-known myths include forcing a female Selkie to remain in human form by finding and hiding—or worse, destroying—her seal skin. Selkies are a part of Scottish folklore, specifically lore originating from the Orkney and Shetland Islands.

My Selkie hero in *Dragon Fury* was born under the sign of the ash tree. He's a free thinker. Imaginative, intuitive, and innately artistic, he's inspired by nature. Others may view him as emotionally detached, but he has a rich inner life and little need for interaction with either Selkies or humans.

Raene, my Selkie heroine, was born in early June under the sign of the Seahorse. She's a master at adapting to changing circumstances and has a memory like a steep trap.

Most born under this sign crave attention, but Raene has an independent streak and is perfectly happy being by herself.

Hmmm... Two Selkies with fiercely unconventional leanings. Wonder how that's going to play out?

egir's snout broke the surface of a choppy Irish Sea. The sun was vanishing behind the western horizon. What was left of its rays painted the ocean's surface a delicate gold. King of the Selkies, he was used to rising to any and all occasions, but this time he wished he could rewrite history— and his agreed-upon obligation.

A child's dark head popped up next to him. "I'm here," he announced with élan only a two-year-old could muster. "Still don't understand why, though."

"We're meeting someone." Aegir spoke into the boy's mind and nuzzled his neck with his whiskers. If Johnathan had been a seal, he'd have clapped him across the shoulders with a flipper, but humans were delicate—by seal standards.

Not that the boy was precisely human, but he wore a human skin, never mind the magic spilling from him in iridescent waves.

"Who?" Johnathan cocked his head to one side and regarded Aegir from serious amber eyes. "Mother is returning. She promised me."

Instead of answering, Aegir scooped the boy against his chest and held him in place while he covered the distance to a deserted beach on a little-known island in the Hebrides chain. Jonathan snuggled close, and Aegir battled conflicting emotions. He didn't want to turn Jonathan over to his father, but it was time. That had been the agreement. Two years with the Selkies and thence to Angus's care.

There was nothing amiss with Angus Shea. Seer and dreamer, his power complemented that of his son, but in the time the boy had lived among the Selkies, Aegir had fallen in love with him and felt fiercely protective of the youngster. Selkies adored children, and the entire pod had taken turns pampering Jonathan. Everyone pretended today was just like any other to not alarm their young charge, but Aegir wasn't under any illusions. Back at their palace hidden beneath the waves, his kin were in mourning.

Aye, and so am I...

"It is Mother, isn't it?" the boy pressed. The hope in his young voice smote Aegir. Arianrhod had left for Caer Sidi—her special world where she controlled the moon and tides—a few hours before. She'd spent much of her son's first two years by his side but remaining longer was too risky. She didn't want her Celtic kin to know about her fall from grace.

That her absence had gone mostly unnoticed for as long

as it had was a small miracle. One requiring stealth and heaping doses of judiciously applied diversion spells.

Virgin huntresses weren't supposed to produce young. Not by normal channels, anyway. Her magical children, Dylan and Lieu, hadn't been in her life for many a long year. Rumors of her dalliance with a coal-black dragon were finally dying down, but if Arianrhod's Celtic kinsfolk got wind she'd birthed a flesh-and-blood child, she'd be laughed out of the Pantheon.

Aegir's belly scraped the shoreline. He let go of Jonathan, who ran nimbly up the rocky beach. The boy was buck naked, but he was used to the chill of the Irish Sea, and the cold didn't touch him. Aegir shifted in a blaze of blue-and-white light. Power crackled around him, adding to the fading rays of the sunset. When he was done, he gathered his pelt into his arms and ran lightly to the standing stones where he usually left his skin.

Jonathan hurried to his side. "I want to go back to the palace."

"I know ye do." Aegir regarded the boy. Dark hair dripping water fell to shoulder level. Power flashed and flared around him, but the boy was unaware of it. Beneath the sea where he'd been raised, everyone was magical in one way or another.

He extended a hand, and Jonathan clasped it. Walking side by side, they headed for another circle of standing stones. Aegir was relieved both beach and stones were deserted. He could have called beastly weather or wiped minds or done whatever was needed, but it was better this way. No human settlements marred the small island. Caves with colorful limestone formations and standing stones were the primary attraction. The occasional tourist hired a boat to visit, but it didn't happen often.

A quick peek into the boy's mind revealed curiosity mixed with apprehension. He wasn't one to whine or complain, though, and he'd already stated his preference, which was to return to the Selkies' palace beneath the waves.

Aegir settled with his back against a stone column and held Jonathan in his lap. Of the four stone circles on the island, this was the largest, consisting of sixteen gray obelisks. Half of them had cross stones resting along their tops. All standing stones were sacred because their energy matched itself to whoever stood among them.

Primitive magic pummeled his mind. At first Aegir resisted Jonathan's attempt to troll for information, but maybe it would be easier to let the lad in. He'd pluck what he needed and ask questions. Not sure if it made him more coward or more fool, Aegir dropped his warding. He hadn't yet found a way to bid the lad farewell.

Jonathan's eyes widened. "Da is coming?" His high, thin child's voice rose in a question.

Aegir nodded. "Aye, lad. 'Twas the agreement."

A shadow crossed Jonathan's face. "What agreement? I love him, but I want to stay with you—and Mother. She promised she'd return."

Aegir shuttered his mind and managed not to make a

disapproving face. He'd heard Arianrhod's farewell. Craven bitch; she'd taken the coward's way out and lied. He looked away, chiding himself. How did anyone—let alone a mother —tell a young child they wouldn't see him again? Maybe not never, but certainly not until he'd grown to manhood.

Ashamed of his rush to judgment, Aegir searched for a way to bid farewell to Johnathan but didn't fare much better than Arianrhod had. "Come here." He beckoned to the boy who'd left his lap and stood a short distance away.

Jonathan shook his head, crossed his arms over his chest, and announced, "I'm going back into the sea."

"Ye can certainly come and visit," Aegir began, still soft-pedaling the truth.

"But I live there." Jonathan's voice rose in protest, and his lower lip trembled.

Aegir blew out a frustrated breath. Left to his own devices, he'd have come up with a version of the truth, titrated so the boy would understand. Maybe. Did words exist to smooth over the harshness of being ripped from the only home the child knew?

A staunch blast of magic turned the air liquid with shades of crystalline light. Aegir was almost certain it had to be Angus, but *almost* was less than a hundred percent.

He flowed to his feet and thrust his body between Jonathan and the source of the power. A shimmery gateway, glowing against the fading day, split the damp, marine air. Angus Shea bounded through. Long mahogany hair, many shades lighter than his son's, was bound low at the back of his neck with a bit of leather. Jonathan had Angus's eyes, though. Amber with golden flecks glowing around the pupils. Tall, rangy, and well-muscled, Angus wore leather breeks, a cream-colored linen shirt, and a deep-blue tartan draped over everything.

Dipping around Aegir, he knelt next to Johnathan and his weathered face split into a warm smile. "I'm here to take you home, son."

"But I am home," the boy insisted.

Angus shifted his gaze upward and stared at Aegir. "Did no one tell him aught?"

"Mother did. She's coming back," Jonathan said firmly. "It's why I must stay here."

Angus gathered the squirming child into his arms, wrapping him in lengths of tartan. Aegir sensed a spell, infused with love and hope, as Angus wove it around his boy. Once he slept, Angus rose to face Aegir.

"Talk to me but be quick about it."

The Selkie nodded. "Arianrhod did tell him she was coming back."

Angus's expression could have curdled new milk. "Aught else?"

Aegir nodded. "None of us could bring ourselves to bid him farewell. He's so young, and he is well loved by my people." He should have stopped there, but a few more words spilled out. "Where will ye take him?"

Angus's mouth curled into a sneer. "Why? Do ye not trust me to care for my own flesh and blood?" Before Aegir could stumble through an answer, Angus went on. "I'd have cared for his mum as well if she weren't so caught up with maintaining her false image."

He squared his shoulders. Jonathan curled against him, still caught up in his father's spell. "We shall be in Ireland. Some Witches there will help me raise him."

"He's always welcome to return to the Selkie pod." Aegir tried for a positive note.

Angus seemed to consider the suggestion but shook his head. "Nay, not for a verra long time. He will mourn for your people, Aegir, and for his mum. I will keep him safe, but I will also do what I can to erase his memories and ease his passage into a different life."

Aegir bristled. "And how is that different from what the Celts did to you? Ye've hated them for cutting off your knowledge of who ye are and whence ye sprang."

"They used me, and they still are." Angus's tone was harsh, grating. "I'm shielding my son from pain. The two have naught in common."

Aegir knew when to back down. He'd led his people long enough to recognize when a battle was lost. Inclining his head, he murmured, "As ye will, Angus. Know that the sea people were ever friends to you. Naught about that has changed."

Angus bowed back. His next words held a formal note. "Thank you and your kin for providing a place for Arianrhod to birth and nurse our child."

"Be sure Johnathan knows." Aegir looked away. "If not

now, then when ye deem the time is right. He is not done with his days in the sea."

Angus shifted Jonathan so he held him with one hand and placed the other on Aegir's shoulder. "I canna do that. He'll be better off believing he was always with me." He narrowed his amber eyes. "I'm a seer, and I have seen naught beyond his tenth year. If ye have knowledge, ye must tell me."

"Nothing to impart beyond my intuition and wishful thinking," Aegir replied. "I'm far from a seer. We utilize the Druids to look into the future on our behalf."

Angus sharpened his gaze. Aegir held it, willing Angus not to dig deeper. To divert the seer, he asked, "What about Jonathan's magic? It has already manifested and will only grow stronger."

"I will teach him my talents as best I can, taking care to hide my efforts from the Celts. Goddess knows I doona wish them to conscript him as they did me. Time alone will tell what he inherited from his mother. I bid you farewell."

Aegir returned the farewell and bit back further words. What was the point? The boy had Arianrhod's magic. It shone around him in shades of violet and gold. Either Angus was blind, or he was still so disappointed by Arianrhod's refusal to reveal their love, he discounted evidence of her power in their child.

Aegir clasped his hands behind his back and watched Angus step through the gash in the ether he'd used as a gateway. He should have told the seer his boy was ocean-marked, but he hadn't had the heart.

Even now, he could summon Angus back. Telepathy would still reach him.

Aegir swallowed a bitter taste, trudged back to his skin, and retrieved it. The real reason he hadn't disclosed Jonathan was ocean-marked was he hadn't wanted Angus to obliterate that bit of knowledge as well. When Selkies valued someone, they put their mark on them. It ensured they'd return to the sea someday.

It also ensured they'd be able to breathe underwater. Not that such a thing was needed in Jonathan's case. Most magical creatures had no trouble dredging oxygen from seawater. Because the boy had been born in the sea, he'd learned to switch back and forth between air and water from birth. Arianrhod had ventured to the surface with him often during his early months. Air was more her métier than water, but her comfort level beneath the waves had increased over time.

Aegir walked slowly toward the incoming tide. Before he got to the waterline, he spread his pelt on the beach and summoned shift magic. The warmth and prickliness he associated with his seal form closed around him. Usually, he welcomed the transition, but today was a sad day.

For everyone except perhaps Angus.

Jonathan had been ripped away from everything and everyone he'd ever known. Arianrhod's grief had been so palpable, her young son had patted her hand and told her not to worry. Aegir ground his blunt seal teeth together. He should have tried harder to ease the boy's passage. Problem was he didn't see what more he could have done.

How did anyone prepare a two-year-old for such a major change in his circumstances? Though wise beyond his years, and as articulate as a much older child, Jonathan was still very concrete in his thinking. He lacked the ability to grasp that his mum had defied convention and that her rebellion would have a lasting effect on him.

Her too.

Aegir would have had to be an insensitive boor not to sense Arianrhod's distress. He slithered forward until his sleek form was fully immersed in the chill waters of the Irish Sea. It was time to journey to the eastern side of Scotland. Past time. In truth, he should have been there a fortnight ago, but he couldn't bear to leave Jonathan's side. He'd known the boy's tenure was growing short, and he hadn't wanted to miss even an hour of what remained of it.

AEGIR SWAM NORTH. Once he cleared Scotland's landmass, he'd turn eastward. His kind didn't call the land Scotland, though. Its ancient name was Caledonia. He was headed for a chain of islands scattered above John O'Groats. Currently known as the Orkneys, they'd been the Selkies' home base millennia ago.

Aegir's father, Krise, had rebuilt the palace in its current location on the western side of Caledonia hundreds of years before. A rampaging wizard coupled with an effort to escape the beastly weather plaguing the North Sea were the official reasons behind the move, but Krise was nothing if not a diplomat. He hadn't wanted to tell his people he feared for their safety for many reasons, not only the two he'd given voice to.

As Aegir swam, he thought about Scotland—Caledonia— and its two faces. The one humans saw and another magical land named Arcadia. In contradiction to current mythological beliefs, Arcadia wasn't a Greek utopia, but open to any with strong magic. Shifters considered the land sacred along with Witches, Druids, and all others wielding White Magic. Over time, Arcadia had become a haven for those such as him, a break from humans who'd written off magic. No one believed in it anymore. If they glimpsed his head bobbing in the waves, they saw a seal, not a Selkie, and it made him sad.

The redirection of human beliefs had taken a significant notch out of magic-wielders' abilities. Nothing quite like trying to cast spells in the presence of a veritable sea of negative energy. By moving their palace, locating it offshore so to speak, Krise had ensured the continuation of Selkie magic at full strength. He'd played his cards close to the vest, so the other Shifters who continued to reside in Scotland, grumbling all the while about how bad things had grown, never knew Selkies didn't share their problems.

Aegir surfaced to breathe. He'd been fielding a flurry of telepathic summons from the Shifter Council for the past twelve days. The requests had started out polite enough but had escalated to threats about excommunicating Selkies from the council table if they eschewed their responsibility to Arcadia.

Aegir had answered every message, promised he'd be there soon. It wasn't as if Arcadia were in trouble. His visits across the magical barrier were more *pro forma* than necessary.

He'd pointed that out, but the messages had edged from requests to demands. Unable to deal with anything except Jonathan's imminent departure, he'd shunted things off onto Krise. He'd meant to check in with the elder Selkie before leaving with Jonathan, but it hadn't happened.

Probably just as well. He wanted to show up on the island that held a gateway into Arcadia with as positive a mental outlook as possible. Having a bunch of Shifters furious with him would only piss him off.

Selkies didn't interact much with other Shifters for a host of reasons. They were the only iteration of Shifter who spent the lion's share of their time in their animal form. They were also the only Shifter in danger of being stuck as humans if a crafty miscreant lay in wait and stole their pelt.

Back when he'd been quite young, he'd confronted his father, asking why they bothered to keep up the charade of bonhomie when it was patently false. In those days, magic was stronger and far more visible. The rampaging wizard was but one threat. Demons, Furies, Harpies, and other hazards were commonplace occurrences.

Krise had told him they'd be fools to go it alone.

Aegir wasn't sure that was still the case, but he wasn't one to rock the status quo. If Krise and his queen had produced more children, Aegir would have gladly slithered out from under the royal banner. He'd been nonplussed when his father announced he was stepping down. Aegir had done his damnedest to talk Krise into a few more years at the helm of Selkie-dom.

It hadn't worked.

Familiar landmarks slid past; he altered course still lost in thought. Jonathan and Angus would be in Ireland now. Would Angus muck about in the boy's mind before he woke him from trance?

Probably. Otherwise, it would be that much harder to alter the lad's memories.

Aegir shook himself from snout to flippers to tail. He hated the thought of Jonathan's memories being obliterated, but he had no stake where the boy was concerned.

None.

Aye, and I'd do well to remember it.

Looking backward wasn't his style, but neither was hardening his heart and forgetting the bright light the boy had shone, illuminating the Selkies' palace with his quick wit and ready smile.

Aegir would see the boy again. He knew he would; it was foretold according to the Sea Witch. She'd shaken a bony finger beneath Aegir's nose and warned him the boy would be grown to manhood and would carry no memory of his time with the Sea Folk. He hadn't liked her prophecy, but like all divinations, it was seeded with truth.

He swam faster. Not only was he late showing up in Arcadia, he was centuries past prime mating time. Krise had stopped nagging, but Aegir was all too aware he needed to locate a mate. She didn't have to be a Selkie, but she'd have to agree to live among them.

It was a stumbling block for most other types of Shifters, and he couldn't marry a woman with no magic at all.

He broke the surface to breathe and slapped his tail hard in a trough between two staunch waves. He'd have been happy raising Jonathan, but that future wasn't open to him. He needed to buck up, pull his head out of his ass, and produce a child of his own.

One no one could take away from him.

He glanced at the stars. If he added a wee bit of magic to his trajectory, he'd be at his lair in the Orkneys before dawn. Once there, he'd make a beeline for Arcadia, put on his best company manners, and apologize all over the place for being late.

Arcadia didn't need him—or any of the Selkies and other magic wielders who helped keep her safe. Seat of White Magic, it was worth protecting, but the enchanted land had its own resources.

He had no idea who'd come up with the idea of Shifters, Selkies, Witches, and Druids making certain the land was never alone. More than a millennia back, one of the Druid sects had moved there permanently. Aegir had been surprised the rest of them continued to do more than visit occasionally after that, but he was damned if he'd be the one who flew in the face of tradition.

Maybe he'd suggest they loosen up the schedule, though. Not worry so much and threaten drastic measures—like excommunication—if someone happened to be a wee bit late. The more he considered it, the better he liked the idea. It would be a decent beginning. He'd float it past the Shifter Council—once they weren't out to hang his head from a pikestaff.

CHAPTER 2

Raene bent over the large double oven in her bakeshop in Wick, a tiny hamlet on the northeastern coast of Scotland. The township straddled the River Wick and extended along both arms of Wick Bay. Because it was so far north, six months of the year provided extravagant hours of darkness.

Perfect for a creature like her. One who held secrets and aimed to make certain they remained hidden.

Sweat slid down her face, and she mopped it with a sleeve as she rearranged loaves and buns in the oven. The Wedgewood commercial gas range was old and cantankerous. So long as she moved things back to front and side to side, they didn't burn. Not that it would matter much. The village was very small, and she maintained the only bakeshop. If people wanted fresh bread, either they made it themselves or bought it from her.

She straightened and shut the oven door. Jamming a hand into the small of her back she rubbed at the sore places. It was past time for her to shift and slip into the sea. Usually, she closed up her bakery in the middle of January, but this year her closest friend had been nursing her husband through a serious illness.

Raene had known he was dying. So did Ula, but she kept up a brave front. Privately, she'd asked if Raene could put off her annual holiday, and Raene didn't have it in her to refuse.

Everyone assumed she left for warmer climes, returning in early May. If they knew the truth, that she lived in the sea, they wouldn't have believed it. Magic had fallen out of fashion at least a hundred years before. Edged out by science, very little in the way of superstition remained.

Raene had lived a long time. She'd survived eras where those like her were burned or hanged. By employing a combination of stealth and wariness, she'd managed to conceal her dual nature for the most part, except for a fifty-year stint when a man had hidden her skin, binding her to her human body. She'd hunted and hunted for her stolen pelt, but the longer she was separated from it, the weaker her magic grew.

Finally, with her husband on his deathbed, she'd wrested the truth from him as he wandered in a delirium. The temptation to run back to the sea was overwhelming, but Rolf had treated fairly with her—if she discounted the way he'd tricked her out of her skin. After checking her pelt was where he'd said, she'd eased him out of this world, hastening his passage with magic to put an end to his pain.

Once he was gone, so was she.

Years passed—a whole lot of them—before she ventured ashore again, and she picked the other side of Scotland this time. It was how she'd ended up in Wick. She'd have to leave sooner or later, but she had another decade before that option switched from choice to necessity.

Another peek inside the oven told her today's bounty was done. She shut off the gas and removed her loaves and buns. She'd already put out a sign letting the villagers know that after today, she'd be gone. A grief-stricken Ula had hinted about perhaps traveling with her, but Raene forestalled her friend by listing out dozens of mythical kinsfolk she made certain she saw every year.

Ula had patted her on the shoulder, told her all would be well, and commiserated about Raene's holiday not being so much of a holiday after all. Raene hated lying to her friend, but she'd had no choice.

Not unless she skipped donning her seal form for an entire year, and she wasn't willing to do that. The half century she'd spent without her skin had taught her many things, including how critical time in the sea was for her dual nature.

The string of bells over her shop door tinkled. Raene bustled trays of hot bread into the front of the bakery. No reason to arrange the loaves and buns on doilies in the display case. They'd be gone almost as soon as she could ferry them from the kitchen.

The next few hours passed quickly. By eleven in the morning, she'd sold everything edible in the shop. After bidding her last customer goodbye, she hung out her "Gone on Holiday, Back 1 June" sign and twisted the deadbolt to ensure no one else pushed the door open—despite her sign. A steep, winding set of stairs led to her living quarters above the bakery. She didn't need to do much to prepare to be gone, and she'd catch the train that left at two.

That way, anyone who was interested would see her leave town. And no one would notice her exit the train at its next stop because by then she would have cloaked herself with magic.

Excitement thrummed through her. The sea was her natural environment. She'd ended up wearing her human form most of the year through a combination of capitulating to an era unfriendly to magic and taking pains to never, never be separated from her pelt again. Being rejected by the local Selkie pod played into her decision too.

She hung her apron over a hook and stripped out of the white smock and pants she wore when she baked. Raene never bothered with underthings. They'd come into fashion long after she was born. Goose bumps dotted her naked arms and legs, and she hurriedly tugged a pair of black gabardine breeks from her old-fashioned dresser and put them on over her stockinged feet. Stout tan boots followed. Once she'd laced them, she pulled a beige woolen sweater over her head and a plaid woolen coat over that. It wasn't raining, but she wrapped a length of wool around her bright hair anyway.

She double-checked the latches on the two upstairs windows and grabbed her battered old valise. Her skin was waiting for her a few kilometers south of Wick, shrouded by spells atop spells, in one of the many caves dotting Scotland's rocky coastline. No ship—not even one as modest as a rowboat—could penetrate that section of coast. She'd have to teleport there, but it was easily done.

A glance at the clock on her bedside table told her she had plenty of time to walk to the train station, but it would be good to lock up and get going. The phone rang, jangling and discordant. She ignored it and trotted lightly down the spiral staircase. It was still ringing when she let herself out the door, turning to lock it behind her.

She'd had an answering machine for a while but hated having to remember to check it. In the end, she'd gone with keeping her life as simple as she could and donated the annoying electronic device to a secondhand shop. Ten minutes later, she stood at the train station's window, offering up money for a ticket. She always bought one all the way to Glasgow. It was the only time she ever wasted money, but she had to make her travel plans look real.

Boarding document in hand, she went to sit in the small station. The train would show up in about three-quarters of an hour. By the time she got on and staged her exit, darkness would be well on its way.

Once she'd settled in to wait, she let her mind range wherever it wished. Not a luxury she generally indulged in. Her mother was half human, half Selkie. She was magical, but she couldn't take seal form. If she knew who Raene's father was, she'd been very closemouthed about it. Raene had questioned her nine ways from Faery but had never gotten any answers.

No one had been more surprised than she the storm-tossed, cloudy night when she'd been walking a deserted beach on the Isle of Skye. She'd felt odd all that day. Antsy and not right in her head. She ran a fever and had escaped into the night to let the chill air caress her body. After leaving her clothes beneath a handy boulder, she'd run barefoot on the beach, feeling like she was doing something dirty, something wrong, but not caring.

As soon as she dipped one bare foot into the sea, heat shot from it, igniting her entire body. If she'd truly been engulfed in flames, it wouldn't have felt any different. A ripping, gnashing, tearing sensation blasted through her. Bones broke, skin stretched and reformed, sprouting a thick, reddish fur. With the last of her hands before her arms shortened and her fingers turned to flippers, she felt her elongated snout.

Before the transformation totally died away, she'd plunged into the sea, delighting in her effortless transit through first shallow and then deeper water. If she'd still had human vocal chords, she'd have laughed the first time she surfaced when she blew salty spume over a meter into the air.

Raene understood what had happened. Her magic manifested. She was not quite eighteen and realized her father had to be a pureblood Selkie since three-quarters blood was a bare minimum required to shift. In her imagination, he was a Selkie prince or maybe even a king, but one with a jealous wife. She and her mother always had money, so maybe the prince/king had paid her off handsomely to keep her mouth shut.

Figuring out how to hide her skin after that first shift had been a challenge. Magic was far from second nature, and it took her many tries before she was satisfied no one would make off with her pelt. How it had simply materialized would remain a mystery.

The train's strident whistle cut into her thoughts, and she rose to her feet and snatched up her empty valise. It was a prop, but she tried to create the illusion of normalcy. The train chugged to a stop, and she showed her ticket before boarding.

Raene took a seat near the back of the second car. Once the train lurched forward, she wove webs of magic around herself. *I'm not here* and *don't look here* spells mixed with a simple concealment casting. Since she'd kicked open the door to her memories, she wondered where her mother was. She'd left her in the northern reaches of Norway more than a hundred years before.

Her mum hadn't been nearly as thrilled with Raene's news about taking seal form as Raene expected her to be. It had been the beginning of the schism that eventually separated them. By then, her mother had taken up with another man, a purely human one. It seemed like a bad idea to Raene, and she'd quietly pointed out a few of the problems. After that, her mother told her it was past time for her to strike out on her own. While Raene was still reeling from the rejection, her mother had said something curious, called Raene ocean-marked without explaining precisely what it meant. Afraid it was some arcane curse, Raene hadn't turned that rock over to peer beneath it.

She exhaled sharply. Her stepfather had to be long since dead, but she'd never heard from her mother again. The Selkies had a pod that traveled from the North to the Irish Sea and back again, but when she'd approached them, they'd not been overly friendly. She never knew why, but assumed they looked down on her because her blood wasn't pure, and she'd never had any formal instruction in how to employ her magic.

Or maybe they sensed she was ocean-marked, and it was even more of a malediction than she'd imagined. Regardless, the pod had been her first stop after she'd gotten her skin back, and she hadn't been in the mood to kowtow to anyone's weirdness.

Or criticism.

They hadn't wanted her, and she hadn't stuck around to argue the point.

She'd done all right on her own. Figured out what she had to. She watched the station placards change as they passed small settlements. Rather than pulling the bell cord for a special stop, she waited until the train steamed into the next station to the south before slipping unnoticed out the door.

She assumed no one remarked on her egress since no one spoke with her. Raene struck out on foot, head down, walking quickly. Once she cleared the hamlet's borders, she ducked behind a boulder and left her valise in an unobtrusive spot. She'd come back by this place to collect it in a few months. If it was here, great.

If not, she'd buy another.

Darkness closed in with the coming night. Once it was complete, she summoned a teleport spell, visualized her cave, and hoped the muted blaze of light from her magic wouldn't bring anyone running.

It shouldn't. The nearest farm was at least a kilometer away, and she hadn't seen any stray sheep out this way. In the space between two heartbeats, she transported to a spot a few meters in front of her familiar cave. Always cautious, she stilled herself and took a deep breath, ready to flee at the first hint of anything amiss. She'd know if anyone had been here, even if it was months before.

The only thing that bounced back to her was the salt tang of the sea. A smile sprang to her face, and she hurried forward, intent on trading her clothes for her skin. Raene had to duck to enter the cave. She kindled a mage light, and its golden glow played around the rock walls slick with moss and lichen. Not much grew this far north, but mosses and lichens were ubiquitous. They grew everywhere.

"I knew you'd come." A wavery voice, not much more than a breathy whisper, rustled from the shadows.

Raene stopped dead. She'd know that voice anywhere. "Mother?"

"Aye, and who else would be able to track you by smell?"

Raene hustled deeper into the cave, brightening her light. The reek of decaying flesh rose up, slapping her in the face. "How long have you been here?" she demanded and fell to her knees next to her mother's emaciated form. Kari lay wrapped in Raene's skin, which explained why she hadn't sensed her mother's presence from outside the cave.

"Long enough. I'm dying, daughter. Naught anyone can do to alter that, but I wanted to speak with you while I still could." Her gaunt face took on an expression Raene remembered. Part resignation, part defiance. Part understated humor.

"Let me get you something to eat and drink." Raene cradled her mother's head, settling it in her lap. Her red hair, once the same color as Raene's, had lost its rich russet patina. Streaked with silver, it fell lankly around her shoulders. Her turquoise eyes were rheumy and unfocused.

"Don't bother," her mother croaked. "I've very little time left. I expected you a month ago, perhaps more."

"I was delayed, but I'm here now." Raene didn't see the point in taking up any of the few moments remaining to her mother with the story of Ula's dying husband.

"Aye, that you are, sweetling." Kari's lids closed for a moment. When she opened her eyes, she said, "I've a tale to tell, but 'twill be shorter than I'd planned. I fear I haven't the strength for more than a little—" A rattling cough shook her thin frame. Blood-flecked sputum dotted her lips and chin.

"It's okay, Mum." Raene pulled a handkerchief from a pocket and wiped her mother's face clean.

Kari shook her head weakly. "Nay. 'Tisn't. When I was young, I fell in love with a Selkie, but you'll have already guessed that part. His name is Gregor and he was married to a Selkie queen. He feared she'd kill me if our affair was discovered. When I became pregnant, he pushed me to abort you. I refused to even consider it."

More coughing racked her thin chest, and Raene held her closer. Power from her skin pulsed, and she understood it was the only thing keeping her mother on this side of the veil.

"I ran away," Kari went on, her voice barely above a whisper, "but he found me. By then, my belly had grown large. He was angry, but he also understood. He spun magic that would end my life if I disclosed the secret of your birth. He also made certain we'd have enough money. It was kind of him."

"Quite the motivation to remain silent," Raene murmured, thinking horrible thoughts about her father. Far from being kind, he'd threatened her mother with death.

"Aye." Kari nodded. "I hoped you wouldn't be able to shift. If you were merely magical, you wouldn't draw attention. Not so much, anyway. And you'd have been safe from Gregor—if he chose to look for you."

"It's all right, Mum. Truly it is. I love you. You did the best you could by me."

"Nay. I failed you in so many ways. I was afraid if I taught you more than rudimentary magic, it would backfire, and Gregor would think I'd broken my agreement. My fear made me a bad mother. For that, I am truly sorry. In a backward way, he was certain he was being generous. That my dying from his magic would be far less painful than what his wife would do to me, but I was never convinced about that."

"Ssht. Hush. It's fine." Raene lay next to her mother and gathered her close. Her body encased in the seal pelt was already cold as death. "Thank you for making the effort to find me."

"Och, I've known where you are for a long time, but I've left you alone. What good could possibly have come from me hanging about?"

Raene felt the bitter bite of tears. "I'd have taken care of you, Mum. We could have lived together. I have a bake shop, and—"

"Aye, I know. 'Tis proud I am of you, daughter."

Kari's next inhalation rattled. The one following, rattled louder. Raene held her mother as death first stalked and then claimed her. Once Kari breathed her last, Raene stood and carried her mother's almost weightless form to the sea, placing her in the surf. The woman had been all but dead for days, maybe weeks. She'd only held on long enough to make certain Raene knew about her father.

She crouched next to the shore and raised her voice, asking the goddess to accept her mother and ease her into the life to come. Water from the incoming tide washed over her boots. By the time it rose to ankle level, the salty wind had dried her tears.

Raene straightened and made her way back into the cave. The mage light never left her side as she removed and folded her garments, stashing them behind a pile of rocks. Naked, she picked up her pelt. It still smelled like her mother. The good smells of lavender and vanilla and wildflowers. The skin's magic had obliterated the sweet rot of death.

Feeling sad and empty, yet free in a way she'd never been before, Raene carried her skin to the shoreline. Her mother's body was gone, so perhaps the goddess had heard Raene's plea. After draping the skin around herself, she waded until the cold water hit her mid-thigh before summoning a blast of shift magic.

The transition to seal no longer caused pain, and it happened far faster than it had the first time. Shielded by a nice layer of blubber, she wasn't cold any longer. The tide ran against her, but seals were strong swimmers, and it took very little energy to move herself beyond the pull of the incoming tide.

Was Gregor part of the local Selkie pod?

Should she look for him?

She dove deep, surrounded by the tumultuous North Sea. The wisest course would be to leave well enough alone, but damn it, she didn't want to. Her mother had suffered. Because of Gregor's threats, she'd gone to her grave believing herself a terrible mother.

Raene told herself she was reacting, not thinking clearly.

I'll give this a week, she promised herself.

If I've still a notion to track him down after that, give him a piece of my mind, I will.

She swam due north. The Selkies had an organized group

somewhere between the Orkneys and the Hebrides. It was the pod that had rejected her. If she could locate them, which shouldn't be hard with a bit of magic, she could ask around.

Discover who Gregor was and where she could find him.

In case she decided to look for him, after all.

If she'd been human, she'd have rolled her eyes. She was deluding herself if she thought she wouldn't chase down the father she'd never met. It was mostly a matter of how her hunt would play out and whether it happened this season or next or the one after that.

Selkies didn't have last names. She'd adopted Cameron since it was the same surname Kari used. Perhaps she'd do well to rename herself, or just stick with Raene. If she were subtle, she could find out a lot without disclosing a thing about her motives.

Or herself.

Her mind wandered as she cleaved through waves, catching the odd fish that ventured near enough to be easy pickings. If Gregor turned out to be somewhere on land, she'd need clothes, which might pose a problem...

I'll figure things out as I go.

Her annual swim usually took her south, sometimes as far as the continent. This year would be different. She'd remain in the North Sea until she either had answers or decided she no longer needed them.

CHAPTER 3

*A*egir had bowed and scraped and apologized until he was blue in the face. But he'd been right about things blowing over fast. Shifters might be quick to anger, but they were equally quick to forgive. He chalked it up to their dual natures. Not much point holding grudges on sea or land. Both had a mellowing effect.

Back on the tiny Orkney Island where he'd established a comfortable lair, he strolled along the shoreline enjoying a new day. Arcadia was close. A few steps away beyond an enchanted barrier. He was plenty near enough to satisfy everyone. The Druids would let him know if they had need of him. Because they were immortal, they didn't require robust magic. He was unclear about how they lived forever, but it had something to do with merging their essence with trees and other plants.

He inhaled deeply, savoring the rich scents of wet rocks,

sand, and sea. For the moment, it wasn't raining or sleeting, but thick, gray clouds promised precipitation at some point. Probably sooner rather than later.

He grinned to himself. The British Isles were nothing if not damp, but he wouldn't trade them for anywhere else in this world or others he'd visited over his lengthy life.

He caught the flash and flare of magic fifty meters offshore. Had to be another Selkie enjoying an early dip. Wondering which of his kin were out and about this morning, he paid out a thread of seeking magic. He didn't want the Selkie to know he was spying on them, so he kept it unobtrusive.

Aegir frowned. He'd been right about the Selkie part, and he ascertained it was a female, but he didn't recognize her. Scarcely possible, since he knew every Selkie in this part of the world. They were all his subjects. He reeled in his magic, uncertain what to do next. He could let it go. That was by far the most prudent course, but he owed it to his kinsfolk to determine who swam in their waters. From time to time, another pod challenged theirs for sovereignty.

That hadn't happened for over three hundred years, and he hoped to hell it wasn't happening now. Damn Krise, anyway. His father was far better suited to dealing with an emergent war than he was. Aegir unwrapped the tartan he'd swathed around himself and plucked his pelt from where it lay hidden by magic. Moments later, he was swimming toward where he'd felt the unfamiliar magic.

He'd be pleasant but firm. Find out who the intruder was

and see them on their way. He rolled his mental eyes. That strategy would work fine—so long as the unidentified female wasn't a spy or the forward guard of a much larger group.

He swam a little faster, choosing a course that would intersect hers. He didn't mask his magic, but if she was aware of him, she didn't show it. No surreptitious glances over a shoulder when she surfaced to breathe. She appeared to be heading for the island directly northeast of the one he'd claimed. Aegir thought about it. As far as he knew, that island —barely more than an atoll—was so small no one else bothered with it.

The other Selkie, still oblivious to his presence, surfaced again, blowing salty spume. This time, she remained above the waves long enough to glance about. Aegir's first tendency was to duck beneath the swells. So long as she remained unaware of him, she wouldn't titrate her behavior, and perhaps he'd learn why she was in his waters.

But it felt sneaky and underhanded, so he held his position, swimming along with his snout above the waterline. Her gaze zeroed in on him. He stroked toward her. She was attractive with a well-formed head and large, liquid eyes the color of raw sapphires. Her reddish pelt was thick and lush, and he couldn't help but wonder what she might look like in her human form.

After a brief hesitation, she pushed through the water in his direction. Had she recognized him, despite him not knowing who she was? More likely, she had a message to deliver and he fit a description she'd been given.

Damn it. This wasn't looking particularly promising.

He blew water out both blowhole and mouth. The hard truth was he hated conflict. If he had to call in reinforcements, the sooner he got it done and this problem behind him, the better he'd like it. He barked a greeting, holding a neutral tone and hoping against hope his assessment of why the Selkie female was here was wrong.

She barked back and switched to telepathy. Seal vocal chords were incapable of human speech. *"Who are you?"* she demanded.

Aegir steeled himself. She wasn't shy on guts. Good she was checking, but her intent was clear enough. He waited until he was only a meter away and used his flippers to position himself so he faced her. *"I am Aegir. King of this Selkie pod. Who are you?"*

Rather than answering him, she asked another question. *"Well, Aegir, Selkie King, do you have a subject named Gregor?"*

Aegir shook water from his snout. What an odd question. *"Nay, I doona. Why? Is he someone ye seek?"*

"Aye. He is my da."

Aegir did a quick scan, keeping his magic low key. The female had to be several hundred years old. *"How is it ye lost track of him?"*

"I never knew him at all." She tipped her snout at a defiant angle.

Aegir sensed now was a time to tread gently. *"Then why seek him now?"*

"I only just discovered who he was."

It made sense. Aegir considered offering his assistance. He was curious about the female. *"Ye never told me your name."*

"Aye. 'Tis true enough," she agreed affably.

He tried again. *"I ken all the Selkies in this region and many from other pods. Why have I never met you?"*

"I spend most of my time in my human body."

Frustration beat a path through him. He wasn't used to Selkies sidestepping his queries. *"'Tis fine and well."* His tone wasn't nearly as friendly. *"What should I call you?"*

She slithered back, placing more distance between them. *"Why must you call me anything?"* Before he could reply, she went on, *"Names presume we will get to know one another, and I doona plan to remain here long."*

Aegir straightened his spine and rose until his head and neck were visible above the waves. He infused his next words with steel—and compulsion. *"So long as ye swim in these waters, ye owe me allegiance. My request is simple. I am not requesting your firstborn or a blood oath of fealty. If ye refuse such a simple thing as your name, I'll be forced to assume ye've something to hide."*

She bared her teeth at him and hissed, *"I owe you nothing. You're not my king."* With a toss of her tail, she flipped over, turned, and made for the open sea.

Aegir didn't stop to consider his actions. He barked a spell. A golden length of netting draped around the female's thrashing form. She growled and snarled, biting at the strands, but they were impervious to her efforts. Aegir waited for her to go limp, give up. Once she did, he'd neutralize his casting. By Poseidon's balls, all he wanted was her name.

And right now, he'd settle for her acquiescence, recognition of his sovereignty in these waters. He was starting to not give a drowned crab if he ever saw her again, but he'd taken a stand, and he couldn't back down.

She was clearly tiring. One of her flippers was bound up in the netting and had become useless. *"Tell me your name, lass, and I'll let you go,"* he urged.

"Is this how you rule?" she sneered. *"By being a bully and throwing your weight around?"* The other flipper snagged, and she started to sink.

Damn it! Could this be going any worse?

Aegir swam beneath her, supporting her body with his own. His next words came hard. He wasn't in the habit of apologizing to anyone. *"I'm sorry."* He dismissed his casting, but it took a few moments before the part of the net trapping her flippers disintegrated.

Once he was certain she wouldn't drown, he surfaced and just looked at her, uncertain what to say. She balanced on her stomach, flippers extended, head bobbing with the ocean swells. He'd expected her to swim like a mad thing in an effort to escape, but she didn't seem in a hurry to leave.

"Are ye all right?" he asked at last.

She lifted her head. *"Aye. Thank you for asking."*

He regarded her. She was difficult and prickly and downright rude, but he didn't want to swim off and never see her again. Despite her less than stellar traits, she intrigued him.

"Do ye have a pod of your own?" he asked.

"Nay. When last I tried to join this one, someone chased me off."

If he'd been human, he'd have raised both eyebrows. *"I never heard about a lone Selkie requesting admittance to our pod."*

"How long have you been king?"

"A verra short time. Less than five years."

"That explains it. This happened long before."

Talking with her raised more questions than her clipped responses answered. *"I would like to know more about you, Selkie No-Name,"* he said and raised a flipper to point toward his island. *"If ye'd like, I have a dwelling just there. I offer food and drink."*

"In exchange for information," she said archly.

"Aye, 'tis generally how things work," he agreed.

"I'll think about it," she said, and added, *"Thank you,"* as an afterthought.

"Doona think too long," he cautioned. *"I am only here for a fortnight, and then I must return to my home."*

"But you said it was over there." She mimicked where he'd pointed with her own flipper.

"Do ye know aught of Arcadia?"

"Nay. What is it?"

"The magical elements of Caledonia, the land now named Scotland. They exist just beyond the boundaries of human imagination."

"So there's another Scotland?"

"Aye, lassie. Not so much another Scotland, as an enchanted land beyond its borders. I am bound to spend some time every year making certain naught befalls Arcadia. This year, I was late."

Curiosity streamed from her in waves of brilliant blues and greens. Aegir capitalized on what felt like the slightest of upper hands. *"If ye wish to know more, ye know where to find me."*

Turning, he swam fast and sure toward his island. He hoped she'd follow—now that he had information she wanted. Maybe they could trade. Why was she so protective of her name? They held power, but surely she knew he meant her no harm...

Or maybe not so surely. His knee-jerk reaction had trapped her with a magical net. He'd probably frightened her. Except she wasn't scared enough to blurt out her name. He admired her spunk. No one had stood up to him for a long time, and the "Yes, my lieges," grew terribly stale after a while.

Between where he left her and his beach, he ran the name Gregor through his memory banks. It rattled about, hitting a sour note or two, before he came up with a couple of candidates. One he'd met on a borderworld. The other had been highly placed in a pod to the north of Russia. Years back, that particular pod had swum in the North Sea, but for unknown reasons, they'd pushed farther and farther north and east.

He reached his island and shifted on the beach. Before he hid his skin in its usual spot, he scanned the water, hoping for a glimpse of red fur headed his way. Disappointment speared him when nothing beyond waves met his scrutiny. Convinced he'd done all he could to lure the elusive female, he walked along a path he'd cleared from the beach to his cave. Constructed with cleverly woven charms, it showed itself only to him. Anyone else viewing that stretch of shoreline would see boulders blocking their path.

Aegir nodded to himself and dismantled the illusion that protected his privacy. If Selkie No-Name showed up, she was already skittish as a newborn eel. He didn't want her to encounter any additional problems.

On the hunt for intel about Gregor—in case the female decided to trust him—he raised his mind voice. *"Krise."*

His father hated being disturbed for anything shy of a tsunami, and even that had to be sufficiently severe it would affect the underwater palace with its colorful grounds and schools of fish.

Aegir wasn't exactly expecting a reply, and he'd pulled on black sweatpants and an oversized fisherman's sweater before Krise's crisp, *"What?"* reverberated in his head.

"Do ye know aught of the Siberia pod?"

"Nothing new. Why?"

Aegir considered how much to reveal. He could ask if his da remembered the lone female. But if he did, Krise would connect the dots. If he'd sent the Selkie packing, he'd had his reasons.

"I'm waiting," Krise prodded. He was a good listener—so long as someone was imparting information. Patience had never been his strongest suit.

"Does Gregor still lead the Siberia group?"

"Pfft." Krise snorted derisively. *"Only because he married into their royalty."*

"He can't be that incompetent," Aegir pointed out, thinking Gregor had held the position for many years.

"Of course he could. 'Tis a job no one wants. Ye've made that clear enough."

Aegir winced. He hadn't exactly embraced Krise's retirement, but shirking his duty as the heir apparent had never been a serious consideration.

"Why the sudden interest in the Siberia pod?" Krise's question held pointed edges.

Aegir didn't have a decent answer, so he switched tactics. *"Do ye recall any Selkies who've breached our waters? Unfamiliar ones?"*

A long, drawn-out breath filled his head. *"Ye mistake diplomacy for riddles. Ye ran across a Selkie who's not part of our pod. Ye suspect he may be from the next closest pod, which happens to be the one in Siberia."*

"Close enough."

"I'm still not understanding what ye're wanting," Krise said, but at least the sharply annoyed tone had left his voice, replaced by mild curiosity.

"I'm not certain, either," Aegir muttered mostly to himself.

"It is only one Selkie?" Krise asked.

"Aye, just the one." Aegir didn't correct his father's assumption the Selkie was male.

"Let me know if that changes."

Before Aegir could reply, Krise was gone. He didn't blame his father. A single strange Selkie didn't pose any particular problem—unless they were spies for a rival pod. He was almost positive the female had no such affiliation. She appeared focused on finding her father.

He mixed up a drink of crushed kelp, honeycomb, and milk he extracted from anemones. A sprig of rosemary and another of cumin added a hint of spiciness to the nourishing mixture. Usually, he hunted while he was in the sea, but this morning the female's presence had diverted him. He considered teleporting into John O'Groats for lunch, but decided to wait.

He'd hoped the other Selkie would follow him, but she hadn't shown any sign of materializing. Drink in hand, he wandered back outside and settled on a sandy spot, looking out to sea. Dark clouds were spitting a chilly rain. If he remained here very long, his clothing would end up soaked, but he could dry the garments with magic if they grew too uncomfortable.

He scanned the waves. Tipped with white, they rolled in, breaking to foam on the beach. Maybe he should have taken a firmer stance with the mysterious Selkie.

Aye, and that would have worked about as well as throwing a net over her did.

She'd been correct when she'd said she owed him nothing.

He walked to the island's other side. Water dripped down his face and neck; he scarcely noticed it. Should he grab his skin and return to the water? He drained the last of his drink, considering his options.

Not that he had very many.

He wanted to know more about the other Selkie. She clearly didn't share his curiosity, though. She'd said she spent most of her time in her human form. That seemed odd to him. Every other Selkie he knew passed the lion's share of their time in the sea.

Selkies were nothing if not linked to their heritage, yet she'd had no idea who her father was until recently. Only one explanation made sense. Gregor had stepped outside his mate bonds. The penalty for infidelity was severe. Gregor's wife would have had grounds to banish him from their pod. No wonder Selkie No-Name hadn't known about his identity.

He'd been so lost in his thoughts, he hadn't been watching either waves or beach. A seal's bark snapped his head around. He'd been expecting a garden-variety seal, or perhaps another pod member with a problem, who'd chased him down to kick options around.

The russet pelt was unmistakable. Not many seals were that color. His mouth stretched into a smile before he could stop himself, and he hurried to where the Selkie was using a combination of flippers and her stomach to move from sea to beach.

Aegir crouched in front of her. "Thank you for trusting me."

"But I don't," she replied in telepathy. *"I need two things, Selkie king. A robe and for you to leave me while I shift."*

"I can put your skin next to mine for safekeeping."

Laughter hooted from her in a series of sharp, pointed yips. *"No one knows where my skin is except me. No one."*

He held up a hand, palm facing outward. "I meant no ill will, but I understand. Back in a moment with a blanket. 'Twill be warmer than a robe." He hurried up the beach. She'd clearly been tricked, forced away from her skin. Goddess only knew what had happened to her during those days—or maybe as long as months or years. If he found out who'd harmed her, he'd make certain they died a miserable death.

When he returned, a patterned woolen blanket folded and slung across one arm, she'd already shifted. He caught a glimpse of high, firm breasts, long legs, and a thatch of spiky red curls before she snatched the blanket and wound it around herself. Hair the color of ancient sunsets spilled to waist level. She had an arresting face with starkly defined bone structure. A high forehead and carved cheekbones were set off by eyes that sparkled turquoise with gold and silver flecks around the pupils.

Aegir was staring, but she was gorgeous, and it was hard to rip his gaze from her. "Thanks for trusting me," he said again, stammering a little.

"But I don't." Her voice was low, rich, musical as she repeated what she'd already said telepathically.

"Then why'd ye leave the sea?"

"I would hear more of this Arcadia. How can I find it? What purpose will it serve once I locate it?"

"That conversation willna be short. Would ye come within? I can offer simple refreshments."

She shook her head. "No. I don't know you. I'm safer out here."

He bowed low before straightening. "I willna harm you. I've apologized for the net. Ye caught me unaware, and I reacted. 'Twas wrong of me."

"Will you tell me of Arcadia, or not?"

"Aye. Are ye always this single-minded, lass?"

The corners of her full mouth curved into a half smile. "When I want something."

Aegir started to ask for a quid pro quo—like her name or how she'd come by the knowledge about Gregor being her sire—but he might do better if he didn't begin with bargaining. She was ready to bolt in a heartbeat. He saw the hesitancy in her gaze.

"Long ago," he began, "at the beginning of the world, Druids carved out a place for themselves in what is now Scotland. They're guardians of animals and the natural world, plus they're immortal, so their interest in this tiny bit of the world ensured it wouldna fall to evil spirits, demons, or other hellspawned beasts.

"Arcadia is the bastion of good magic. I believe it predates the world, but I'm not certain. Some of the Druids moved from Scotland to Arcadia a verra long time ago and set themselves up there. They built a castle and continued to watch over animals and trees. Under their care, Arcadia developed healing energy. Perhaps 'twas always there, but they brought it out, made it more apparent."

Interest lit her face, and she leaned slightly closer.

He didn't blame her. Magic made for fascinating tales. "Over time, other beings who wielded power discovered the Druid's private enclave and its healing aspects. We would visit there to renew ourselves and recover from traumatic events."

"This healing, how long does it take?" she asked.

"Depends on what ye're healing from." He narrowed his eyes in speculation. Scanning her with magic would answer many of his questions, but she'd take it as intrusive, an invasion of her privacy.

"Too bad Mother didn't know about it," she murmured.

"I could bring her here," Aegir offered.

"Too late. She's dead."

"I'm sorry."

"Me too. We weren't close this last century, but at least now I understand why."

Aegir waited for her to clarify her statement, but she didn't say anything further. When the gap in conversation was starting to feel uncomfortably long, he said, "Since ye're here, maybe ye might want to..." His words ran down. They didn't know one another well enough for him to suggest she might benefit from Arcadia's healing energy.

"Is this"—she spread her hands to both sides—"Arcadia?"

"Nay. Where we are just now is Scotland."

"How do you travel from here to there?" Before he could

answer, she added, "I thought you said you were here to protect Arcadia. How can you protect it if you're not there?"

"I'm close enough, the Druids could call on me if they had need." He took a measured breath. "Many of those with White Magic spend some time here. So there is always at least one of us close by. The Shifter Council coordinates things, and it's based in John O'Groats."

"Shifter Council, eh?" She skewered him with her direct gaze. "Sounds impressive, but I bet some of them are part of your pod."

He offered a sheepish grin. "Nay. We spend as little time as possible on land. Actually, we're quite territorial, and the next nearest pod is north of the Asian continent." He stopped shy of mentioning that the father she sought was probably there. The omission was pure selfishness on his part because he didn't want her to leave. Not yet, anyway. Not until they'd gotten a chance to know one another better.

She closed her teeth over her lower lip and frowned. "Who actually has the final say about Arcadia? You or the Council?"

Aegir laughed. "The Council. Ye give me far more power than I lay claim to. If I feel verra strongly about something, I might take a stand, but it hasna happened yet. Ye ask a lot of questions, and then pile more on the heap afore I can answer them all."

"Sorry. It's one of my many failings." Her smile was infectious.

"Back to Arcadia. If ye wish to travel through the barrier, I can show you what ye must do. 'Twill require ye trust me for a short time."

"In what way?"

"Ye must speak your name to enter."

Her smile widened. "Raene. My name is Raene."

CHAPTER 4

Raene regarded the other Selkie. If he meant her harm, he'd cloaked his intent, buried it so deep she couldn't tease it out. He was comely. Wet hair, black as midnight, streamed down his body. He was built like an athlete, tall and slabbed with muscle visible even through his loose-fitting clothing. But his eyes were the best part. They changed color, reflecting the many moods of the sea. At the moment, they were a deep, mossy green, with silvery highlights.

She was almost certain theirs had been an accidental meeting. She hadn't been taking care to conceal herself, and he'd sensed her magic and come to investigate. If he was truly king to his people, it was a very liege-like thing to do. As they talked—and it was mostly him offering her information about Arcadia—she started to relax.

And she felt stupid for being so intransigent about

withholding her name. Granted, names had power, and a canny sorcerer could use her name to locate her skin, but Aegir was another Selkie. If anyone understood how critical her pelt was, it would be him.

"The portals to enter Arcadia are located in a few key spots," he continued after telling her she'd have to trust him to pass the boundary. "This island holds one of them, which is why I settled here. Follow me. I'll teach you the incantation needed to cross the threshold."

"Will you come too?"

"Only if ye wish me to."

Raene nodded, her mood suddenly serious. She hadn't undertaken much that was magical over the course of her life —other than shifting to her seal form. "My blood is not pure. Will it matter?"

"Nay. Ye're more Selkie than human, or ye'd not be able to shift. 'Tis all that matters. Arcadia's borders are open to all who wield White Magic."

"I'm guessing there's dark magic," she murmured.

"Aye, lass." He lowered his voice. "Everything has an opposite, and so a balance is achieved. But Black Magic is verra real, and a potent threat. 'Tis why we protect Arcadia, though the land has ways of caring for itself unless it is beset from too many sides."

He started walking toward the island's high point; Raene fell in behind him, digesting what she'd heard. Midway there, he stopped dead, turned toward her, and held up a hand, fingers spread in the universal sign to wait. Magic sparkled and flared around him, turning the air incandescent. She felt the bite of power, like miniature lightning bolts, shoot through the air toward Aegir. Even though she wasn't the target, a few nipped her on their way through.

A worried expression replaced his earlier smile. "There is trouble," he said. "I must go, but if ye remain here, I'll complete the instructions to enter Arcadia upon my return."

"What kind of trouble?"

"Fae and Black Witches teamed up. They're attacking Arcadia's protections. If we canna stop them, they may breach her borders."

"Who's we?"

"Myself, other Shifters, and several resident Druids."

Raene didn't want to hold him up, but she needed to understand. "Last question. Promise. What happens if Arcadia's barrier is ruptured?"

His handsome face turned grim. "Its magic will leak out, and humans will die. The magic that nurtures us will kill them, and 'tisn't a pretty death, but a long, slow painful one."

She'd heard enough. Maybe because she'd lived among humans, she valued them and didn't want any to suffer unnecessarily.

"I want to help."

"Are ye trained as a warrior?"

Not unless he counted whipping recalcitrant dough into line. Raene thinned her lips. "Nay, but—"

He raked a hand through his wet hair. "Please. I canna risk

splitting my attention. Magical battles play out quickly. I'll return afore ye know it."

Raene offered what she hoped was an agreeable expression. "I'll watch closely while you craft magic to cross the boundary." She didn't bother to add she'd be right behind him.

Aegir's attention was clearly elsewhere. He bent the magic still shimmering around him into a shiny arc, chanting low in the Selkie's language—a combination of Gaelic and Latin with a few other bits and pieces she'd never been able to tack down with any precision.

That she knew the language at all was courtesy of her insistence. Her mother hadn't wanted to teach her anything about magic, let alone the Selkie's language. Her one brush with them after getting her pelt back convinced her that her mother had been right. Learning about Selkies was worse than a waste of time.

That was then, though. Perhaps her rusty linguistic skills were about to become useful.

She waited for a reasonable interval, perhaps five minutes, after Aegir vanished in plumes of magic-imbued smoke before mimicking the bones of his casting. It rose to her command. Not quite as quickly as it had responded to the same spell from him, but she'd been worried it wouldn't work for her at all.

She might not have shaped much magic, but what little she'd done had convinced her there was a nexus, an intersection point where the type of spell and who was summoning it came together. Either there'd be sufficient power to fire the casting.

Or not.

Her skin prickled with an electric sensation so strong the fine hairs at the back of her neck stood on end. The scent of the sea tinged with ozone and rocks heated by the sun filled her nostrils. Odd since the sun in the British Isles rarely grew warm enough to create the baked-stone smell. The only reason she even recognized it was from a trip to Greece several years before.

Raene waited. A threshold had formed for Aegir, and he'd stepped through. Despite power swirling around her, no gateway showed itself. She reached deeper, threw more magic into the mix. The gray day faded to darkness, and her belly tightened with fear.

Had she done something wrong?

If she reeled in her magic, could she undo it, or had her spell reached the point of no return? Something with black feathers and a sharp beak flitted past the edges of her peripheral vision, followed by an even larger scaled creature. Feeling spooked, she cut the flow of power, but nothing changed.

She'd entered what looked like a no-man's land. No nice, clean, shiny portal for her. Raene dunned herself for a fool. Aegir had made it look easy, but magic was unique to the wielder. The same spell from her had yielded different results.

So different, she had no idea where she was. The stretch

of rain-swept beach was gone as was the island dotted with scrubby bushes, driftwood, and rocks. A tunnel formed before her. Long, dark, and daunting, it was her only choice. To make certain, she turned in a full circle. Walls hemmed her in on every side but one. She didn't trust they were real, so she touched one. It smoked beneath her finger but didn't give way. She'd been hoping her hand would punch through, proving it was only illusion.

The magic that had her in its grasp was an independent entity. She'd withdrawn her own power a few minutes before, and it hadn't made a whit of difference. "Steady," she said out loud to calm herself. It didn't have much of an effect. Facing the tunnel, she took a deep breath and blew it out before stepping tentatively forward. The path beneath her feet was solid.

A single note sounded, followed by another. The notes formed music she could see in the darkness. A riot of musical runes in every shade of the rainbow drew her forward. She did her damnedest to hang onto her sense of outrage and caution, but the tune had a hypnotic effect, calming in a weird way.

Black shaded to daylight, and the tunnel fell away traded for a verdant landscape. Sun shone warmly in a blue sky dotted with fluffy clouds. The British Isles occasionally looked like this, but not often. She was still wrapped in the length of woolen blanket Aegir had given her. Beneath its folds, she started to sweat.

It was tempting to leave the blanket. More than tempting.

She unwound it and discovered a skirt and blouse loomed from undyed cotton. Where had they come from?

"Och, and let's focus on the important part, like where I am," she muttered.

Raene folded the blanket and stood with it in her arms. If she laid it down, would she ever find it again? She placed it on a flat stone and set magical markers. If they worked properly, they'd guide her back to this spot. A flock of birds, black with mottled grey across their breasts, flew past chittering like mad things. Two squirrels chased each other up a nearby tree.

A quick scan told her she was in a forest, one where the trees were old. It meant she'd either left the UK entirely or traveled backward in time to when trees grew thickly across Scotland from the Irish Sea to the North Sea.

She shook herself from head to toe. She should be petrified, frantic to return to the small island in the Orkney chain where Aegir lived—and she'd left her pelt—but curiosity won the day. The earth beneath her bare feet was warm, soothing. Power flowed into her, thick and sweet as honey. Had she stumbled into Arcadia by accident? Did the enchanted land present differently to different magic wielders? It made sense. If one of its purposes was to heal wounds, it followed that not everyone would seek the same absolution.

Raene pressed forward. She should be hysterical, working her arse off figuring out how to return to where she'd concealed her pelt, but worry and her current situation were incompatible. She couldn't worry here, and she wasn't certain whether to laugh or cry about it.

The music that had drawn her still played. She couldn't see the glowing runes any longer, but the melody had morphed from single notes to a fully complemented orchestra. She stopped at a babbling brook, crouching by its banks long enough to cup water into her hands and rinse her face. A quick taste told her the water was pure and sweet, but she hesitated before drinking. In some enchanted worlds, drinking or eating anything bound you there. She had no idea how she knew, but she was fairly certain wherever she was held no malevolence toward her.

Nothing obvious, anyway.

"I have to remain alert," she lectured herself before swallowing several mouthfuls of water from the rushing creek. If she was wrong about the eerie world being harmless, she might have sealed her fate and made it impossible to leave.

She tried to make herself care but didn't get very far.

Time became meaningless as she wandered in and out of thick, ancient tree boles. The magic surrounding her was clean and older than the beginnings of the world, though how she knew remained one more of today's many mysteries.

An even bigger one was why she wasn't trying harder—or at all—to find a way out.

Something Aegir had said rattled in the back of her mind. He'd been summoned to deal with dark power, but how could evil gain a toehold in a place like this?

Maybe this wasn't Arcadia. Perhaps she'd been transported to her own private Eden, a spot she might never leave. The music swelled, but this time she didn't pay attention to it.

"I can't stay here forever," she announced to a passing group of buzzing bees. They kept right on flying.

Her head seemed clearer. She visualized where she'd left the blanket and turned back the way she'd come. Less than twenty steps brought her to the flat stone with the blanket folded on top of it. Twenty steps, when she'd taken hundreds moving through the forest. It wasn't possible, not in a world where physics principles applied, but anything was possible here.

She should have been alarmed. Instead, a sense of peace filled her. She hadn't been at one with the world in a long time. Maybe not ever. Wrapping the blanket around herself, she held an image of the spot she'd left on Aegir's island. It formed with no fanfare at all. No discernable magic. No dark tunnels. No floating runes.

One moment, she was in the blue-sky world. The next Scotland's ever-present rain pelted her head and shoulders.

Aegir was perched on a rock, regarding her. "Better?"

"I didn't know anything was wrong," she sputtered, "but, yes, I'm better."

He angled his head to one side. "Ye've courage, lass. Ye might have waited for me to return."

"I might have," she agreed and drew the blanket more

tightly around her. The clothing that had proven so useful in the other place had disappeared. "Was I in Arcadia?"

"Of course. Where else might ye have gone off to?"

"I have no idea," she said a bit stiffly, wondering if he was making fun of her.

"Would ye care to learn the proper incantation? One matched to your energy?"

Heat moved from her chest over the top of her head. "Guess the one you used isn't an all-purpose casting," she mumbled.

"I was in a hurry. It was the fastest way to move me where I needed to go. The Druids had already reached for me, so I borrowed from their residual energy to teleport."

Raene made a face. "I'm surprised it worked for me at all."

"Arcadia sensed your need. And so it allowed you entry. Magical realms are picky about who crosses their borders." He paused to take a measured breath. "I told you earlier, each person's experience is unique. Give it a day or two afore ye assess what happened to you."

She remembered why he'd left her. "The Fae and Witches, did they stop whatever they were doing?"

"Permanently."

Raene opened her mouth to request clarification, but if Aegir and the Druids and other Shifters had killed the miscreants, she didn't want to know. She settled for saying, "But it's so peaceful there. How could anyone sustain dark magic in such a place?"

"Easily—if their hearts were bound to evil to start with.

But it did require several of them consolidating their wickedness to create an incident." He jumped off the rock and crooked two fingers her way. "Come with me. We'll complete the lesson I'd began when I was called away."

Raene fell into step next to him. "I didn't see Druids. Or anyone at all. Just birds and animals."

"As I said, lass, Arcadia bends itself to your energy. If ye'd required Druid support, they'd have found you."

She held silence, falling behind Aegir as the path narrowed. When they got to the island's high point, he halted and pointed at an oblong mound between two standing stones. "This is the easiest entry point." He focused his gaze, now more blue than green, on her. "I realize I dinna come this way, but as I said, I rode Druid energy past the barrier. 'Tis thicker there, but not impossible to cross. This will be easier for you because ye already found your way."

"It was more like it found me."

"Aye. It tuned in to your need. Come stand just here." He scribed an X in the wet dirt with a small rock. The skies had made a full commitment to rain, and it sluiced down his body, making his clothing cling to the muscles she'd known were there.

Raene stopped looking at him and complied, positioning herself in the indicated spot.

He continued in the Selkies' tongue. Sweet and lyrical, it commanded the veils to part while promising she would hold Arcadia's secret, never revealing its presence to anyone unaware of its existence.

"But you disclosed it to me," she murmured.

He broke off the incantation long enough to narrow his eyes at her. "Aye. 'Tis my right as Selkie king to do so."

She absorbed the remainder of the incantation—the one matched to her energy—in silence, memorizing the words. It wasn't difficult, almost as if they wanted to be inscribed in her mind.

Aegir swept one hand up and to the side. "Try it now, while 'tis still fresh in your head."

"Is there a special way to return?"

"Ye seem to have managed it." He offered half a smile.

"Aye, but I managed to get there too, and with a very different spell than what you just taught me."

His smile broadened incrementally. "Good observational skills."

She didn't bother to tell him those same talents were essential to what she did for a living. "You didn't answer my question."

"The way back shows itself to you when Arcadia is satisfied ye're done there."

"Come with me. I'm curious if it looks different when you're there." Raene winced at her forwardness. The man across from her was a king. Surely, he had better things to do than play companion to her. "Sorry," she mumbled. "That was presumptuous of me."

Before he could reply, she began the incantation he'd taught her. The same gateway she'd noticed earlier formed; she stepped through. No dark tunnels. No dancing runes. No music. Not yet, anyway. It was as if she'd stepped directly from the obscure island in the Orkneys into another world.

The place she stood looked different from where she'd been before but smelled the same. Water still dripped from her face and the ends of her soaked hair. Arcadia's sun was welcome. A flash and a shining spot off to one side shaped itself into Aegir.

Her face grew warm, and she looked away. "You didn't have to come with me."

"What if I appreciated the opportunity to act as your guide?" He raised one dark, arched brow.

A pleased feeling fluttered behind her breastbone. She peeked beneath the blanket. Sure enough, the same skirt and blouse were there. She removed the blanket, folding it. "Last time, I left this and set magic to indicate its location."

"Caution is never wasted."

"Where did the clothes come from?" She placed the blanket on another convenient rock and added a much more subtle magical marker.

"As I said. This place senses what ye require."

"So if I were hungry or thirsty—?"

He nodded at her unfinished question. "It meets all your needs."

She shoved her hair behind her shoulders. "Does anyone ever just decide to stay?"

"Aye, but Arcadia willna allow it. The only permanent residents are the Druids."

She wanted to ask why, but it was one of those

questions that probably didn't have an easy answer, or even one at all. Aegir started walking. She caught up with him. The countryside was verdant, just like Scotland. Birds chirped, and small rodents chittered out of direct view.

Raene opened her magical senses, not wanting to miss anything. A layered view spread in front of her third eye. Timeless power anchored this place, magic so ancient it had probably been part of the making of the world. "This has always been here," she murmured.

"Always," he agreed.

A sense of rightness flowed from the dirt beneath her feet like a tide of warm nectar. Occasionally, she sensed different energies, but they faded nearly as quickly as they appeared. "We're not the only ones here."

"There are others," he confirmed.

"Why can't we see them?"

"They are here to heal."

She remembered her earlier visit. She'd been alone then. "Where are the other entry points?"

"Now that ye've been here, ye'll sense them. They have a particular pull, but only when ye need to be here. There is only one Arcadia, and many who wield magic."

"How come I never knew about this place?" She stopped walking and waited for him to turn to face her.

"The same reason the Selkies dinna know about you. Ye've chosen to live as human."

She squared her shoulders. "I approached your pod after

a long stint without my skin. I got the distinct feeling I wasn't welcome."

"We can be an insular lot." He pressed his lips together. "Mostly, a strange Selkie is cause for alarm. Pods keep to themselves. Occasionally, a rival pod tries a coup, and the first sign is a Selkie we don't know. Rather like a scout getting the lay of the land."

"I had no idea."

"Of course not. Your mother was part human, aye?"

Raene nodded. "Half. She fell in love with a Selkie, and I was the result."

"We mate for life. How is it ye only just recently discovered your father's name?"

"He already had a mate." Raene rolled her eyes. "Guess infidelity isn't common with the Sea Folk."

He drew his dark brows into a thick, disapproving line. "Damn near unheard of. We have strict penalties for such things."

"I found that out too." She sucked in a tight breath. "My mother was waiting in the place I keep my skin. For a long time. Long enough, the magic from my pelt was the only thing keeping her alive."

Understanding flickered across his expressive features. "That was the sadness I sensed in you."

"Aye. She died in my arms, after telling me about my father. Apparently, he put a type of geas on her. One that would have meant her death if she'd revealed his identity."

Aegir fisted a hand and punched the air in front of him. "I

canna even begin to list how many ways that was wrong of him."

Raene shrugged. "Maybe so, but I want to find him, anyway. No magical threats are hanging over my head."

Two men in dark robes sashed with colorful bands shimmered into being. Raene assumed they must be Druids. Both were tonsured with sharp-boned faces. Reprimand shot from their eyes. "We just balanced her energy," the blue-eyed one said, directing his words at Aegir.

The Selkie king bowed. "I have not undone your work. The disturbance ye felt in Arcadia's energy came from me."

"Not entirely," the brown-eyed Druid corrected him. "Some of her sorrow has returned, accompanied by anger." He turned his attention to Raene. "Do ye require more healing?"

"No. Thank you for asking."

Aegir bowed. "Apologies for disturbing the energy flow. Raene and I will continue our conversation back on Earth."

"Doona go far," the first Druid cautioned.

"We're not certain our earlier...problem is completely resolved," the other Druid added.

Aegir drew back. "Of course, 'tis. They're dead."

"Other complications have surfaced." Without explaining further, the Druids faded from view.

"Damn it." Aegir turned and walked back the way they'd come, moving at a much faster clip.

Raene visualized where she'd left the blanket and beat him to the clearing. She'd just draped the length of wool around herself when he showed up. "Nice use of magic," he said.

His approval warmed her, and she took a chance and scanned him with the power she'd already summoned. He, too, carried an undercurrent of sorrow. It might have been why hers was so apparent to him. She waited until he'd parted the barrier and they were on the other side to blurt out, "What happened to make you unhappy?"

"Doesna matter." His features developed a shuttered look, but he didn't deny her assessment.

She started to place her hands on her hips, but it wasn't compatible with the blanket, so she settled for crossing her arms over her chest. "I talked with you."

"So ye did." His soft words were at odds with the furrows marking his forehead. Aegir's head snapped up. Breath hissed through his teeth.

"The Druids want you back already?" she guessed.

"Aye."

Raene drew herself up to her full height. It still placed Aegir a few inches taller, but she wanted him to take her seriously. "I'm going back with you. Hunting for Gregor can wait. Besides, you called it earlier when you said magical battles don't last long."

The corners of his mouth twitched but stopped shy of a smile. He moved behind her, dropped his hands atop her shoulders, and began to chant. The feel of his magic surrounding her was heady, but she focused on the task ahead. She wasn't a warrior. Far from it, but there had to be a way she could help. She had good instincts, and magic ran strong in her.

Between the two, she'd make herself an asset.

Realization slapped her hard. She double-checked her reality but came up with the same conclusion.

Desire to be accepted by a pod was driving her. She'd never recognized it before, but maybe Arcadia had opened her eyes to her true nature. Before she could sort it out further, they crossed the threshold and the sounds of battle—swords and armor clashing—battered her ears.

CHAPTER 5

Aegir had been pleased Raene wanted to accompany him. And worried. He could have ordered her to remain behind, but didn't have the heart. Besides, she wasn't one of his subjects, and she was likely to ignore his wishes, precisely as she'd done last time. Sincerity shone from her, but he hadn't doubted her stated desire to go with him. Not after she'd cared enough to look within and seen his unrest. Giving Jonathan to his father had been far harder than Aegir imagined it would be. Not that he didn't trust Angus to keep the boy safe, but knowing the seer meant to erase the boy's memories of his years with the Selkies hurt.

A lot.

Aegir had hoped—nay, he'd *assumed*—Jonathan would want to visit. Scarcely an outcome if the boy didn't remember him or any of the rest of the pod. One of Angus's ongoing grievances was with the Celts, who'd wiped his early memories. He still had no idea about his origins. That he would do the same to his own son defied credibility.

Even though Aegir hadn't imagined this particular development, he didn't have to dig too deep to understand. Far simpler to erase memories of a mother who had competing priorities than to explain how Arianrhod had lied to her kinsmen—the Celtic pantheon—choosing not to tell them about her son. Because Jonathan's memories of his mother were tangled in his memories of the Selkies, there wasn't a way to eradicate one and leave the other intact.

Angus had been resolute when he'd come for his son. Arianrhod had been desolate as she fled to Caer Sidi. Surrounded by so much angst and misery, Aegir hadn't dissected his emotions. Easier to hang onto annoyance at Angus than to examine how much he'd miss the boy's bright light and his burgeoning talent. Magic ran rampant in Jonathan. How could it not with a seer for a father and a goddess mother?

He jerked his attention back to the present and crossed the boundary into Arcadia amid the escalating sounds of battle. Worry displaced his sorrow about the boy. The Druids wouldn't have summoned him back this soon unless their need was dire.

Raene had already shed the blanket. In place of the simple skirt and blouse she'd worn before, she was encased in light armor. Arcadia clearly believed she'd need its protection. She angled a brow at him, tapped her mail-clad chest, and asked, "Which way?"

He crossed the space between them and gripped her forearm. "Stay behind me, lass, until we see what we face. From the sound of things..." He didn't finish his sentence. Didn't have to. She understood. He had a feeling not much escaped her keen mind. She was an intuitive magic-wielder, unaware of how she employed her considerable gifts, but reliant on them just the same.

He hurried toward where the clash of magic joined the rough sounds of steel on steel. Must be Fae, rather than Black Witches. Many of them favored swords. Unlike most magical creatures, the Fae were relatively insensitive to iron. He extracted power from the land—and the sea. Opening channels deep within himself, he drew magic into his body, shaping and forming it into a weapon that arced between his hands.

Better to be ready. Even the few seconds it would take to craft a defense might mean Raene sustained harm. Keeping her safe was important to him, although he didn't fully understand the why of it. They broke through dense tree cover into an open spot. The enchanted world was a veritable shifting sea of elements that never looked the same way twice. It appeared the trees had withdrawn a safe distance to provide a killing field—and keep them and their saplings out of danger.

At least fifteen Fae were ranged in a ragged line swinging blades of varying types that glittered beneath Arcadia's sunny skies. The two Druids from earlier had been joined by half a dozen others. Badly outmatched, they focused magic in swirling funnels to deflect the swords. No one was seriously injured. Not yet, but blood dripped from jagged rips in the Druids' robes. Its hot, metallic smell felt wrong in what had always been a place of peace.

The Fae firmed up their line and ran lightly forward, carving from left to right and back again. The Druids fell back a few paces. They were too few to mount an effective defense, but they'd fight until they were too wounded to continue, and the Fae knew as much.

Aegir sent magic in a circle to double-check, but he was the only non-Druid fighting on their side, not counting Raene. If the Druids had raised the Shifter Council telepathically, they'd yet to send reinforcements. He edged back into the forest with Raene sticking close to him. He thinned his lips into a harsh line. The wise path would be to wait for more warriors to show up, but waiting wasn't an option. Not with the Fae advancing with blood in their eyes.

At least Raene was following his orders.

So far.

That might change. He didn't know her well enough to make any predictions.

He aimed to position them across from the Druids and catch the Fae in a deadly crossfire. He tried not to look right at the Fae. Most were far from beautiful in their native form, but they employed glamours designed to force the eye their way. Once you looked at them, they could exert power over you.

"Do not let them capture your gaze," he told Raene, switching to telepathy.

"Even I know that much," she mumbled, not bothering with mind speech.

Magic built behind him, subtle but with strong roots. Good. She was readying herself.

Two of the Fae, stunning men with long, flowing hair of silver mixed with gold, surged forward, sabers swinging so fast the blades were a blur. Dressed in old-fashioned garb, they wore leather breeks and shirts with sleeves that belled out at the bottom. So similar they might have been clones, they chanted a compelling refrain in a language Aegir didn't recognize.

He closed his ears to it since it felt damned near as hypnotic as their dark eyes. Fae were a scourge. Far worse than they'd been a few centuries before when magic roamed free. As things stood, they blamed everyone—magical and human alike—for what the world had turned into. He supposed they figured if they killed everyone off, they could resurrect an environment more to their liking.

The attacking Fae balanced on the balls of their feet. Small silvery flecks glistened around them, looking harmless enough until one zapped past Aegir and buried itself in a nearby tree. The tree groaned piteously. Sap shot from the hole, washing the dart out.

"Watch out!" Raene's voice was soft, a contrast to her grim warning.

He feinted sideways narrowly avoiding a volley of the insidious bits of evil. Raene ended up next to him. "Those barbed things, they're coming from the ones not actively fighting," she hissed.

"Drop back, and I'll ward you." His voice was gruff.

"You'll do no such thing," she said, indignation clear in her tone.

One of the Fae angled his blade, slicing sideways. The targeted Druid moved fast, but not quickly enough to avoid losing a finger. Magic formed around his injured hand, glowing golden. He must be beyond agony, but he didn't say a word.

Druids never used weapons, but jets of magic flew from their upraised hands as they spat words in Gaelic. Power words designed to assist their cause. The Fae blades sizzled when Druid magic crashed against them. One turned black. Another burst into flame. A Fae on the sidelines tossed fresh swords at his companions.

Aegir sidled past the perimeter of the trees. They were outraged by the disturbance that had dared cross Arcadia's borders. It wasn't terribly sporting of him, but he loosed a volley of power at the Faes' backs. His magic formed a bevy of dark blue spears, seawater sharpened to a razor edge.

A sharp intake of breath next to him suggested Raene had never considered such a use for her magic, which was a lot like his. She was a quick study. Moments later, a second batch of spikes in a slightly lighter blue raced toward the Fae. By now, they'd turned into a hissing, snarling batch of pissed off Faeries.

They bolted to a spot where they faced Aegir and Raene squarely, murder glistening in the depths of their eyes.

Behind him, the trees soughed, their leaves rustling menacingly. Would they help? Aegir dared hope so.

The Druids didn't look much happier than the Fae. The golden glow had formed a glove around the one Druid's injured hand. Aegir considered telepathy, but Fae magic was far more potent than either his own or the Druids' Earth-based enchantment. They'd intercept any communication.

Two of them batted at places the backs of their shirts had caught fire, courtesy of Aegir's darts, or perhaps Raene's. Done with standing in his shadow, she'd placed herself by his side, hands raised and power flowing smoothly from them.

The air thickened with the reek of expended enchantments. Selkie magic carried the varied scents of the sea; Druid power was rich with the smell of freshly turned earth. He'd always thought Fae magic should stink, be as foul as they were, yet it wasn't. Wildflowers, heather, and ancient moorlands under a summer sun mingled into a pleasing mélange.

The Fae didn't remain between Aegir and the Druids for long. Clearly understanding they'd lost the upper hand, they leveraged their superior numbers to split forces. Four flanked him and Raene. The remaining eleven faded out of sight, reappearing behind the Druids.

Aegir rested a hand on a nearby tree bole, urging, encouraging. If the trees truly had a stake in this—and they well might since Fae were not their friends—now would be an excellent time to make a move. He didn't linger near the tree, returning his full attention to the peril they faced.

The Fae nearest him twisted his lovely face into a sneer. "Return to the sea, Selkie king. We have no grievance with you."

"Aye." Another Fae, this one female with hair the color of a rusty sunrise and a stunning body wrapped in a richly embroidered sky-blue dress, stepped closer. "Go now and we will forgive your attack. And allow your companion leave to depart as well." She sent a pointed look winging Raene's way.

"Leave me out of this," Raene snarled. "I can get myself out of here."

Aegir swallowed surprise. There was more to the woman standing by his side than he suspected, or perhaps she didn't fully comprehend the range of Fae power. He aimed his words at the nearest Fae. "I canna comply. This land is sacred not just to my people, but to all magic wielders."

"Pah. Ye're weak," the male retorted. "We have no such haven, and we live forever."

"Aye, and just look at you." Aegir screwed his face into a disapproving expression.

"What is that supposed to mean?" The female Fae spat the words.

Aegir watched the Druids out of the corners of his eyes. They'd come up with shields from somewhere. Maybe they'd built them on the spot with magic, but it gave them something to parry the Fae swordplay. Eleven against eight were better odds, but still not good.

The trees' thick canopy rustled louder in an unseen wind. It was the only warning before the trees rushed forward as if no longer tethered by roots. Reaching with branches that had developed hooked protuberances, they snatched up the Fae as if they were a passel of rag dolls and shook them.

Magic sheeted from the skewered Fae, turning the air black and gray shot with threads of red and silver. An unholy screeching ran through the clearing from the highest note on the scale to the lowest and then back again. The heather and moorland scent developed undernotes of rot.

A look of wonder flitted across Raene's face, and she fell to her knees, head bowed in supplication. She didn't remain there for more than a moment before rising. "Goddess bless the trees. I've only seen them do this once before."

"They rarely come to our aid, lass," Aegir replied.

The four Fae who'd circled them had vanished. He wasn't certain when they left, but it had to be after the ones still dangling thirty meters above the ground were nabbed.

The Druids stood in a semicircle and raised their clear, pure voices in song. Aegir recognized it. The Gaelic prayer honored the Earth from which they drew strength. Blood streamed from the captured Fae, wetting the ground. One by one, they disappeared, accompanied by a splatting sound as if they'd been sucked into some cosmic vacuum cleaner.

He waited, Raene by his side, until all was quiet. The Arch Druid walked heavily to where Aegir stood and bowed. "Thank ye for heeding my call, Selkie king."

"How could I not?" Aegir inhaled sharply.

"Will they return?" Raene asked.

The Druid eyed her. "I know you. Ye're who sought healing earlier. Did Arcadia give you what ye needed?"

She nodded solemnly. "It did. Thank you."

He inclined his head. "Ye are new to this place and its customs. The land helped you, so now ye must return the boon."

"I will help any way I can."

Aegir was proud of her. She wasn't trying to wiggle out of anything.

"She lives mostly as a human," he informed the Druid.

Raene curled a hand around his forearm. "I will adjust things so I can stand watch here. How often do you need me?"

"Once a year, child," the Druid replied, "for one turn of the moon."

"I return to the seas for longer than that, anyway." She frowned. "You didn't answer me. Will they return?"

"Not anytime soon. We hope." The tall, tonsured Druid twisted and retrieved a blade that had dropped when the trees stepped in to mete out their own brand of punishment. A quick glance reassured Aegir that the trees were only trees again, rooted firmly to the earth as if they'd never moved at all.

He barked a command in the Selkies' tongue, and the rest of the blades slithered across the ground to form a heap at his feet. They clanged and clattered, having a hard time lying still.

"Would ye like me to remove them from Arcadia?" he asked the Druid.

"Aye. We have no use for weapons as ye well know."

"Nor do we," Aegir said. "Magic is quicker and cleaner, and metal is...difficult for many of my people, but I can bury them in the sea. Make certain they're never raised against us again."

All around him, the trees began to rustle and sough again. The Druid narrowed his eyes. "We owe them for their assistance."

"It's a blood boon they need, isn't it?" Raene raised one russet brow.

"It is, indeed." The Druid looked as pleased as Aegir had ever seen him. Detaching a small blade from a sheath, he handed it to Raene. She turned toward the nearest tree, sliced the blade across her palm, and gripped the tree's rough trunk.

Power thickened around her, accompanied by the astringent salt smell of the sea. The air turned silvery as the tree accepted her offering. Aegir hurried to her side, took the knife, and repeated her actions. He wanted to ask how she'd known, except she said she'd seen the trees spring into action before.

He handed the dirk to the Druid and inclined his head. "If ye have no more need of us, we shall return to my island."

The Druid leveled his dark gaze on Aegir. "Ye were late arriving."

Aegir nodded. "True enough, but I shall remain until we are certain the Fae have given up their foolishness." He tried to look away, but Druid magic held him in place. He met the man's direct stare. He did not want to explain himself. The why of him being late was his affair and his alone.

He would select who to reveal it to, and it was none of the Druid's affair.

Insofar as the Druids were concerned, all creatures with magic should play a role protecting Arcadia, yet most didn't even know about the enchanted land. He was fairly certain the Celts were aware of its existence but didn't view preserving it as their problem. Most of the Celtic gods had their own special worlds, much as Arianrhod ruled over Caer Sidi.

Angus might not be aware of his origins, but Aegir knew them all too well. Angus's da was Cathbad, a Druidic seer who'd fallen out of time and memory at least a thousand years before. If this group of Druids realized the ancient seer's spawn was near at hand, they'd move heaven and earth to co-opt his presence, holding him on Arcadia and claiming him as their kinsman.

Aegir clamped his jaws tight together. The Celts relied on Angus's prophecies. They'd fight tooth and nail to hang onto him. The end result wouldn't be pretty. He'd consulted with his own father, and both he and the prior Selkie king were in full agreement. Angus wasn't their problem, and the Selkies would do well to steer clear of the whole, tangled mess.

His knowledge might have been a bargaining chip. A big one, but he couldn't have used it to convince Angus to leave Jonathan's memories alone. Doing so would have placed both himself and his pod at grave risk. If it had been anyone but the Celtic gods who'd shanghaied Angus, Aegir would have told him the truth. It didn't require seer ability to determine how such a move would play out, though.

Angus would jump through time and return to Cathbad—taking Johnathan with him. The Celts, beyond furious at losing their favorite lackey, wouldn't rest until they ferreted out who'd spilled the beans. Wouldn't take them long, not with their powerful magic.

Once they'd singled out Aegir, his life would be forfeit—or they'd turn him into a slave—and they might well wipe out his pod while they were about it. Depended how livid they were...

Power probed the edges of his mind. He held it at bay easily.

The Druid narrowed his eyes. "Keep your secrets, Selkie king. As long as ye honor your vow to keep Arcadia safe from harm, I require naught further from you."

Raene cast a questioning glance his way.

Before she could ask anything, he nodded at the Druid assemblage and aimed for a formal note when he said, "I'm as close as your call should need arise."

Amid murmured thanks, he gestured at Raene and walked toward where she'd left his blanket. Her energy pulsed beside him, warm and accepting, but he could feel her mind brimming with things she wanted to ask.

As was common with Arcadia, they reached the blanket far more quickly than on the journey away from its location.

Raene wrapped the length of finely woven wool around herself. Her forehead furrowed in thought.

"This is so strange," she murmured.

"What is?" He prepared magic to move them to Scotland's side of the barrier.

"How clothing comes and goes here." She stood taller and met his eyes with hers. The turquoise was more silvery in this light. "And the magic is so thick, I breathe it with every movement of my lungs."

He angled his head, regarding her intently. "Do ye find it unpleasant?"

"Nay. I'm beginning to view my power as a mostly untapped resource."

"'Tis, indeed, but ye've lived primarily as a human. They doona value what they canna explain."

She snorted. "It's worse than that. It frightens them. I've taken great pains to hide anything out of the ordinary."

"What do ye do, lass?"

She grinned. It lightened her features and made her unbelievably lovely. "I run a bakeshop in Wick."

He grinned back. "Splendid!"

"Why? What'd you have in mind?"

He opened his mouth to reply but shut it equally quickly. He'd been about to propose she teleport home and whip up some scones, but she owed him nothing. For him to assume otherwise would be wrong.

Now, if she offered to make them pastries or a meal, it was another matter entirely.

"Well?" she urged.

"Nothing." He focused the power he'd summoned. "Let's leave afore something else happens on this side of the veil."

"Good idea." She placed a hand lightly on his arm and rode the coattails of his magic to the island he'd laid claim to.

CHAPTER 6

Raene was so full of magic, she felt it each time she swallowed, each time she blinked. Every muscle movement, no matter how slight, reminded her of the enchantment she'd been a part of when the trees had joined the battle. How could she ever return to her bakery? Her simple life there—one she'd been more-or-less satisfied with—would feel flat, dull, uninspired.

I have a few months, she reminded herself. Not all problems required immediate solutions. Riding herd on her magic had never been a problem before, but maybe that was because she'd never used it much.

With Aegir's power surrounding her and her own pushing for recognition from within, she basked in waves of light shimmering around her as they came out in the same spot they'd left: the island's high point.

"Do you always return to the same place?" she asked.

He shook his head. "Ye control the travel spell, same as any other one. Arcadia has many gateways. We could have exited from any of them, but as the Arch Druid pointed out, I need to remain close enough to return quickly."

She pulled the blanket closer around herself. A chill air blew up off the North Sea. Not having clothes was an inconvenience, but she'd left hers in the cavern where her skin had lain.

He must have divined her thoughts because he said, "I havena much here, lass, but there is a robe if ye'd like to wrap yourself in it. 'Tisn't as warm as the blanket, but mayhap more convenient since ye can sash it."

She looked away, acutely aware of her nakedness beneath the blanket. "I never worry about clothes whilst I'm away from my bakeshop."

Interest flared from his eyes, more blue than green in this light, when he asked, "Do ye spend the entire time ye're not in Wick as a Selkie, then?"

"Aye. It's my only opportunity, and I take full advantage of it. I love my seal body. It's difficult to give it up when I return to my other life." Heat rose from her chest and over the top of her head. She'd never admitted how much her time in the sea meant before, not out loud and to another person, but then who would she have told such a thing to?

Approval flowed from him. She was still surrounded by his magic, and she felt it as keenly as if he'd used words. "Come with me. I'll find that robe for you. Ye willna have to keep hanging onto the edges of the blanket."

Part of her wanted to stay and spend time with him, but she had a mission. Finding Gregor was important, now that she had a name. "How hard will it be to locate my da?"

Aegir frowned. "Why do ye wish to? He broke our laws. If ye show up and identify yourself, his pod may kill you."

She took a step back and licked at suddenly dry lips. "I don't understand. He's who broke your covenant. Why would they take it out on me?"

"They know him. He's their prince, married to their queen. They'd assume ye were lying to discredit their liege."

"But they could use magic to determine I'm his daughter," she protested.

"They could, but they probably won't. Selkies are a rather reactionary lot. We live practically forever, and we enjoy sameness. 'Tis part of the allure of remaining in the sea. It's constant. A known quantity."

Aegir moved close enough to drop his hands onto her shoulders. "How old are you, lass?"

She screwed her face into a wry expression. "Never ask a lady her age."

"Fair enough, but ye've gone this far through your life without laying eyes on your da. 'Tisn't as if he'll claim you as heir to his line. He has other rightfully born children."

Sorrow arrowed into her heart and burrowed further, entering her soul. The truth was stark and harsh, and it hurt. She battled the quick stab of tears. Gregor had been a bastard to her mother. He'd set a spell that would have meant her death if she'd revealed his identity.

Raene forced herself to hold Aegir's direct gaze. "It makes no sense. I owe him nothing, yet I wish to see for myself who he is. Mum wasn't some simpering fool. He must have been special for her to take him into her bed."

Aegir moved to her side and guided her down a well-worn path. She assumed it led to the home he'd built deep within the heart of the island, but she didn't fight him. Not knowing who'd sired you would leave a serious hole in anyone's world, and she didn't apologize for her desire to meet her da.

Something he'd said reared up and slapped her. She came to an abrupt halt. "You know my da." It wasn't a question. Aegir had said as much when he'd revealed the existence of other rightfully born heirs.

He stopped and turned slowly until he faced her. "Aye. 'Tis an unusual name for a Selkie. He rules the next nearest pod."

"Where is it?" She started to place her hands on her hips, but the blanket slipped down her shoulders and she caught it before it bared too much of her.

"Come with me. Let me get you that robe, and we'll have something to eat—" he began.

"Where is the next nearest pod?" She inserted spaces between the words and didn't move.

Aegir narrowed his eyes. "I propose a bargain."

"What might that be?" She bit down hard on her lower lip. He had what she needed. It would save her oodles of time, and—

"Ye will accompany me to my dwelling. We will eat and

talk. Once I'm convinced ye're not going to run off half-cocked and get yourself killed—"

"That's a pile of crap." She punched the air with a fist. The blanket slipped precariously down one shoulder, but she ignored it. "You don't rule me." Another jab at the air when what she wanted to do was rain her fists against his chest.

"Nay," he agreed, "I doona." He took a measured breath. "But we've become comrades in arms. We've shared Arcadia, and it has created a bond betwixt us. I care about what happens to you, lassie."

"Don't lassie me," she hissed.

"Ye dinna let me finish a little bit ago," he inserted smoothly, not ruffled by her ire. She supposed kings got a lot of guff from their minions, though, so he must have had practice deflecting pissed-off Selkies.

"Once we've recovered from the battle with the Fae, I'll accompany you to Gregor's pod. We willna remain long, only till ye're satisfied." Before she could say anything, he continued. "Ye willna reveal aught about yourself. I'll merely say ye're my subject, and no one will look any deeper."

"I scarcely require an escort." She shook herself and repositioned the blanket. "I've been on my own for a long time."

"Aye, in this instance, ye do, indeed, require an escort," he corrected her. "Remember what happened when ye approached my pod? They dinna exactly welcome you with open flippers."

"Why didn't they?" she countered.

"I already told you, but it bears repeating. Lone Selkies are often spies for rival pods."

Her eyes widened. She'd heard him the first time but hadn't absorbed the implications. "Internecine warfare is common among us?"

"Not common, yet not so rare as all that, either."

Raene narrowed her eyes. "Why are you offering to help me?"

"Because it's important to you."

His words were so simple, and yet so powerful, they slammed into her like an out-of-control train. No one had done anything for her since long before she'd left her mum's home. A host of conflicting emotions battled for ascendency. Gratitude. Relief. Shame. Sorrow.

"I shouldn't require help," she mumbled. It was tough to talk around the thick place in her throat.

"Och, lass. We all need assistance at one time or another." He hooked a hand under her forearm and began walking again.

They continued down the hill and around a bend to an opening in a rocky cliff. It was cleverly concealed by magic and so unobtrusive she'd never have noticed it unless she were looking. A low tunnel opened into a rounded cavern lit with magical globes suspended in the air at strategic intervals. It was warm within, and the crackle of a fire drew her gaze to a hearth crafted out of a rocky wall. The flames must be magical because there was nothing much to burn on the island.

Colorful cushions were scattered atop a thick, patterned rug. An alcove held kitchen accoutrements. Aegir vanished behind a curtain at one side of the cozy space, and she walked to the ledge holding a couple of pots, various herbs gathered into bundles, and an icebox. She pulled the door open and peered within. Cheeses and other items that weren't immediately identifiable lined the small space.

"Here you go." Aegir tapped her shoulder. When she turned, he held out a woolen robe lined with shearling.

"But this is too nice," she protested. "Besides, then you won't have anything to relax in."

"'Tis fine. Take it, please." He pressed it into her hands and walked to the hearth, crouching in front of it with his back toward her.

Raene recognized he was offering her privacy. She let go of the blanket and slipped her arms into the plush robe's sleeves. It felt heavenly against her skin, and it held Aegir's musky scent. She belted it around herself. "I'm decent. You can turn around."

She folded the blanket and bent to place it on top of a cushion.

He rose and turned slowly. A smile spread across his face. "Looks better on you than it ever did on me. What did ye find in the kitchen? I can go fishing if we're thin on provisions. And I'm happy to cook for us," he hurried on. "No need for ye to trouble yourself with—"

She cut off his flow of words with a gesture. "I like making food. It's why I chose to open a bakery. Do you have flour?" At his nod, she continued. "I can make us biscuits with cheese in them. Fish would round out a meal nicely."

He bowed, sweeping one arm to the side. "Back verra soon. Fish are easy."

She grinned. "Aye, because you'll take to your seal form."

He laughed along with her. "Ye know me too well, lassie, and we've only just met." Still laughing, he trotted smartly out the door.

She felt a flare of magic with his unique signature all over it, and understood he'd shifted. Too late, she realized, he'd said he had flour but hadn't told her where. She tried telepathy. It wasn't second nature to her, so she hoped he'd hear.

"Bottom of the stack of bins," floated back in response to her query.

Raene scanned the tidy counter. Aegir had taken advantage of a natural stone shelf and built around it. A cone-shaped affair maybe two-feet high sat in a corner on the floor. She squatted in front of it and pulled the door open. A blast of heat puffed out.

She shook her head in amazement. She hadn't been aware Scotland had much in the way of geothermal activity, but Aegir had harnessed the earth's power to create an oven. She'd wondered how she'd manage to bake biscuits, but the answer was right in front of her.

Rising to her feet, she located a bowl, found the flour, and grabbed a wheel of cheese and butter from the icebox. This time, she looked more closely and located a block of sea ice melting in a ceramic bin. She'd known the apparatus was an old-fashioned cold box, but years had come and gone since she'd seen refrigeration that didn't come courtesy of gas or electricity.

As she worked, shaving bits of cheese with a sharp knife, and mixing everything with her hands, she wondered how Aegir and his pod did things in their usual environment. Did they live beneath the sea? She assumed they did, but seals had to breathe, just not very often.

The pump handle delivered seawater, and she rinsed dough debris off her hands. She needed a bit of liquid for her dough, and salt water would serve two purposes, so she sprinkled in enough for the mixture in her bowl to hold together. Another search yielded a large, cast-iron skillet. She shaped the biscuit dough, pressed it into the pan, and slid it into the oven. Since she wasn't certain of the temperature, she'd have to keep a close eye on things.

She was just rinsing her hands again when Aegir hustled inside, his hands full of two good-sized fish, their scales still shiny with droplets of ocean water. He crinkled his nose. "Mmm. Smells wonderful. Ye located the oven, I ken. Mostly, I wanted you to know I'm back. I'll just dress these and put them on a barbeque affair I rigged near the cave."

"What are you burning for fuel?"

He chuckled, looking young and carefree for a moment. "Magic, lass. What else?"

She wiped her hands on a square of terrycloth hanging

from a nearby hook. "Is that what powers the oven?" She nodded toward its corner.

"Aye. What did ye suppose created the heat?" He furled his brows.

"Geothermal activity. The oven is on the floor, so I assumed you'd found a way to take advantage of what lies beneath."

"In a manner of speaking, I did. I crafted a funnel to pull heat from the liquid layer just beneath the earth's crust. Doesn't require much energy from me to keep it ready whilst I'm here. I cut the flow afore I leave."

The smell of baked bread sent her scurrying to oven level. When she opened the door, the biscuits were indeed done. Each sat in a pool of delicately melted cheese. Raene folded the terrycloth to make a hot pad and drew the skillet out of the oven.

"And now it smells so delectable," Aegir said, "I'll have a hard time forcing myself back outside to cook the fish."

"If you cleaned them, we could cook them in the same pan," she suggested.

He sent an approving glance skittering across the expanse of the room. "Grand idea. Back in a flash. Ye might want to poke your head outside. It finally stopped raining, and the sunset is glorious, but it willna last for long."

Raene followed him out of the cave. Breath caught in her throat. The sky was alight with reds and oranges with burnished golden edges. Aegir had moved to the shore and was hunkered down to split the fishes' bellies.

"Thank you," she said. "It's gorgeous."

He glanced up at her. "I thought ye might enjoy it. Scotland's skies aren't always gray."

Raene laughed. "Only maybe 80 percent of the time, but it makes the other twenty that much more memorable." She stood watching the sunset until the colors began to fade. Aegir had been right. The entire display didn't last more than ten minutes. She shivered. His robe was warm, but an icy breeze blew off the turbulent sea.

"See you back inside."

"Aye, lassie. I'm nearly done."

She hurried into the cozy cavern and moved the biscuits to the stone ledge after brushing it off. By the time Aegir returned, the pan was empty and ready for the gutted fillets, and she'd chopped some herbs for a garnish. A pat of butter on top of the herbs, and she pushed the skillet back inside the oven.

Dusting her hands together, she said, "Won't take long. Fish cooks quickly."

He moved past her to the pump and got the water flowing to wash his hands. She tossed the terrycloth square his way.

"Would ye care for spirits with our meal?" He hung the towel back on its hook.

"Are they crafted with magic as well?" she asked with a smile. It was hard not to smile around Aegir. His aura shone around him, brilliant with color.

"Och, I'd love to claim full credit, but my Selkie kin keep this place stocked. All of us spend time here supporting

Arcadia. I may have built this cavern, but the others all use it."

"I'd love a glass of something," she said and bent to check on the fish. It was bubbling. Almost there, but not quite. "I'll get plates ready for us. I found them whilst I was hunting for the skillet."

He opened a cupboard she hadn't noticed before because it blended in with the dirt and rock walls and drew out a bottle and two tumblers. She split two biscuits each for them and spread butter between the layers. The pastries smelled so good, she couldn't resist sampling a few crumbs.

"I saw that," he called from in front of the fire where he was arranging cushions and pouring amber liquid into glasses.

"Had to make certain I wasn't about to poison you," she pointed out, managing to keep a straight face.

When she peeked this time, the fish was done. She set the skillet nearby and transferred thick chunks of Arctic Char to their plates. Balancing a fork on one, she crossed the room and handed it to Aegir before returning for the plate she'd made for herself.

Raene sank to the cushion next to Aegir's, picked up her glass, and said, "Slainte!"

He clicked his glass against hers and drank. She did as well. When she dug into her meal, she realized how long it had been since she'd eaten. It was a challenge to take her time, not plow through her meal like a pig before a trough.

"These are amazing, lass." He waved a corner of a biscuit at her before popping it into his mouth.

"They did come out rather well," she said. "Perhaps the magical oven added something to them."

Aegir snorted. "Aye, well if that's so, it never happens to what I place inside. I'll have to have a chat with…well, with something."

Raene got up and retrieved two more biscuits, dropping one on each of their plates when she returned. "There's so much I want to know, it's hard to pick a place to begin. First off, what does ocean-marked mean?"

He angled his head to one side. "And who mentioned that phrase to you?"

Raene clenched her jaw, preparing herself for the worst, for hearing it was the curse she'd feared. "Mum. She told me I'd been ocean-marked after my first shift."

Aegir nodded. "'Tis a good thing. It means the Selkies have put their mark on you, and that ye'll feel an urge to return to the sea."

Breath swooshed from her. "Is that all? Can it be so simple?"

"Aye, lass. What did ye suspect it meant?"

Raene rolled her eyes. "Because Mum said it, and she was obviously upset about me shifting, I assumed it was some kind of curse." She took a measured breath. "Moving on here. Do you live beneath the sea?"

"Aye. My pod has a palace of sorts on the western side of Scotland a few leagues off the Hebrides chain. Because 'tis underwater, it's simple enough to add to it if we require additional space. Coral is verra accommodating."

"It's made of coral?" Wonder filled her, along with a desire to see a Selkie palace.

"And stone. And magic."

"How does that work?" She leaned closer. "Not the magic but traveling back and forth to the surface to breathe."

"The magic takes care of that part. Whilst we're within the palace, or even close enough to see it, we're able to breathe underwater."

Raene chewed and swallowed the last bit of fish on her plate and considered what he'd said. "Does it work that way for all Selkie pods?"

"Aye, and for other magical creatures who visit us. Until early today, we had a small boy who'd been with us since his birth."

Understanding ran through her. "The child I saw in your mind. The one you…" She faltered. "All I could see is he's no longer with you. Did he die?"

"Nay, lass. Although, that might have been easier. His father came for him. 'Twas part of a bargain struck long ago. He would spend his first two years with us—and his mum."

"I did see a woman. Surely, she went with the boy and his da."

Aegir shook his head but remained silent.

"How could any mother—?" she began.

He placed a hand over one of hers. "Doona ask, lassie. Some secrets must remain so."

"You're still sad. You'd rather have kept the boy. Raised him."

"All true, but not within my control. What else would ye like to know?"

She drained the rest of what had turned out to be a fine, old brandy from her glass and held it out for more. "Why do Selkies prefer to be in their seal form?"

"'Tisn't a short answer for that one."

She leaned back, balancing on an elbow. "We have time. At least I think we do. Unless the Druids sound the alarm bells again."

"I propose a trade." His blue-green eyes twinkled.

Her body came alive, intensely aware of how close he was to her. Not that she'd been immune to his raw sensuality before, but something in his tone got her blood flowing. "What kind of trade?"

"Once I'm done, I would hear about you."

Raene held a neutral expression, but disappointment cut deep. She got hold of herself fast. What had she hoped for, anyway? That he'd be so overcome by her charms he'd want to bed her? He was the Selkie king for chrissakes. He probably had hot-and-cold running women vying for the opportunity to share his bed.

"If ye'd rather not—"

"I've nothing to hide," she said. "And my story's not as interesting as all that. Of course, I'll tell you what little there is to know about me." Her tone was clipped, not quite as warm as she would have liked, and he shot her a look she couldn't interpret.

He tipped the decanter into his own glass. After a quick trip to the ledge for more fish and another biscuit, he returned to his spot next to her. Raene reminded herself he was only here for now, and perhaps tomorrow. Once he'd escorted her to Gregor's pod, he'd walk out of her life.

And she'd eventually return to her shop in Wick. While she never actually looked forward to picking up the threads of her human existence, this time it would be far harder.

Och, I need to get over myself.

"Is aught amiss?" he asked.

"Nothing at all. Now, about why most Selkies remain in the sea…?" She left her thought unfinished to encourage him. This was the best opportunity she was likely to have to find out about her seal nature, and she'd be a fool to waste it mooning over what could never be.

He set his empty plate aside and arranged his cushions so he faced her squarely, rather than the fire. "Unlike other varieties of Shifters, Selkies are born in seal form in the sea…"

CHAPTER 7

*A*egir didn't want to intrude, but it was hard to hold himself back from scanning Raene's mind. Something had changed in her a few moments before, but he had no idea what spawned the alteration in her mood. Perhaps he could risk a quick examination if she was more focused on the words flowing from his mouth than on his actions.

It was a pretty big "if." He'd have to wait and see. She'd asked a question that cut to the heart of what it meant to be a Selkie.

"Not only are we born in the sea. Were it not for the Celts, we'd have remained there, rarely if ever bothering with our human bodies." He took a breath and a deep swallow of brandy before continuing. "The Celts are a meddling lot, and they've done naught but grow worse with the passage of time. Long ago, when humans still believed in magic, they worshipped the Celtic gods, and the pantheon drew a part of their power from that adulation."

Raene propped an elbow on one knee and supported her chin with a hand. "Hold up a moment. I had no idea the gods were anything beyond the purview of mythology. Beyond that, I wasn't born in the sea, but at home. Or so I've been told."

Aegir smiled. "Ye were there, but not in such a way as to remember the conditions of your birth. Your mum, she was half human?"

"Aye, she couldn't shift, and the lack always caused her sorrow."

"I ken her pain. The sea would have sung to her, called her, yet no matter how hard she tried, she wouldn't have been able to produce the transformation. Ye may not know this, but ye were born in the sea, and ye were a seal when born."

"But how could she have raised me? Fed me?"

"I dinna say ye remained in your seal body. Like as not, ye shifted as soon as she cradled you in her arms. Betimes, it happens so quickly, she may not have realized ye began as a seal. Childbirth is hard, painful. When a woman is immersed in birth pains, she misses things. Plus, she couldna see beneath the water's surface." He hesitated, unsure whether to add what had to be true, but Raene was astute and sensed his omission.

"You left something out. Tell me."

"Gregor must have been there. He'd have had the magic to

coax you from your mum's womb, and the power to ensure ye could shift to human and back again."

Pain inscribed small lines at the corners of Raene's eyes. Aegir wanted to comfort her but didn't know how. He'd given her new information, but she'd have to come to terms with it on her own. Nothing he could say would ease her path.

"So he was there, but then he left?" She turned her liquid gaze full on him.

"Aye. If not him, then the Selkie who served as midwife for their pod, and I doubt it would have been her since Gregor had many reasons to hide his dalliance from his subjects. How old were you when ye first remember shifting?"

"Eighteen."

Surprise shot through him. "That old? 'Tis unusual."

"I wouldn't know. Mum wasn't nearly as excited about it as I thought she'd be. She'd always wanted to become a seal, so I assumed she'd be thrilled for me. Instead, it was the beginning of the end of our relationship." Raene hesitated. "When she was dying, she told me she was afraid for me. Worried that me shifting might attract Gregor's attention."

"I can see how it would be a concern."

"Enough about Mum and me. Go on." She took a swig from the brandy, a determined expression on her face. She'd kicked this door open and would see it through. The respect he was developing for her took a giant leap forward. Selkies tended to look down on the ones who chose humankind over the Sea Folk, but Raene had substance—and courage.

And she'd never had anyone to teach her about her Selkie blood. Until now.

It took him a moment to remember where he'd left off with the Celtic gods. "Aye, lass. So the Celts grew restless. They'd have left Earth if aught better awaited them on the borderworlds. Many did leave, but most returned. There are a few exceptions, like Arianrhod."

"Which one is she?"

"The virgin huntress who rules the moon and tides." Aegir took a measured breath. "Turns out the virgin part is so much tripe, but 'tis neither here nor there. She has a special world within this one named Caer Sidi. 'Tis where she cares for the moon and ensures its pull on the tides."

Raene closed her teeth over her lower lip but remained silent. Aegir was grateful. He didn't want to lie to her, and he wasn't sure exactly what she'd seen in his mind. She did say she'd seen a woman, so perhaps an image of Arianrhod had been there, along with Jonathan and Angus. Not that she'd know the woman with floor-length silver hair and mismatched eyes clad in hunting leathers was the virgin huntress.

"The Celts were lonely," he went on. "Even absent human prayers and offerings, they had power to burn, and they coaxed us from the sea to have magical beings to talk with beyond themselves. Other Shifters exist, but their magic pales in comparison with ours."

"Is that why they're human most of the time, and hardly ever in their animal bodies?"

He nodded. "Have ye met any?"

A soft smile played around her mouth. At least she didn't look as if she'd been gutshot the way she had after he'd delivered the news about her da. "Aye. I grow restless sometimes and wander the moors beyond Wick. When I'm there during the dark hours, I've met wolves who aren't wolves, hawks and eagles who were more than they appeared as well.

"Did ye ever speak with them?"

"Nay. But I sensed what they were. Magic shimmered around them, and if I looked from a certain angle, I could see their human shape. I have another question for you."

"Go ahead." He steeled himself, hoping it wasn't about Arianrhod. He'd been an idiot to use her as an example.

"When did all this happen, with the Celts?"

Her question was easy, and many degrees removed from anything personal. Relief coursed through him. "Long ago. Magical folk are tied to the makings of the world."

"It couldn't have been all that long. Humans only stopped believing in magical goings-on around the middle of the nineteenth century or thereabouts."

"True enough, but the Celts laid the groundwork for controlling the Sea Folk a thousand years before by seducing our women." He sucked in a tense breath. "We produce very few children. Part of that is because we are so long-lived, but we are also not very fertile. In any one pod, 'tisn't unusual for a century to pass without any births. The Celts promised us children, and matings with them did produce new Selkies, but Selkies with slightly different magic."

"Makes sense. From a genetic perspective," Raene murmured.

"Aye, but no one knew about such things back then. The infusion of their particular brand of magic made it far harder to refuse them when they called us from the sea. The song of the sea is strong, but so is Celtic power. In the end, 'twas simpler to acquiesce to the Celts, even though it meant more time on land. The transition dinna happen all at once, ye ken. But over hundreds of years, we gradually ended up where we are today."

He paused, turning something over in his mind before adding, "They havena been nearly as present these past fifty years—give or take a few. At least not with my pod. We've seen so little of them, I was wondering where they'd gotten themselves off to."

"Intriguing. What else would I have learned if I'd grown up in a Selkie pod?"

"How to employ your power. The history of all other types of magic wielders." A thought occurred to him. "Ye said ye've seen the trees rise in defense afore. When did that happen?"

A conflicted expression marred her even features. "At the time, I didn't understand." She looked at the glass she held rather than at him. "I was taken captive by a man who knew about how vulnerable we are without our skins."

A guttural noise, more growl than anything else, burst from him. "Tell me where to find him. I'll—"

Raene waived him to silence. "He's dead. I was wife to him for close to fifty years, and he wasn't an evil man—other than how he came by me in the first place. He told me he'd watched me enter and leave the sea for months before deciding he couldn't live without me. It was only then he visited a local hedge witch, and she's who gave him an incantation to locate my skin."

"Still. It wasna right. If he wasna already dead, I'd hasten his egress from Earth. How'd ye escape?"

"I wrested secrets from him whilst he lay dying—including where he'd hidden my pelt. My magic had weakened greatly without it, yet he was so ill, what little I had left was sufficient."

She blew out a breath. "You'd asked about the trees. When I didn't have time to change bodies and play in the sea—or it was broad daylight—I'd taken to swimming in a loch close to where I'd hidden my skin. Willows grew thick about the water as they're wont to do. Though I remained human to swim, the nearness of my skin was reassuring. One day, I felt a disturbance from the far side of the loch. It was horrible, and my connection to my pelt blew up in front of me."

Aegir moved a hand to her arm. "Go on, lass."

"I was stupid. I should have run, but instead I swam as fast as I could for where I'd left my skin. By then, the trees had closed around Rolf, and I couldn't sense my pelt at all."

"I'm surprised the trees dinna kill him."

"They would have, except the witch must have prepared him—or else he figured how to outsmart them himself. By then, he'd built a barrier around my pelt, crafted from Black Magic. The type wicked witches employ. And he'd hidden himself within its folds as well. The trees couldn't penetrate it. Judging from what I saw today with the Fae, Rolf must have constructed his safety net before the trees attacked."

"Ye said ye couldna sense your pelt."

Raene bobbed her head. "Aye, but it had to be in the middle of that stinking, hideous dark magic. For one thing, that was where I'd left it. I'd heard stories of Selkies' skins being taken, but I had no idea how long it would be before I was whole again."

"What happened next?"

She shrugged. "Eventually, the trees retreated. It was only later I learned if I'd shared my blood with them, they'd have tried harder to protect me. I raced to Rolf, except then I didn't know his name, and demanded my skin. I punched him and kicked him and bit him, but he sloughed it off and dragged me away from there to his village. It was a different one from mine, not that anyone would have stepped forward to help even if they'd known what transpired. It was the 1800s, and women had no rights at all."

"I'm so sorry." His heart beat harder. Trapped between outrage and horror at what she'd suffered, he'd have done anything to erase her pain. Had she been part of a pod, they'd have hunted for her when she didn't return. And they'd have moved heaven and earth to locate her skin and see her reunited with it.

She sat straighter and pulled her arm out of his grip.

"Don't be. He was kind to me—once I stopped trying to run away." She skinned her lips back from her teeth. "I'd have poisoned him in those early months, except then I'd never have found out where my skin was."

"But you knew," he protested. "It was next to that loch."

"Same as I thought, but 'twas the first place I looked when I ran away, and it wasn't there any longer. Or perhaps the dark power had finished its job hiding it from me." She turned her hands palms up. "All I know is 'twas in a far different spot when I finally reclaimed it. The Black enchantment must have run its course because my pelt called to me once I was close."

Aegir shook his head. "I suspect the enchantment was linked to Rolf. Once he was gone, it would have departed as well."

"He wasn't quite dead when I found it. I had to make certain he'd told me the truth before I hastened his death." An uncomfortable expression rippled over her even features. "He was dying, anyway. I didn't rob him of more than a few days of life."

"No one is finding fault, lass. Least of all me." Aegir extended support, letting it flow from his mind into hers. "He deserved far worse than he received. If ye'd been part of a pod, they'd have punished him for his crimes."

"I guess those are things I would have learned if I'd grown up with someone who knew about Selkie magic—or magic at all." Her words were wistful.

"Aye. But 'tis never too late to begin. Power runs strong in you, and ye've an intuitive grasp of how to maximize it."

She frowned. "How could you know that? We've only just met."

"We fought side by side. No quicker way to take a man's mettle—or a lassie's—than in battle." He offered a smile. "But I may have cheated, a little."

The corners of her mouth twitched. "How's that?"

"I'm used to looking within our kind. Sorting what I need to know, and your spirit is pure and resilient."

Color stained her cheeks, and she looked away. "Thank you."

He still hadn't figured out what had bothered her from earlier, nor had he had an opportunity for a bit of surreptitious sleuthing. Whatever it was, she seemed to have moved past it, and he didn't want to upset her all over again by bringing it up.

"Anyway," she went on. "Once I had my skin back, I took to the sea and remained there for a long time. That was when I found your pod, but they made it clear they wanted me to leave. So I wandered and swam with no particular aim or goal other than a determination no one would ever separate me from my skin again."

She drained the remnants of brandy from her glass. He offered the bottle, but she shook her head. "I've had enough. Eventually, I emerged from the sea, but in a different spot. The Orkney side rather than the Hebrides, where I was originally from. That was when I settled in Wick and eventually got my bakery going."

Raene got to her feet and picked up the plates, carrying them to the pump.

Aegir sprang upright and ran lightly to her side. "Leave those. I'll take care of them." He gathered the remaining biscuits and bent to return them to the oven, cutting the flow of magic that kept the enclosure warm.

"I should go."

He tried to mask the dismay that punched him in the guts. He didn't want her to leave, but he had no hold on her, either. He aimed for a neutral tone. "Where will ye go?"

She shrugged. "Not sure. Is your offer to accompany me to where Gregor is still, uh, good?"

"Of course. I gave my word."

"How long before you don't have to stick so close to Arcadia?"

"Perhaps a fortnight."

"I'll return then." She started for the entry.

Aegir stared after her. She couldn't just walk away, yet she was doing exactly that. He, who'd always planned out his every move, threw his carefully scripted life aside and ran after her. She was already outside by the time he caught up and called her name.

She stopped but didn't turn around. "Did you forget to tell me something important? Don't worry. I'll leave your robe far enough up the beach the tide can't get it."

He reached out, desperate for the touch of her, but

stopped before his fingertips grazed her shoulders. He had no idea what he was asking for when he said, "Please."

Something about the tone of his one word, part entreaty part prayer, must have startled her because she did turn then, her brows drawn into a worried expression. "Is something wrong?"

What to say? How to tell her why he'd run after her when he wasn't certain himself? He opened his mouth, but nothing emerged. He'd become so adept at hiding his true feelings about everything, the only phrases that sprang to his lips were platitudes. He'd actually begun to tell her all was well, and he'd see her soon, but he didn't need to be out here for that.

"I—I doona want you to leave." He choked the words out, and they sounded garbled over the rush of the sea.

She angled her head to one side. "I don't understand. Why not?"

His heart beat a tattoo against his ribcage. He had to tell her the truth, not some trumped up story. Besides, what could he possibly come up with that made sense. He did touch her then, placing a hand lightly atop her shoulder. "I like you, Raene. Ye're different, and I want a chance to get to know you better."

There. He'd gotten at least some words out.

He waited, but rather than smiling or looking pleased, she closed her teeth over her lower lip. "It's not a good idea."

"Why not?"

"We have two very different lives. I'm not about to spend more of the year than I already do in the ocean, and you're not going to take up residence in Wick above my wee shop. Besides," she plowed on, "you're the Selkie king. Doesn't that mean there are lots of women waiting in the wings to be queen? Obviously, I wouldn't know such things, but isn't Selkie royalty determined by some kind of birthright?"

"Nay. Other than a king, the only other leadership in a pod is its council, and it's comprised of twelve Selkies who are elected every four years. The council advises the king, and if he's wise, he listens to their advice."

"Is there ever a queen, not linked to a king?"

"Nay. Unless the king in question died an untimely death. Gregor's pod had a widowed king who died, leaving a daughter. ''Tis how Gregor became a prince by marrying her." He hesitated before adding. "At the time, many of us thought two royal deaths strange. Selkies are long-lived, and to lose both a queen and then the king within a short timespan seemed...unlikely."

"Did anyone investigate?" Raene drew her brows together.

He shook his head. "I know not. It wasna my pod, and what I just shared falls into the realm of gossip passed from one Selkie to another."

"Doesn't seem fair. Not about Gregor so much, but about there not being queens unless a male relative dies."

"Patriarchies are as old as time. Not that they're right, but our system predated 'equal rights' by millennia." Aegir raked hair back from his face and shook it over his shoulders. He tipped her chin up with an index finger so she had to look at him. "I've never married. Never met anyone I wanted to spend my lifetime with. Coming after you was hard for me, ran against my better judgement, but I did it anyway."

"Why?"

"Because ye've become important to me. Too important to let you go without making certain ye ken how I feel."

Raucous trumpeting sounded from a distance but grew rapidly closer.

"What the hell is that?" Raene scanned the cloud-laden darkness with magic that shone about her in a silvery mist. "Are we in danger?"

Excitement filled Aegir as he, too, scanned the skies. "Nay, lass. No danger. Not for us. 'Tis a dragon, and I suspect it's seeking me, otherwise it wouldna have left Fire Mountain."

"A dragon?" Raene's voice turned into a high-pitched squeal. "Impossible. They're not real."

"If we are, why can't they be?"

"I don't know. What's Fire Mountain?"

"Does this mean ye're staying?" he asked.

"Are you fucking kidding me?" She laid a hand over the one he still had on her shoulder. "Leave and miss my only chance to see a living, breathing dragon?"

He laughed. "Love your honesty, lassie. I'd rather ye remained on account of me, but I'll take any concession I can get."

Raene clapped a hand over her mouth. "I'm sorry. I didn't mean to hurt your feelings. My social skills are way more than rusty. They barely exist."

"Doona fash. I was teasing."

The beat of powerful wings joined the dragon's roar. He could see the creature now, a massive blood-red dragon with spinning golden eyes, and it was headed right for them. "I know her," he told Raene. "'Tis Tarika. She's actually a dragon shifter. Her human half is Britta Kilkerran, Countess of Cumbria."

Raene moved to his side and gripped one of his hands. She was probably scared, but he welcomed her touch no matter how it came to be.

Still bugling like a mad thing, the dragon touched down lightly a few meters away. He walked close with Raene by his side and bowed. "Welcome, Tarika, and Britta as well."

"I started with your pod." The dragon's voice was rich with echoing overtones. "Your sire told me where ye were. Ye must come. There are problems."

Aegir bowed again. "I canna. I am bound to Arcadia for some days yet."

Fire spewed skyward. Aegir was grateful it hadn't been aimed at him and Raene. "Your sire will be here soon enough to take over. Ye must come with me now."

"Why?"

"Do ye question me?" More fire lit the night sky.

"No, Mother of Dragons, and one of Fire Mountain's First Born." He kept his words low and respectful.

Raene edged off to one side, pulling her hand from his. "I was just leaving."

"Think again!" Another blast of fire, except this one hit

the beach a meter in front of Raene's bare feet. "Ye're a Selkie. Ye're coming too. I can carry the two of ye."

"Carry?" Raene squealed. "I can't ride a dragon."

"'Tis a great honor, lass," Aegir told her, thrilled and excited almost beyond words at the prospect of flitting through the skies on Tarika's broad back.

"We're wasting time. Get on," Tarika commanded. "Now."

"Will we need our skins?" Aegir asked.

"Aye. Give them to me, I shall keep them safe while we fly."

"I can't," Raene sounded frantic.

"Ye must," Aegir told her. "It's not wise to anger a dragon by refusing a direct command."

To set an example and, hopefully, establish trust, Aegir retrieved his skin from behind its enchantment and handed it to Tarika. He went to Raene, who looked as if she'd frozen in place. "Lass, the dragon doesna want your skin for nefarious purposes. Wherever we are going, we will need our seal bodies."

"I know. I'm scared, but I'll get it."

He felt the bite of Selkie power, and Raene marched to Tarika, pelt thrown across her arms. She didn't say a word as the dragon took her skin.

Tarika puffed steam until Raene was surrounded by it. "That ye've trusted me speaks well for you, little Selkie. I shan't betray your faith in me."

"I hope not." Raene turned back toward Aegir.

He gripped her hand and hustled around to the dragon's side. "She's huge. How do I—" Raene began.

Tarika twisted in an athletic maneuver that belied her bulk and lifted Raene, tossing her sideways as she instructed, "Grab my horns."

Aegir focused a blast of magic and rode it to the dragon's back. Raene sat, legs splayed and hands holding onto the dragon's neck horns so hard her knuckles were white. He settled behind her and wrapped his legs and arms around her trembling body.

"It will be all right," he whispered in Raene's ear.

"Of course it will," Tarika trumpeted. "No one's ever fallen off me. Not yet, anyway."

Aegir waited for the rush of air as the dragon lifted off. He'd said enough. Questioning Tarika wouldn't bring answers any faster than she wanted to provide them. Raene was still shaking. He wanted to reassure her, but the dragon would hear telepathy as easily as she'd picked up on his last attempt at comfort.

Instead, he opted for a wee bit of history. Surely, it would please Tarika to hear him relate the saga of her people.

"Long ago, afore Earth existed," he began, "the dragons made their home in Fire Mountain..."

CHAPTER 8

aene pried her eyes open sometime after the dragon left the ground. Air swooshed past, but something about the architecture of the dragon's wings protected her and Aegir from the worst of the slipstream flowing past them. Heat rose upward from Tarika's scaled back, warming her.

Turning her pelt over to the dragon terrified her, but it was done. No going back. Besides, the dragon had no use for a Selkie wife, so maybe she was safer than she believed.

After she remembered to breathe, her sense of teetering on the brink of fainting receded. The unbroken beat of dragon wings coupled with Aegir's story about the first dragons had a steadying aspect. Fire Mountain was a borderworld, separated from Earth by a barrier only dragons or those given dispensation by dragons could cross. Apparently, the Celtic gods were an exception to that rule. A

117

land of heat and light, it consisted of a ring of active volcanoes and caves. Within one of them lay a single spring. It was sufficient for the dragons and the herds of wildebeest who provided food for them.

Raene relaxed, leaning back against Aegir. The way he'd surrounded her body with his own was tantalizing. She'd been thrilled—and surprised—when he'd asked her to stay, but she hadn't been playing hard-to-get when she'd refused. She'd had time to assess the attraction she felt for him. Everything she'd told him was true. Their lives were too different. Beyond that, his kin would never accept her, an outsider, as their liege's mate.

She drew herself up short. He'd only said he wanted her to remain so he could get to know her better. He hadn't said one word about marriage or mating or anything permanent. For all she knew, his interest didn't run deeper than a roll in the hay. He said he'd never married, but surely he'd had dalliances.

The dragon had been silent since ordering them to mount her. They flew high enough, clouds floated beneath them and the night sky was shot with millions of stars. Black and beautiful, it tugged at Raene's soul.

Behind her, Aegir cleared his throat and said, "Tarika. I could be of greater assistance were ye to give me an idea where we're going and what ye expect of me."

"Ha!" The dragon blew flames that lit the night. "A curious man."

"I admit to curiosity." Aegir's reply was smooth and edged

with the tiniest bit of compulsion. "But I'm worried too. Is this a task where I shall need to put out a call for reinforcements?"

"If I needed brute strength, I'd have tackled this with other dragons." Smoke joined the fire eddying from her open mouth. "We have all agreed with Danu's covenant."

"Aye, we have. Which part concerns you?"

"The prohibition against genocide."

Where Aegir's body had been fluid behind her, it firmed as he sat straighter. "Which race of magic-wielders are ye considering annihilating?"

"Yours."

Any pretense of ease Raene had developed departed fast. "Why Selkies?" she demanded. "What did we ever do to dragonkind?"

"Probably better if I handle this, lass," Aegir whispered into her ear.

If he hadn't been sitting between her and the whirling abyss below the dragon, she'd have told him to go to hell and run off into the night. As things stood, she didn't have that option. Anger and fear twisted her stomach into an unpleasant knot.

"Are ye going to let him run circles around you?" Tarika demanded.

"Um, are you talking to me?" Raene managed to push words past her dry throat.

"Who in the goddess's name else would I be talking to? 'Tisn't as if there's much of a choice."

Rather than delve into Tarika's question, Raene repeated her earlier query. "Why Selkies. What did we do?"

"Stole a dragon youngling."

"But that's scarcely possible," Aegir cut in. "We canna get to Fire Mountain without your express dispensation."

"True enough," Tarika huffed. "The young dragon has always been a handful. He discovered a spell to split the veils and left our world. By the time we discovered his absence, many days had passed."

"How old is this missing dragon?" Raene asked, assuming it would be something like a human toddler.

"Only ten years, as we count them, so twenty of yours," Tarika retorted.

Raene started to say the dragon could take care of himself but thought better of it.

"The dragon ran off and joined a Selkie pod?" Aegir's words were edged with incredulity. "How?"

"The same way as any magical creature can breathe beneath the water when in proximity to one of your castles," Tarika snapped back.

"Not exactly what I meant," Aegir said in as neutral a tone as Raene had ever heard from him. "Dragons are fire-bound. Selkies are ocean-marked. I'm not seeing the attraction. Sure, he can breathe underwater, but he can't play with his fire."

"Aye, well, ye'll have to ask him—assuming the Selkies will return him."

Something about her tone caught Raene's attention. "You've already asked, haven't you?"

A blast of fire was followed by. "Of course. I always try the simplest route first. Why involve others unnecessarily?"

"Wait a minute," Aegir broke in. "Ye asked for your youngling back, and someone refused? Who would be so stupid?"

Tarika brayed what might have been bitter laughter. It was hard to tell. "Which is precisely why ye're here."

"Is he your child?" Raene asked.

"Nay, but as one of the First Born, I'm tasked with maintaining order and safety for all dragons."

"Did ye draw the short straw on this mission?" Aegir asked.

"'Twas my turn," the dragon replied.

"I'm glad ye have a system." Understated humor ran beneath Aegir's words. "We have them too, but they rarely work as designed. Which pod has your youngling?"

"The one nearest you. We're nearly there. I figure ye must know them."

Raene stifled a gasp. Before she could say anything, Aegir tightened his hold on her. She recognized it as a warning to keep quiet but didn't understand why. Tarika's earlier comment about letting the other Selkie run circles around her rose to taunt her.

Raene held tighter to the dragon's neck horns. "You might not want to bring me along, if that's the case."

"Why?" Tarika's question held a clipped quality.

"Because I'm an illegitimate daughter to the liege for that pod. No one knows about me."

"He does." The dragon puffed smoke.

"Aye, but I've never seen him."

"Let's see," Tarika mused. "As I recall, Selkies take a dim view of mating outside the bonds of marriage. Is that still true?"

"Aye, 'tis," Aegir answered.

"The penalty used to be something like death or banishment," Tarika went on.

"It still is."

Dragon bugles filled the night sky until Raene let go of the horns to clap her hands over her ears.

"I don't understand." Raene turned her head to talk with Aegir.

"Ye just handed her leverage to get her youngling back." Aegir didn't look pleased.

"What's wrong with that?"

"Your own life may be forfeit. Instead of Gregor's. We've covered that ground."

Raene swallowed hard. "I don't understand." But then what he'd told her earlier flashed through her mind. About how Gregor's pod would do away with her—the evidence— before harming their liege.

"Never mind." She blew out a tight breath.

The dragon wasn't bugling anymore. "Never fear, Selkie. I shall see to your safety," Tarika said in somber tones. "Ye've just given me a bargaining chip."

"Don't take this wrong," Raene said, "but how certain are you that your young dragon will want to return?"

"Och, he probably doesn't, but this isna about what he wants. 'Tis about loyalty to his kind and doing the right thing."

Raene started to say she hoped that type of reasoning worked better with dragons than humans, but decided she'd be better served to remain silent. The dragon had to be ancient beyond reckoning. Surely, she knew what she was about.

"We will ensure your safety," floated through her mind in an unfamiliar voice.

"Who are you?" Raene asked.

"Britta. Tarika's human shifter mate."

"I don't understand," Raene sputtered. *"You're two different, uh, people?"*

"Indeed we are. When my body is primary, the dragon resides within me."

"They're not like us." Aegir had obviously been listening in. "We are the seal and the seal is us. We have a single consciousness, where they maintain two."

Fascination gripped Raene. *"Do you always agree?"* she asked Britta.

A cascade of silvery laughter filled her mind. *"Of course not."*

"Enough," Tarika snapped. "We shall arrive verra soon. I will land, and then we will enter the water."

"Bad idea," Aegir said.

"Explain yourself." Tarika's words could have etched stone that had been scorched by her fire.

Behind her, Raene heard breath hiss from between Aegir's teeth. "Your primary weapon is fire, Madame Dragon. Underwater, that weapon will become useless. Selkies are far more maneuverable in our home environment than you, primarily because ye're so much larger."

"Instead of telling me why it won't work, come up with a better strategy." Tarika sounded as if she were holding tight to her temper. Raene assumed no one ever stood up to her, questioned her, or challenged her proposals.

"I will summon Gregor and whoever he chooses to accompany him. He canna refuse me. We will meet in a spot on land of our choosing, not his."

"I knew there was a reason I brought you along, other than in case my negotiations slid off the rails." The dragon laughed, puffing steam into the dank night air.

Raene scanned the horizon. Grey lined the eastern sky. It wouldn't be night much longer. Unbelievably, she'd grown comfortable astride the dragon. No longer worried about falling off—or being tossed aside—she'd relaxed enough to delight in the impossible.

Not that there was anyone she could tell, but she wished her mother was still alive. Kari's eyes would gleam with keen interest, and she'd mine for details, so she could reconstruct what dragon-riding had been like. Sadness for her recent loss filled her with regrets for all the misunderstandings.

At least I got to see her, hold her, before she died.

A rocky coastline spread before them. Raene leaned to

one side, picking out aspects of the barren land. "Where are we?"

"Siberia," Aegir answered.

A surprised-sounding gasp burst from her. They hadn't been flying all that long. Either Tarika had made far better time than the fastest jet, or magic played a role in their journey. Probably the latter.

"I'd have had a hell of a hard time getting here on my own," she murmured.

"The only way would have been to teleport," Aegir agreed. "For that, ye'd have required a destination."

She twisted her head so she could see him. "Which you would have supplied."

He offered an equivocal expression without actually answering her.

"Hold tight," Tarika instructed moments before she banked hard right and circled to land. The transition from airborne to an icy shoreline happened faster than Raene had expected it would, but this was a dragon not an airplane.

Aegir's magic built around them. She'd grown used to the feel of his power with its salt scent of the sea and leaned into it without thinking things to death. He moved them to the ground. Absent the dragon's heat, she began to shiver.

"Aye, lass. 'Tis cold here on a summer's day, and we're far from summer."

"I can fix that," Tarika turned and puffed steam until it surrounded them. Along with the steam, Raene's pelt fell into her arms. Aegir collected his as well.

He batted the thick steam aside. She peered through the hole he'd made and saw ice-crusted water extending many meters into the ocean. The ice had frozen in waves that matched snow sastrugi decorating the beach in spots. Jagged black rocks rose behind them.

He frowned. "There's a cave not far from here. I've met with Gregor and others from his pod there."

"Why not in the sea?" Raene asked.

"More of an equal playing field. My father was liege then, and 'twas his idea to hold a meeting on shore rather than in the center of Gregor's power."

"I always liked your father," Tarika observed. She made shooing motions with her taloned forelegs. "Where is this cavern? Sooner we get there, the sooner we can summon him."

"This way." Aegir narrowed his eyes. "I was trying to figure out if ye'd fit within."

"If not her, then me," Britta spoke up.

The dragon tilted her head back and painted the sky with fire.

"None of that." Aegir's tone was sharp. He followed it immediately with, "Sorry, First Born. I'm not planning to tell Gregor ye're here—until he shows up. If I do, he'll put two and two together immediately—particularly, since ye've already tried to get your youngling back—and he might refuse to leave the sea. 'Twould be verra unfortunate. Akin to throwing down a gauntlet challenging my pod to warfare."

The dragon's protective cocoon of steam had dissipated. Raene's teeth began to chatter. "The cave?"

"Over there." Aegir pointed at the rocky crags. He set an enchantment around his skin. Raene did the same before they set off toward the cliffs.

Her feet had turned to chunks of ice. She'd have sold her soul for a pair of fur-lined boots. Or any shoes at all. She was almost too cold to be relieved to have her pelt back in her possession. They covered the distance to the band of cliffs quickly. One moment, she saw Aegir, the next he'd vanished between two impossibly tall boulders. Made sense the entrance would be hidden by magic. She opened her third eye and followed the trail he'd left. The air turned brilliant with shades of blue and green around her. The scents of sunbaked clay, rosemary, and cactus flowers joined the kaleidoscope of hues.

Raene was nearly through the opening when a tall, well-muscled, red-headed woman joined her. Though she was naked, she wasn't shivering like Raene. A set of golden eyes brimming with humor regarded her.

"Well, Selkie, do ye not have questions?"

"You must be Britta. Did all those wonderful scents belong to your shift magic?"

The same silvery laughter she'd heard before surrounded Raene. "Aye, 'twas my magic, and I am Britta. Tarika may have fit within, but she'd never have made it through this opening."

Raene battled an inane desire to bow her head to the regal

creature with red curls that fell to arse level. Instead, she hurried inside. A mage light bobbed next to Aegir, illuminating the interior of a sizeable cavern. The walls were covered with iridescent lichen. Water dripped down from the ceiling, forming pools along the sandy floor.

Aegir bowed low, going to a knee before he rose. "My lady. 'Tis been many a long year since we've met."

"That it has. Good to see you, Aegir, although I could wish for more auspicious circumstances."

"Me as well." He stood aside and tilted his head at a series of chests lined up against the wall behind him. "The Selkies keep clothing in those. Ye might wish to avail yourself of their contents."

"Convenient," Raene said and strode past him hoping she'd find something warm for her feet. They'd hurt like hell when blood came back into them, and her Selkie side was pushing hard for freedom. It had layers of blubber—and no human feet to worry about.

Whoever stocked the chests had a methodical soul. One held trousers. Another sweaters and jackets. The third held boots in enough sizes, she located a fur-lined pair that fit perfectly.

Britta had joined her. "I'm not cold, but humans have an odd sense of propriety when it comes to me remaining naked."

"Selkies as well?" Raene asked and quirked a brow.

"Och aye, they're the worst." Britta laughed again and moved on to the chest with trousers.

"If I'd known where we were headed," Aegir told Raene, "I'd have insisted ye take something more of mine than the robe."

"It's all right." Not blessed with Britta's lack of modesty, she'd pulled pants on beneath her robe and turned toward the wall to layer on a sweater and thick woolen jacket. Last, she tugged a hat over her head and ears.

"Are we done with the fashion show yet?" Tarika's voice blatted from Britta, accompanied by smoke and fire.

"Stop that," Britta told her bondmate. "We doona want it to stink of dragonfire in here."

Aegir knelt before a cold hearth. There wasn't a stick of wood in sight, which wasn't surprising since trees probably didn't grow in this cold, barren place. Rocks lined the firepit, and he coaxed them to life with magic until they glowed a deep red.

He stood and dusted his hands together. "There. That should help explain any residual fire smell. Is everyone ready?"

Raene nodded and then asked. "Should I, um, cloak myself somehow?"

"What do ye think?" Aegir asked Britta.

She tilted her head to one side, regarding Raene. "Well, this Gregor person surely willna be expecting his daughter, yet one of those with him may well be suspicious enough to scan us with magic. To be safe, I'll include her in the spell I spin about myself. The one that will shield what I am from Selkie curiosity."

"How long will it take?" Aegir asked.

"Moments. Go ahead and summon your kinsman."

A snort burbled past Aegir's lips. "I willna make it sound like a summons, and I hate to acknowledge such as him as kin."

"If that pesky Selkie gives us any trouble at all about my dragon"—Tarika commandeered Britta's vocal chords again—"ye can kiss those fancy clothes goodbye."

"Och aye, léannan." Britta's voice was soothing. "Doona shift afore ye must."

"I make my own decisions," the dragon retorted.

Raene wondered what it would be like to share a bond with something that ancient. Or that powerful. The specter stole her breath, and her wits. She was more than happy with her seal. She and it were one and the same. No arguments. No dual consciousness. Only a single point of view.

Aegir returned to the fire and knelt once again. He held his hands in front of him so the palms faced one another and curved his fingers, creating unbroken arcs. He chanted low in Gaelic, and something like a display formed between his cupped hands.

In the center, a black Selkie with silver markings took shape. "Aegir. To what do I owe the pleasure of your presence in my cave?"

"'Tis been too long, Gregor. I bring tidings. Would ye meet with me?"

"Of course. Join me in the sea, brother. My palace is always open to you." Long whiskers twitched.

Raene stood off to one side, hopefully beyond Gregor's field of vision. What would he say next? This father of hers who was worse than no father at all. Whenever she thought about how he'd threatened her mother with death, anger swamped her.

"Easy." Britta breathed the word into her mind. *"I have a harder time masking strong emotions."*

Until now, Raene hadn't felt the link with the dragon shifter because her magic was subtle. *"Sorry."*

"Better," Britta murmured. *"Hang onto the place ye are right this moment."*

"I would love to accommodate you," Aegir told Gregor, "but my wife is with me."

"So? Surely, she can enter the sea as well. We've quite a banquet laid out. You'd be our honored guests."

"Too kind of you." To his credit, Aegir managed to look chagrined. "My wife isna one of the Sea Folk." He took a breath and dove into a lie so blatant Raene's eyes widened. "My pod no longer welcomes me, and I would talk with you of many things, yet not via telepathy. As ye well know, we could be overheard by fell things. I am recently returned from Arcadia and a battle with the Fae."

Gregor wrinkled his snout in what might have been consternation or a frown or any one of a hundred other things. Raene hadn't spent enough time with Selkies to read their expressions.

"I understand, brother. I shall arrive shortly with a few of our kinsmen."

Aegir inclined his head. "Thank you, brother. I appreciate your willingness to accommodate my needs."

Gregor barked laughter. "I'm looking forward to meeting the woman who lured you from our fold. She must be something."

"Gentle seas, brisk wind, and plentiful fish," Aegir responded as he substituted a Selkie greeting for responding to Gregor's snide implication.

"Same to you," Gregor said.

Next to Raene, Britta drew more magic. Less subtle this time, it shimmered about her. When it settled, she was blonde, blue-eyed, and had a vixenish look.

Aegir brushed his hands along his sides, dispelling his impromptu screen. He twisted to face them. "Sorry, but I had to come up with something quickly. Ye'll be my wife?"

Britta laughed. "Of course. He'll have no way of knowing my people call me the Iron Maiden."

"Och, I'd forgotten that." Aegir rolled his dark eyes.

"And I shall be her Selkie handmaid," Raene said. "If you have such things."

"Ye can be her lady's maid." Aegir addressed his next words to Britta. "Could ye thicken up the enchantment around Raene?"

Power settled over her like a mantle. When she glanced down at herself, her hair had turned black, and her skin was a deep, coppery shade.

"Now we wait," Aegir said.

"Not for long," Britta countered. "They're nearly here."

*A*egir did his damnedest to appear relaxed, normal. Britta moved to his side, once he straightened from his crouch, and slipped a hand in his. Next, she rested her head on his shoulder. She was a good partner in crime, and an excellent actress. He began to let himself believe they could pull this off.

Once Gregor and his minions showed up, the dragon would swathe the cavern with magic. If he remembered anything about Tarika, no one would leave until she got her dragonling back.

The air grew liquid with the salt scent of the sea and the soft, mossy touch of Selkie power. Gregor had never been particularly strong magically, but he had a ruthless side that more than made up for his lack. The Siberian pod had once coexisted with his own in another segment of the North Sea.

They'd only moved thousands of kilometers to the east after Gregor took the helm.

Aegir had never understood why, and Krise had told him not to question good fortune.

He curled the edges of his mouth into what he hoped looked like a welcoming smile. Britta leaned in toward him and whispered. "Och, and shall we invite him to a threesome?"

It broke through Aegir's tension, and he laughed. "Now there's a thought, lass."

Shimmery waves rolled through the cave. It had grown warmish from the hearthstones, and Aegir was glad for Raene. Her lips had begun to develop a bluish cast outside, and her feet had turned white. She hadn't complained, just hobbled inside the cavern and dressed quickly.

Salty spray joined the multihued magic swooshing through the cave. He dialed up the lumens in his mage light to make certain nothing snuck through with Gregor and scuttled into one of the many dark corners to hide. Small, wicked things could do a great deal of mischief, and were damned difficult to catch since they could move fast.

Goblins, gremlins, Faeries, elves, and leprechauns could be especially nasty, and who the hell knew what Gregor kept for pets these days.

Gregor took shape first. He was powerfully built with black hair that spread across his shoulders. Shrewd, close-set dark eyes scanned the cave. He didn't bother with a smile, but that was Gregor. Never one for social niceties, the Selkie considered most everyone less than worthy of his consideration.

In short order, three more Selkies shimmered into view. Aegir knew two of them. Johannes and Viko were Norse brothers with white-blond hair and ice-blue eyes. They sported muscles even more impressive than Gregor's.

Gregor covered the distance between himself and where Aegir stood with Britta molded to his side. He raked his gaze over Britta and offered a lecherous grin. "Well, I can see why you captured Aegir's attention."

Aegir looked meaningfully at Gregor's swelling phallus. "Get dressed, man. I'll not have my wife subjected to your lechery."

The other Selkie laughed and patted his cock. "I'm sure she's used to male attention. Aren't you, honey?" He started to reach for Britta, but Aegir blocked his effort.

"Get dressed." The command could have scraped glass.

"You're scarcely in a position to bargain," Gregor noted. "Didn't you come specifically to join my pod?"

"We'll discuss it," Aegir said coolly, "once ye're dressed."

The other three Selkies had been bent over the clothing chests. None of them had done more than drag trousers over their damp legs. Johannes and Viko nodded at Aegir. He nodded back.

"Who are you?" he asked the Selkie he hadn't recognized.

"Brock."

"How is it we've never met?" Aegir pressed.

Gregor hadn't made any move to cover himself. "You don't

know every Selkie," he told Aegir. "I imported Brock. He came highly recommended."

"For what?"

Brock pushed his shoulders back. Red hair streaked with silver fell to midback, and he trained very green eyes on Aegir. "I am master magician to this pod. I ensure no harm befalls us."

Aegir narrowed his eyes in the man's direction, thinking he couldn't be much of a magician if he'd missed the undercurrents of dragon magic eddying through the cave. Britta had done a fine job masking her true nature, but anyone worth their magical salt—a master magician, for example—could have sniffed her out.

He risked a quick scan with his own power and nodded pleasantly to conceal his dismay. Brock might be wearing a human face, but something wicked and ancient lay beneath. He wanted to warn Britta, but perhaps she'd already figured it out.

"And who is this?" Gregor's dark eyes zeroed in on Raene.

Huddled next to Britta, she'd kept her face hidden.

"My maid," Britta replied in crisp tones. She'd adopted an American accent with overtones of the South.

"Perhaps she's up for a spot of fun." Gregor chuckled. "Gets boring with the same faces day in and day out."

Aegir pushed shock and revulsion from his mind. Had things changed so much in this pod that Gregor was obvious about cheating on his mate?

"Come on, sweetheart. Be a sport." Gregor sidled closer to

Raene, nostrils flaring. "She's no maid. What's one more cock?" He wrapped a hand around his jutting appendage.

Aegir stepped between them, bristling with barely controlled rage. If he didn't watch it, his anger would get the better of him and he'd land a punch in the middle of Gregor's lecherous smile. "I dinna bring my wife and her maid for your entertainment," he gritted out.

"Fine, mate." Gregor moved back a couple of paces. "I'll have plenty of time to...explore these two once you've joined us."

Aegir pressed his mouth into a thin line. He could keep the charade going, or they could dive right into why they were here. Movement caught the corner of his eye. Brock was edging away from the lighted areas of the cavern. His glamour had slipped a little, enough to reveal bulging green eyes, a long snakelike tongue, and pointed teeth, all of which vanished as soon as Aegir looked his way.

"What the hell?" Aegir blurted before he could stop himself.

"Whatever are you referring to?" Gregor asked.

Johannes and Viko flanked their liege, eyes trained dead forward in thousand-yard stares as if they'd been hypnotized.

Britta unhooked her arm from his and stood straight. Power flared, so bright Aegir squeezed his eyes shut. The smell of sunbaked clay nearly choked him as robust power poured through the cavern. He pried his eyes open as fast as he could and saw a pulsing crimson vortex surrounding the cave's perimeter with Tarika dead in its center.

Brock had given up any pretense of humanity. Where he'd stood was a creature unlike anything Aegir had ever seen before. A leonine head with a tawny mane of fur surrounded a reptilian face. The huge green eyes were squarish, and a forked tongue slid in and out of the thing's mouth. It's lower body was more equine than anything else with four squat legs. Each ended in a pointed black hoof that looked as if it could do a lot of damage.

Rather than trying to escape as Aegir had predicted, Gregor stood tall, head thrown back. "If you wanted to declare war, there are more direct ways." He scrunched his face into a frown. "Is the dragon shifter truly your mate? Now, that would be a coup. I've heard they're into sex any way they can get it."

"Silence!" Tarika roared, punctuated by a staunch blast of flame.

"You stand on my ground," Gregor countered. "I'd watch those commands, if I were you."

"And I'd watch stealing what belongs to me and Fire Mountain," Tarika retorted.

Raene had moved next to Aegir. She threw her shoulders back and regarded her father with bitter eyes. Britta's disguise still cloaked her. "What a bastard you are." She spat the words.

Aegir caught her eye before she said anything that might reveal who she was.

The leonine creature suddenly sprouted wings. Long and green, they didn't match anything else about him. What the hell kind of magic stood behind such fluid shifts? Could the thing take an infinite variety of forms?

Tarika spun to face the winged horror and blasted it with dragonfire. Aegir expected it to go up like a torch, but the fire sloughed off its hide, frittering to nothing. It's mouth spread in a simpering grin displaying double rows of razor-sharp teeth.

"Where'd you really get him?" Aegir shot the question at Gregor.

"Hell. Where else? All the really good monsters come from there." Gregor tossed his head back and laughed uproariously as if he'd made a wonderful joke.

The thing Brock had morphed into took a step toward Tarika, observing her through narrowed eyes. She spread her wings, fanning the air, and stared back. Usually, no one could meet a dragon's whirling gaze and not get swept up in its spell, but the winged horse-lion wasn't having any trouble.

It feinted left and then back to the right.

Tarika wasn't wasting any more fire on it, but she never moved her gaze from the abomination. Black-rimmed lightning exploded around it. When the lightshow cleared, a miniature version of Tarika faced off against her. It opened its mouth, and a gout of fire emerged, hanging suspended in the air in front of it.

"Shield yourselves," Tarika warned just before the whirling maelstrom circling the cavern moved inward. It slid harmlessly past Aegir and Raene before forming a barrier around the thing that had been Brock, Gregor, and the Norse brothers. Sparks flew when a sword materialized in Gregor's hand. Power sheeting from the blade had a greasy, wrong feel about it.

"This is why ye moved away from the North Sea." Aegir skewered Gregor with the full force of his outrage. "Ye parlay with evil."

"We all do," Gregor replied coolly. "I'm just more obvious about it." He sliced from side to side until a gap opened in the vortex. Johannes and Viko ran through. Gregor joined them as the gash swooshed shut with a cry like a hunting falcon who'd just sighted prey.

"Isn't this cozy?" Gregor, who was still buck naked, sashayed toward Aegir and Raene. "Brock will keep your dragon shifter entertained while I make short work of you."

"Aye, I never liked you, either," Aegir sneered while casting about for something he could use as a weapon.

"I must admit to curiosity about why ye came, but the dragon clinches it. She must want her young one back. The old bitch is certainly persistent. I'll give her that." More peals of malevolent laughter told Aegir how far Gregor had sunk into madness.

"Ye have no right to dragonkind." Aegir kept his tone mild.

Gregor shrugged. "Brock found him for me. We'll break his mind, and then he'll serve as a weapon for us."

Raene had darted back toward the clothing chests. Good. She'd be out of harm's way. Aegir lifted both hands and summoned power, letting it flow into him from the earth beneath his boots. Other magic threaded itself with his.

Raene's. She was helping.

Brightness flashed and flared as he rocked on the balls of his feet, light and nimble. Gregor swung his saber. Aegir jumped over its trajectory easily and sent what should have been a killing blow directly into Gregor's chest. The other Selkie—or whatever he was these days—stumbled back a few paces but recovered fast.

He dove forward, blade slashing downward this time. Aegir leapt aside, missing the blow, but not by as comfortable as margin as before. His heart rate accelerated. This would be a fight to the death. One of them wouldn't walk out of here.

So far, Viko and Johannes had done nothing but stand on either side of their liege. Were they even capable of independent thought, or had Brock bewitched them somehow?

Fire flew back and forth between Tarika and the faux dragon, amid bellowing and strident cries. The air thickened with steam and smoke until breathing became difficult. He couldn't pay any attention to the dragons, though. Gregor was warming to his swordplay role. Remaining out of the path of his blade was taking all Aegir's stealth and speed, with a magical assist layered over everything.

He hoped Raene had taken cover near the floor of the cave where breathing would be easier. The sword whistled past. He jumped and twisted midair, but it still caught the edge of his upper leg, slicing cleanly through trousers and flesh. The wound stung and burned far more than it should.

Poison.

The blade must be coated with poison. Aegir sent a river of magic to create a barrier between his body and where the sword had cleaved through his flesh. Fury burned a path from feet to head. He dug deep and threw magic at Gregor's head, aiming for his vulnerable eyes. One burst from its socket. The other caught fire.

Good! If the bastard couldn't see, evading his sword would become much easier. Gregor screeched, a high, thin cry, and his body arched like a bow before falling to the ground. Aegir stared and bolted forward, willing his gaze to pierce the murk filling the cavern.

Her glamour gone, Raene straddled Gregor's back. Her face had twisted into a rictus of agony as she plunged a dagger into his back, withdrawing it and sinking it time and again. "I'm your daughter, you son of a bitch," she shrieked as she drove the knife home.

Akin to marionettes that had just been animated, Johannes and Viko rushed them from either side shrieking imprecations in an Old Norse dialect.

Aegir swept up the sword that had fallen from Gregor's hand and hefted it. He may have known both men, but whoever they'd been had departed long since. One mighty swing separated Viko's head from his neck. Blood geysered, coating everything in its path. Aegir twisted to deliver the same blow to Johannes, but the Selkie fell to his knees.

"Please, Master. Deliver me from evil."

His face was downcast. Aegir said, "Look at me."

When Johannes raised his face, it was drawn into a mask

of pain. "Being dead would be an improvement over how I've had to live. Do it."

"Can ye be redeemed?"

The Selkie's blue eyes sheened with agony. "I don't know, but I shall try my damnedest."

"We are too few to squander ourselves." Aegir dropped the blade and snarled, "Do not make me sorry."

"I won't, Master."

"I am not your Master. Selkies bow to no one."

Aegir turned his attention to Raene. Tears streamed down her face as she stabbed the lifeless body of her father again and again. Blood splattered her hands, arms, and face. He knelt behind her and held both her arms. "He's dead, Raene. Stop."

"I can't." She surged forward, but he held her in place.

"Tarika needs our help. Get up. Ye can mourn later. Where did the dirk come from?"

"It was in the shreds of Britta's clothing. Pah." She spit on the bloody mess between her legs. "Mourn that piece of dung. Never. The world is a better place now." She looked square at him and grinned, showing bloody teeth that made her look wild, feral. "I've avenged Mum. Wish she was here so I could tell her."

"She knows, lass. Believe me, she knows."

Dragon bellowing rose in intensity. The smoke was even thicker now.

"Get out of my way," Tarika commanded, her words teeming with compulsion only a true dragon could command. And she was one of the First Born of dragonkind.

Aegir rose to his feet and dragged Raene upright with her still clinging to the dirk. Through the smoke, he could make out the faux dragon. It was on fire and burning merrily. Whatever warding it had mustered must have failed. It morphed back into the leonine creation and then into Brock.

His red and silver hair was a smoking ruin, and his skin blistered. He held out both hands. "I concede, Madame Dragon." His tone turned silky. "You must not kill me. I'm the only one who knows where your young one is."

Short, hard blasts of laughter pulsed from Tarika. "Are ye so stupid, ye doona understand I can find my own without any help from anyone. Even if my youngling is buried deep within your wicked power, I will find him. Ye doona deserve to live, Hellspawn."

"Send me back. Um, please." He batted at a spot the flames had worked their way down to bone on his forearm. "I promise—"

"Promises from the likes of you are worthless," Tarika proclaimed just before a rolling gout of fire ignited around what was left of Brock. It burned hot and fast, leaving a pile of cinders where he'd stood.

Aegir glanced at Johannes. The Selkie crouched right where he'd been before. That he'd made no move to escape to the sea told Aegir all he needed to know. Evil couldn't corrupt everyone, and Johannes had retained enough of his Selkie nature to resist complete contamination.

Tarika huffed steam and magic. The air cleared. "By all the dragons who ever flew," she trumpeted, "'twas far harder than I anticipated. The demon had grown strong because he was borrowing Selkie magic from Gregor and the other two hand over fist."

Aegir draped an arm around Raene who was weeping silently, still clasping the dagger. He squeezed her shoulders and then let go to walk over to Johannes. "Get up," he instructed.

Johannes rose unsteadily to his feet, keeping his gaze downcast.

"Talk," Aegir said. "Has the entire pod become corrupted?"

"Nay, Master, uh, Aegir," Johannes said and shook himself from head to foot as if dispelling a heavy weight. "They will rejoice."

"Who will become king?"

"I know not," Johannes replied. "Gregor shared power with no one."

"What of your council?"

"He disbanded it after we moved from the North Sea."

"What of the queen? Or his children?"

Johannes shook his head. "She died of shame. His children fled. No one has heard from them in the last hundred years."

Aegir raked his sooty hair back from his face. Selkies did best within their familiar pod formation. He placed his hands on Johannes's shoulders. "Return. Tell them what has happened. If no one wishes to lead, your sisters and brothers are welcome to join my pod until a new leader takes up the mantle."

"Ye can tell them yourself," Tarika spoke up. "We must enter the sea. 'Tis why ye brought your skins along. Once I'm closer, I will know where my dragon is, and I will bring him home."

"Quite a lesson for him," Raene muttered.

"Aye." Tarika laughed bitterly. "I bet adventure-boy never puts so much as a claw outside the boundaries of Fire Mountain for the next ten centuries."

"Will he be all right?" Raene pushed her shoulders back until they were square and looked at Tarika.

The dragon nodded gently. "Aye. We dragons are a tough lot. Thank you for caring enough to ask."

Aegir unzipped his jacket and laid it aside. "Ye doona have to accompany us," he told Raene.

"I'd rather be with you than holding court with that." She jerked her chin at what remained of Gregor and shook her head sadly. "How could Mum have ever fallen for him. He's rotten through and through."

"He wasn't anywhere near this wicked in years past." Aegir reassured her as best he could. "He was always high-handed and arrogant, but this full-blown swan dive into evil is fairly recent. It happened long after he threatened your mum with death if she revealed his infidelity."

"How's your leg?" Raene angled her gaze to his shredded breeches.

"'Twill be all right." He stopped shy of mentioning the poison. He'd caught it in time, and it was oozing from the wound. A dip in the sea would complete the healing process.

A sharp blast of magic laced with silver, gems, and gold announced Tarika's shift back to Britta. The dragon shifter shook out her red mane and strode to Raene, wrapping her in her arms. "All will be well," she crooned. "Ye did the only thing possible under the circumstances. 'Twas right and fitting he die by the hand of one with his blood. It ensures he willna enter the *Dreaming* but will wander forever, lost in Hell's halls."

"Thank you," Raene mumbled.

Britta let go of Raene and held out her hand. The dirk jumped into it. "'Tis a magical weapon, and it sensed your need. 'Twas why ye found it within the ruins of my clothing. 'Tis always with me when I am in my human body. Tarika gifted it to me long ago, and it somehow survives the shift."

Aegir shed the remainder of his garments. Once Raene and Johannes were naked, he led them outside to the icy shoreline. He dropped the enchantment around his pelt; Raene did the same. He called enough shift magic for both of them.

Johannes was on his own in the latter department. Aegir assumed he had a spot where he usually hid his pelt.

Britta waded into the ice-shrouded salt water next to the Selkies. Her lovely face was set in grim lines. "Let's get this over with, shall we?"

Aegir barked at her, ducked beneath an ice floe, and swam

for where he felt the Selkie pod's magic. Raene had been strong and brave and resolute. Before, he'd asked her to stay because she fascinated him, but now he was falling in love with her.

Aegir put the brakes on hard. She'd just lost her father. He was dead by her own hand. If he approached her now, she'd assume he felt sorry for her. He swam faster. He'd have to pick a better time. One not tinged with loss and death and battle-guilt.

Would such a time ever exist again?

He didn't want to think about it, but he had little choice. Evil was rising. Had other pods fallen prey to its pull? He'd consult with the Druids on Arcadia once they returned. Seers, one and all, perhaps they'd hold the answers he sought.

Beyond that, he had no idea how many Selkies were in Gregor's pod. If they all wanted to join his, his existing pod would have to make some fairly serious accommodations.

But he was getting ahead of things. He girded himself. Just because Johannes didn't believe any of the others had embraced darkness didn't mean they hadn't.

"Watch yourselves," he warned.

"Och, as if I hadn't already figured that out for myself," Britta replied.

Raene didn't say a word, just positioned herself slightly behind him. His heart went out to her, but she'd proven herself a warrior today. You didn't coddle warriors. You stood shoulder to shoulder with them and plotted battle strategy.

CHAPTER 10

Raene swam mindlessly, plowing through the chilly water. It wasn't easy to keep her mind clear. If she relaxed her guard for even a moment, she was right back in the cave plunging the knife into Gregor. That it was a magical knife said a whole lot. Yet it hadn't acted on its own. Britta had said it sensed her need and jumped to fulfill it.

Did I hate him enough to want him dead?

The question gave her pause. She'd hated Rolf in those early years, and she hadn't hesitated to cut the last few days off his life once he'd revealed where her skin was. He was dying anyway. Maybe that was why she hadn't lost any sleep over easing him across the veil.

What she'd done to Gregor was cold-blooded murder, though. An act driven by fury and fear. Air bubbled from her blowhole. She let go of the iron grip she had on her mind, determined to replay what had happened. She'd been crouched on top of the shreds of Britta's borrowed clothing sending as much magic as she could to assist Aegir.

At first, he'd done well avoiding Gregor's blade, but either he was tiring, or the sword held otherworldly magic that was getting a feel for his evasive maneuvers. It might have been the twentieth swing or the thirtieth, but she recognized Aegir's reaction was a split second too slow before he did. She cried out before the sword nabbed him, but maybe he was so intent on his adversary, he didn't hear her. Blood spattered, so she knew the blade had bitten deep.

After that, things grew fuzzy. She'd lunged to her feet, a nasty-looking dirk with a six-inch serrated blade gripped in her hand. How it got there was anyone's guess, but she didn't question her good fortune. Instead, she cloaked herself with invisibility. Gregor was fixated on Aegir, and the other two Selkies may as well have been dead for all the good they were doing anyone.

She'd circled around behind Gregor and launched herself onto his back, thrusting the knife deep before he could react. She aimed between his ribs and right into his heart, twisting the blade in a circular fashion before jerking it out to do it again.

And again.

And again.

In a distant part of her mind, she'd known he had to be dead, but she couldn't make herself stop until Aegir put his arms around her and held her back. Had the blade been driving her?

It was a convenient theory, but far too simple, and it ignored her part in Gregor's death. Her hatred may have ignited the dirk's bloodlust, but it had kept right on stabbing, powered by her out-of-control disgust and contempt for the thing that had been her father.

Raene backed up a step or two. She'd sprung into action to save Aegir. He was in trouble once he'd been wounded. No way to maintain the leaps and twists that had been keeping him out of the blade's path.

Raene clung to that last thought. It made the rest bearable. She'd caught the stench of poison from the longsword, but Aegir seemed to have neutralized it. If he'd been cut too many more times, though, he wouldn't have been as fortunate.

She shook herself from head to tail tip. It was over. Done. If the same scenario presented itself, she'd do the same thing all over again. She cared about Aegir. She couldn't have stood by and done nothing while her father sliced him to ribbons.

And Gregor would have done just that. If her father had ever held a scrap of humanity, it was long gone. Every line of his muscled body had bled determination. Determination to kill. Determination to rule.

A chill settled around her heart. She'd been dead set on finding Gregor. All by herself.

What a fool she'd been.

Aegir must have known at least some of what Gregor had turned into. It had to be why he hadn't been forthcoming about the other Selkie's location. And why he'd offered to come with her. Not that he'd really given her any choice. If she wanted to lay eyes on Gregor, her only option—other than thrashing around the seas and hoping for the best—was to go with Aegir.

She'd thought him manipulative at the time, but her world view had shifted radically. He'd been trying to protect her without blurting out an unpleasant set of truths.

No child, not even a grown one, wanted to face evidence their parents were evil. She probably wouldn't have believed Aegir. Would have chalked his assessment up to an old feud, or rival pods, or some explanation other than that he was right.

She turned hard left after Aegir and Johannes. Britta swam next to her, bubbles trailing from her mouth and red hair swishing around her, courtesy of the currents.

"Have you found the young dragon yet?" she asked Britta.

"Aye." The dragon shifter turned golden eyes, shiny with seawater, her way. *"We're heading straight toward him."*

"Does he know we're coming?"

"Nay. I canna break through the enchantment with words. I've tried."

Raene considered asking a few more questions. Things like whether Britta was confident she could rescue the youngster, but she held silence. Tarika shared Britta's consciousness. Between the two of them, if rescue were possible, they'd find a way.

Light shimmered through the waves in blues and greens and violets. Raene moved her head from side to side trying to figure out what they were. Some types of sea vegetation held an iridescent quality, but nothing like this.

A structure came into view, but it was unlike anything she'd ever encountered. White and pink coral had been piled into columns to create partial walls. Within them, magical globes were the source of the light that had caught her attention.

Johannes swam ahead. Aegir waited for Raene to reach his side. *"This must be the Selkie castle,"* she said.

"Aye, lass. Ye've not seen one afore?"

"How would I have?" she replied. *"I've never been part of a pod."*

"Ye might have stumbled upon one. They're not hidden."

"Come with me." Britta's voice held urgency, and she swam quickly parallel with the coral wall. Her limbs churned water, turning into a blur, but Raene had no difficulty keeping up.

Aegir paced both of them. *"Where is he?"*

"Here." Britta sank to the ocean floor and directed magic at it. Sand, dirt, and rocks flew through the water. A chasm formed and grew deeper as she dug.

"How can we help?" Raene asked Aegir.

"Not sure." He swam in a circle around where Britta had created a hole many meters deep.

"Britta!" He made his voice sharp. *"Hold up. Ye'll never get through that way."*

"*But he's here,*" she protested. "*I feel him. Not much farther now.*"

"*We must neutralize the evil holding him prisoner. Once we do that, he'll come to us.*"

Britta stared at the gap she'd opened in the ocean floor. If it ran much deeper, she'd hit the earth's crust. "*So, he's not down there?*"

"*Nay. He is close. Even I feel dragon nature other than yours in this place, but Brock or Gregor layered dark power around his prison. If they hadna done so, yon dragon would have left on his own. What is his name?*"

"*Glaedr.*"

Aegir began to chant, using his sea voice and the Selkies' language. Raene recognized the incantation and joined her voice to his. As they sang together, asking Poseidon and Amphitrite's assistance to rid the sea of impurities and evil, she felt a part of something larger than herself for the first time in her long life.

Rather than remaining on the sidelines or compromising to satisfy part of who she was, she sensed the call of her true nature. It was wild and pure and powerful. Before, she'd felt sad to leave the sea and return to her bakeshop, but now she wasn't sure she'd be able to make the transition.

Aegir had told her Selkies belonged to the sea. It wasn't that she hadn't believed him, but she assumed she was the outlier, the one Selkie who could make her own rules.

Tarika took form where Britta had stood and wove golden strands of power in with their magic. Raene felt the shape and form of the dragon's prison as they drew it from shadow. It hadn't been buried, but behind an eerie enchantment obscuring it from view. A wavery globe of darkness moved toward them, drawn by Tarika's command. It burst when it could no longer cling to the evil that had spawned its existence.

The demon who'd shaped the wickedness was dead, which might have helped. The king and queen of the sea may have aided them too. Raene wasn't certain who or what was tangled in their magic.

A smallish golden dragon with whirling green eyes leapt out of the eye of the bursting evil and lunged for Tarika. She caught him with her forelegs, and he wound his around her as far as they'd go.

Gemstones rained down on the ocean floor. It took a moment before Raene realized both dragons were crying. The fortune in precious stones falling to the sand below were their tears. A mighty blast of magic with dragon stamped all over it shook the water until Raene hoped Tarika hadn't loosed a tsunami. Before the dragon power cleared, both of them were gone.

One of the stones rippled with light. Clear, oblong, and red, it might have been a ruby. It called to her, so she batted it with a flipper until it rose into the water and she flicked out her tongue to catch it. Selkie-hood had a few complications, one of which was a lack of pockets, so she tucked the gem into her cheek. Aegir must have been preoccupied because he didn't mention the blood-red gem.

The ocean rocked and rolled around them for long moments before quieting. She touched shoulders with Aegir and said in her sea voice, "I'm happy for them."

"As am I, lass. I would leave as well, but I must see to the welfare of this pod. Ye can go if ye'd like. I trust ye can teleport back to my island."

"I could, but I'd rather remain. Perhaps I can help in some way."

His whiskers twitched. She wasn't sure what it meant, but he didn't send her away. They swam back around to the front of the Selkie castle. Rows of Selkies trod water, clearly waiting for Aegir. As he came into view, a cheer rose from all of them.

If Raene had been human, she'd have cried. These poor Selkies were finally free. She and Aegir had done a good turn today for more than Glaedr and Tarika.

Aegir held up his flippers, and the crowd quieted. Raene counted at least fifty, perhaps a few more. "Ye owe your freedom to her." He nudged Raene's shoulder with his. "Her name is Raene, and she's who killed Gregor."

The cheering began again. This time with her name on everyone's tongue. Embarrassment swamped her. She'd never been the subject of this much attention, or any attention at all. Unless she counted Rolf stealing her pelt.

"Please. Stop."

Her words didn't make a dent, so she tried again, raising her flippers as she'd seen Aegir do. "Please," she repeated. "Stop. I did what I had to to save Aegir." If anything, the hooting and hollering and barking grew louder.

Because there wasn't any other option, she waited until the crowd settled before saying, "Thank you. I hope to get to know all of you in the days to come."

"Who here was Gregor's current mate?" Aegir spoke up.

"There isn't one. She died of shame, but he may as well have killed her outright," a coal-black Selkie answered.

"Aye, 'twas long ago, that happened," another chimed in.

"I ken the royal line is dead, and the children from their mating long dispersed, but did Gregor not marry again?" Aegir asked.

"Nay," Johannes said.

"None would have had him." A female Selkie glided nearer, disgust clear in her voice.

"Who would lead this pod?" Aegir scanned the group.

No one swam forward.

"Ye have two choices," Aegir continued, still in his sea voice. It was deep, resonant, and his next words made Raene proud of him. "Ye can remain here and govern yourselves as ye will, or ye would be welcome in my pod."

"May we discuss it among ourselves?" the black Selkie asked.

"Of course. Raene and I will be near the cave on shore. We will wait until the moon is low in the sky. If no one comes, I will assume ye wish to remain here."

Without waiting for a response, Aegir turned and swam back the way they'd come. Raene joined him. It didn't seem to take as long to reach the icy beach as it had taken to swim to the castle. They crawled out of the sea in the depths of an

Arctic night. The sky was inky black and shot with millions of stars.

Aegir shifted, so she did as well and stood shivering on the ice-coated rocks while he hid their pelts with magic. The ruby rattled against her teeth, so she spit it out and held it in a closed fist.

"Come on, lass." He held out a hand.

She knew she had to go inside the cave. Had to don the clothes she'd removed or she'd freeze, but she didn't want to see the remains of her father. Chiding herself for being a coward, she slipped and slid after Aegir, stopping when she came to her discarded pile of garments. The cave reeked of dragon, of fire, of expended magic, and of death.

"Get dressed." Aegir's words were abrupt. "I'll set fire to what remains of Gregor. Doona think about this. Remember what it was like riding Tarika, instead."

He was gone before she could thank him. Shivering so hard she could barely get her legs into the warm trousers or her feet into the shearling-lined boots, she smelled fire. Its clean, pure scent chased the overtones of death away.

Raene shifted from foot to foot, directing magic to help warm her chilly fingers and toes. A convenient pocket held the purloined gemstone. Aegir had suggested she focus on Tarika, but when she thought of the dragon, she remembered the flash of gangly forelegs and small haunches as Glaedr launched himself into her arms. Tarika hadn't rebuked him for his stupidity roaming too far from Fire Mountain.

No. She'd just held tight letting the youngling know

without words how much he was cherished. From what she'd seen of the dragon, she would never have guessed Tarika had a tender side, but her tears had fallen as freely as Glaedr's. The ruby—for what else could it be?—pulsed warmly from where she'd tucked it away. Chances were she'd never see another dragon, and she'd treasure her memento of the brief interlude she'd spent with Tarika, Britta, and Glaedr.

Aegir walked from the interior of the cave to join her where she stood beneath its arched entrance. "Give the fire a few moments to do its work," he said. "Soon, naught will remain beyond the same pile of cinders marking the ruin of what used to be Brock."

"How does that work? The fire, I mean. It burns hotter, or has magic in it?"

"Both, lass. Once long ago, 'twas called magefire. 'Tisn't as hot nor as efficient as what dragons produce, but it gets the job done." He positioned himself in front of her and dropped both hands onto her shoulders. "How are ye doing?"

Raene shrugged. "I'm all right. Or I will be eventually." She looked away. "In a very short time, I've moved from barely using my magic to full immersion in archetypal battles. It's a lot to take in."

He nodded, his expression solemn. "I haven't thanked you for saving my life."

"Oh, you'd have figured something out. Or Tarika would have stepped in. Or—"

He moved a hand until it partially covered her mouth. "I was fighting as hard as I could. My magic barely made a dent in Gregor's attack. Tarika was busy dealing with the demon. Nay, lass. Ye did, indeed, save me. Just as ye destroyed your father to do so."

She stood straighter, uncomfortable being reminded about her father, but defiant to her core and ready to defend her actions. "I'd do the same again."

"Och, ye would, eh?" He gripped her shoulder tighter and cupped the side of her face with his other hand.

Raene leaned toward him, drawn by something she didn't understand. She should maintain distance between them because she didn't trust herself with him this close. So much had happened, she wasn't certain who she was anymore. The cheery bakeshop proprietor swathed in an apron that smelled like vanilla and sugar felt like a stranger.

He rubbed his thumb along the line of her jaw. His hand was warm, and magic spilled from him, easing her muddled mind. Maybe because she didn't pull away, he took it as assent because he angled his head and settled his lips atop hers.

The kiss was gentle, tentative. It offered her choices. She could walk away—if she did it now. Except she didn't want to. He tasted sweet, like aged whiskey or confections she browned in her oven. The scent of his magic, wild with the salt tang of the sea, rose around them, kindling all her senses with excitement at the nearness of him.

Raene tried to fight the sensation, but desire for the man next to her ran through her veins like quicksilver. She wrapped her arms around him and crushed her mouth against his, hoping for the thrust of his tongue. He groaned and licked her lips, easing his tongue along the seam between them. She threaded her fingers through his thick, wet hair, loving the feel of him, the contrast between rough, stubbled skin and unruly hair.

She'd never made love with a Selkie. How could she have? She'd mostly avoided human men too. She'd been a maid when Rolf stole her skin, and she'd kept to herself once he died. He'd been considerate—if she didn't count him imprisoning her—and willing to wait until she came to his bed. It had taken a couple of years, but they'd coupled thousands of times after that. The passion on her side had been quick to flare up and equally quick to vanish. She'd never loved her husband, but she'd found ways to not be too unhappy as his wife.

Aegir curled his arms around her, splaying his fingers across her back as he kneaded her tense muscles. She molded her body to his, all too aware of her nipples forming stiff peaks as her breasts were crushed against him.

She felt his heartbeat against her lips when she ran kisses down to the hollow in his collarbone and across to his neck where a pulse was. They traded licking, sucking, and biting as they kissed each other. Salty residue coated his skin, and she licked it up, savoring his taste and how it blended with the sea that was part of her too.

Deep yearning rose within her. She wanted the man covering her mouth with his own. Wanted him with a blind desire that had nothing to do with the heat traveling through her. She hungered for a life with him, one where they'd be together always.

It seemed so farfetched, so impossible, she pulled away from his embrace, her breath coming fast. "We, uh, we should stop." She stumbled through the words.

"Aye, that we should." He circled her shoulders with an arm. "I doona want to. I could kiss you forever and still want more, but the Selkies will be here soon."

"How do you know?"

"I understand my kinsmen. A pod requires leadership, and this pod has been rudderless for too long to imagine." He took a measured breath. "We still have a wee bit of time, and I wish to talk about us."

She shook her head. "Not a good idea."

"Why not?"

She inhaled sharply, nostrils flaring at the nearness of him. "Same reasons as before. You're a Selkie king, and I run a bakeshop." She offered a rueful smile. "Never mind I'm not certain I'll be able to coax myself back there. Not after dragon riding and Arcadia and magical trees and fighting evil."

He smiled, but then his expression grew serious. "I shouldna say aught. I promised myself I'd keep my feelings to myself until ye've had a chance to mourn your da."

She opened her mouth to protest, but he shook his head. "I'm not quite done, lass. Gregor may have been a bastard, but ye need time to absorb all of it. Who he used to be. What he did to your mum. Who he turned into. Why he sold his soul to demonkind."

"For power, why else?" she sputtered.

"My first guess too." Aegir did smile then, soft and sad. "He needed killing, but I'd have spared you the task if I could have."

Raene met his direct gaze, drawn by the changeable hues of his eyes and the silver flecks dancing around his pupils. "What is it you weren't going to tell me?"

"Curious, lass?"

"Aye, that would be me."

He untangled his arm and stood in front of her, tipping her chin up with one finger so she had to look at him. "Ye're amazing. Brave. Beautiful. Resourceful."

Heat rose from her belly and swooshed up her chest and over her head. "You're romanticizing the hell out of me. I'm not anything special."

"To me, ye are. I want you to be with me always."

Her eyes widened. "Not possible," she blurted. "We scarcely know one another. We—"

"We have all the time in the world." He grinned crookedly. "Mostly, I wanted to plant the idea. Ye're a verra special woman, and I'd kick myself forever if ye swam away without me telling you as much."

She was still looking right at him, so she saw his eyes narrow, felt his concentration arrow away from her. Had she done something? She didn't see how, unless the lack of instant capitulation meant all his words were just fancy window dressing to get her to sleep with him.

She'd have done that anyway, but he had no way of knowing.

He bent forward and brushed his mouth across hers, leaving a trail of sparks and heat. "We'll pick up this conversation later. The Selkies are nearly here, and Krise just called me. I'm needed in Arcadia."

"Who's that?"

"My father. The one who was king when the pod turned you away."

Raene winced. "Gee. Can't wait to meet him."

"He's not a bad sort. Old and traditional. He'll have a fit about adding fifty odd Selkies to our pod, but 'tis the right thing to do."

"Your da would have made a different choice?"

Aegir scrunched his forehead in thought. "He'd have come to the same place as me, eventually. But his preference would have been to offer nothing."

"Why?"

"He's not overly fond of change. He gets around to embracing it, but not easily. With this many Selkies, 'tis verra possible at least one of them will cause trouble. 'Twill require work keeping a close eye on them all—without being obvious about it."

"I like you," she said. "Further, I respect you."

"As I do you, lass. 'Tis a decent start."

"How so?" She wasn't certain quite what he meant.

"Anyone can be lovers. Being friends is much harder—and far more important over the long haul."

Footsteps pounded up the beach toward them. Johannes and two male Selkies from Gregor's pod entered the cavern. None bothered to dress, which probably meant they weren't planning to remain long.

Johannes bowed low. "We shall join you."

"Yes." A golden-haired Selkie with clear blue eyes nodded agreement. "Our undying thanks for your kindness. Look for us in about a month."

"Ye're not teleporting?" Aegir sounded surprised.

Johannes shook himself from head to toe. Water droplets flew everywhere. "We all feel we need the purification from a long swim. It's better this way. Your pod will have an opportunity to plan for our arrival, and we'll be better for having a span of time to eradicate Gregor's wicked taint."

"As ye will." Aegir inclined his head. "Ye'll be welcome whenever ye arrive."

The Selkies turned as a group and trotted back outside. She felt the zing of power as they shifted to their sea forms.

"Ready to leave, lass?" Aegir asked, adding, "Doona fash about the robe. The clothes ye have on are far more practical."

"Thanks. I was wondering whether to change, but I can just drape the robe over everything. I'll be ready to go in a moment." She walked purposefully to the pile of ashes that had been her father and knelt next to them. Perhaps sensing she needed to be alone, Aegir left the cavern.

"I'm not sure what to say," Raene began, keeping her words soft. Aegir would hear every one, but she wasn't ashamed of what she wanted to tell her father. "I wish I could have known you long ago, seen the man mum fell in love with." She cleared her throat. "I'm grateful to be a Selkie. Thank you for making it possible, but you were always weak. Too weak to be faithful to your wife. Too weak to withstand the pull of evil with its promise of infinite power."

She took a breath before continuing. "I'm not sorry you're dead. I don't know how I feel about being the one to kill you, but I'm sure I'll work it out."

She searched within herself, but nothing else clamored for ascendency. Empty, drained, but with a sense of closure over a part of her life that had always been a mystery, she rose to her feet and left the cave behind.

Aegir waited, their pelts stretched across his open arms. He gave hers to her and began to chant, summoning the spell to return them to the island with a gateway to Arcadia.

"What happens next?" she asked.

"I doona know but remain alert. Da would not have summoned me were the need not grave."

Alert felt beyond her. She was stumbling with weariness but pushed it aside. Aegir saw things in her she'd never guessed existed. Falling on her face wasn't on the menu. Maybe later, but not now.

"I'm ready." She gave a curt nod. His magic swept them both into its maw. Her mind was a blurry muddle. What she needed most was some time by herself. Swimming time where she let the tides move her as they would and caught fish to fill her belly.

I'll tell him. Just as soon as we're back on the island.

But would she? If he needed her, how could she refuse him anything? If she hadn't been in the midst of strong magic, she'd have buried her head in her hands and rubbed the ache from her temples. She remembered the feel of his mouth on hers. The swell of his cock against her belly. Desire rushed through her, adding to the confused mix of emotions and muddying the waters still further.

Because thinking was getting her nowhere, she blanked her mind. Even he had said she didn't need to make any decisions right now, that they had time. But that was before his father had summoned him home. Would they be embroiled in one battle after the next—until one of them died?

Her carefully neutral mindscape shattered. She'd figure things out. She always had. Clinging to what felt like bogus reassurances because her old life bore zero resemblance to the one she was living now, she waited out the rest of the teleport spell.

*A*egir sensed Raene's unrest but wasn't certain what to do about it. Most of his attention had to remain focused on his spell to ensure they didn't end up in the middle of an Amazon jungle or the Sahara Desert. He'd underplayed both his concern over Krise's summons as well as his da's probable reaction to the news about Gregor's pod.

But Raene had been through plenty, and he hadn't wanted to alarm her. Maybe she could regain some equanimity with his spell cradling her during their journey. Goddess knows, she deserved a break.

Krise would be furious about incorporating Gregor's pod, but there was nothing to be done but ride out his temper. He'd walked away from being king over Aegir's protests, but once the baton passed from one Selkie to another—not always ones related by blood, either—it was permanent.

Krise could rail all he wanted, but Aegir wouldn't rescind

his invitation to the survivors he'd left north of Siberia. To set out on a long-distance swim meant they were committed to doing whatever was necessary to ensure their new home worked out for them. The ocean would remove any residual wickedness.

From those willing to move beyond it.

Aegir shut his eyes for a moment and willed it would be all of them. He didn't want to deal with his da's recriminations if a few bad seeds created problems.

He'd like to have bid Tarika farewell, but dragons weren't bound by Selkie conventions—or any beyond their own. The dragon had what she'd come for. No reason to hang about for a round of goodbyes. A thought rose. He turned it around, looking for holes, but didn't find any.

Evil was rising. He felt it in his bones. Gregor had been an arrogant jerk, but he'd never have succumbed to the dark side of power if it hadn't shown up front and center and tantalized him. The boundaries meant to keep Hell's minions contained must have thinned. It explained the Fae attacking Arcadia, and perhaps a whole lot of other events he didn't know about.

He should have talked with Angus, but he'd been so upset with the seer, he hadn't thought to grill him about current events. The Celts knew a lot, and Angus was their pet errand boy. Where had they sent him lately? And for what reasons?

Perhaps paying him a visit was in order. Him or his da, Cathbad. Locating the ancient Druid—first of their line of seers—might be problematic. Or not. He bet the Druids on

Arcadia knew exactly where the First Seer resided in time. It was the kind of thing they'd keep tabs on. Aegir had met Cathbad a time or two, but so long ago, he barely remembered the man other than that he and Angus could have been twins.

The pull of his island popped them through the veil holding teleport channels separate from the warp and weft of Earth. He didn't have to work very hard once he neared the island because it recognized and accepted his power.

He had an arm around Raene, and she drowsed against him. He did his damnedest to set them down gently. If he managed not to wake her, he'd carry her inside and let her sleep for as long as possible. He'd been vigilant and hadn't sensed anything untoward as they neared the island.

Maybe he'd catch a short break to breathe a little before Krise showed up.

Aegir tossed his pelt behind the same enchantment he always used. When he tried to lever Raene's from her arms, she held tighter. Of course. It was reflexive. Selkies protected their skins at any cost, even while asleep. He swept an arm beneath her legs and carried her and her pelt toward the shielded entry to the cave.

A bleak-and-stormy dawn cast plenty of light, but it was cold and raw. A brisk wind drove rain, sleet, and saltwater across the spit of land. He rolled his eyes and bent his body protectively around the woman in his arms. Scotland's weather was beastly, but the incessant rain yielded greenery in the most unusual spots. He could have lived anywhere, could have relocated the pod once he became king. But it never occurred to him.

Scotland was his home.

He was nearly to the cave when Krise stepped forward. Framed between the two stones that formed the entry point, he stood tall. Years hadn't touched him, and he'd lived through close to a millennia. Snow-white hair streaked with silver fell to his knees. Ropy muscles crisscrossed his tall, spare frame.

He wore his usual: buff hunting leathers that encased his arms and legs as if they'd been made just for him. Who knew? Perhaps he had a tailor hidden in a small hamlet somewhere.

"Took ye long enough." Krise skewered Aegir with his unrelenting gaze out of emerald green eyes.

"Ssht." Aegir shook his head.

"It's okay. I'm up." Raene thrashed in his arms until he set her upright. "I can't believe I fell asleep."

"Who is she?" Krise demanded, directing the question at Aegir.

Raene craned her head around to look at Krise. "I'm right here. If you want to know something about me, ask me not him."

A sputtering grunt passed Krise's lips. "Fine. Who are you? Beyond that, how do ye come to be here with my son?"

She pursed her lips into a sour expression. "I'm a Selkie, same as you."

"Nay. Your blood isna pure."

"Get over yourself, for Christ's sake." She formed a fist and punched the air.

Aegir fought back a grin. No one talked back to his da, but she just had.

"Is this the Selkie ye asked me about?" Krise's tone held patronizing edges. "I assumed it was male."

"Aye. Same one. I dinna give you reason to decide one way or another," Aegir murmured.

"Mmph. Doesn't explain why she's here. Or why ye were carrying her. Explain."

Raene crossed her arms beneath her breasts, squashing her skin against her body. Defiance marked her expressive features, the set of her shoulders, and her lifted chin. "We're just back from a quest to save a young dragon. Along the way, we released a Selkie pod from an evil despot. One who happened to be my father."

"Ye've an active imagination, lass." Krise set his mouth in a tight line.

"What she said is true," Aegir cut in. "All of it."

"This must tie in with the conversation we had recently. The one where ye asked after Gregor's pod." Krise inhaled briskly. "So the lone Selkie was female. Keep talking. If ye're Gregor's daughter, ye must have been born out of wedlock, which means his life is forfeit."

"He's already dead." Raene threw the words at Krise. If they'd been icicles, they'd have shattered around him and come to rest in a pile of shards at his feet.

Both of Krise's silvery brows shot upward in surprise.

"Now there's a piece of good news. He always had a rotten core."

Aegir cringed. It was one thing for Raene to understand her da was a bastard. Quite another to have his shortcomings tossed in her face.

She didn't flinch, though. "I killed him, and what's left of his pod will arrive in a month or so."

"Arrive? Where?" Krise looked thunderstruck.

"Here," Aegir inserted smoothly. It wasn't how he'd have imparted the news, but the barn door stood wide open. No shutting it now.

"But, that's impossible," Krise sputtered. "How many? Wasn't there aught else they could go? Why here?"

"Because Raene and I are who rescued them from unspeakable evil, along with Tarika."

The dragon, Tarika?" Krise's voice tone had raised an octave.

"Aye, the same," Aegir replied.

Krise fell back a pace, but he did clap his mouth shut. For once, he seemed at a loss for words. When he spoke again, he muttered, "I believed the dragon quest was but woman prattle. Ye actually went with Tarika. How did such a thing come to be?"

"We'll tell you the whole story," Aegir said. "But inside. It's cold out here, and I'm wasting magic right and left keeping Raene and me warm."

"I can take care of myself." She leveled her gaze at him, one that had cooled perceptibly.

He didn't blame her. Krise could be a sanctimonious bastard, but he had a pure heart. No way for Raene to know about that part, though. Not the way his da had behaved toward her.

Krise turned and stomped back inside. Aegir gripped Raene's arm and followed him. He'd be damned if he'd allow his da's snarky temper to drive them from what he considered his home.

Warmth from the hearth eddied around them, and Aegir wondered if there was anything to eat that wouldn't require preparation. The biscuits and fish would be gone. Krise, who always ate whatever wasn't tacked down, would have finished them.

"We'll sit and talk," Krise told his son, "while the lass makes us a meal."

Raene—who'd detached his arm from hers as soon as they entered the cave so she could set her skin to one side—spun to face Krise. "Not just no, but hell no. What century are you from? I'm not your servant. I'm not your subject. Last I checked, you're not king anymore. You foisted that off onto Aegir."

"Touchy, isn't she?" Krise was still aiming his words at Aegir.

"I'm not a she. I'm a me. I'm right here. Do. Not. Objectify. Me." Without waiting for a response, she strode to the cabinet where Aegir kept spirits and opened it. Without reading labels, she grabbed a bottle, uncorked it, and drank deep.

Krise followed her, planting himself in front of her and snatching the bottle from her hands. "Now look here, missy."

"No. You look here." Anger blotched her face with patches of red.

"Ye may be a Selkie," Krise went on, "yet ye've not spent enough time with our kind to learn manners."

"Not for lack of trying." She interrupted him. "I asked to join your pod about fifty years back. You turned me away."

"Aye. We turn most lone Selkies away. Ye could have been spying for another pod. Best not to take a chance."

Raene tossed her head and copied his word choices. "Best ready yourself. About fifty potential *spies*"—she emphasized the word—"are swimming your way. My da sold out to evil. He had a demon sidekick, and the Selkies under his care suffered greatly. You have an opportunity to help them. You say I'm rude. Well, maybe I am, but you started it. If people are kind to me, it's easy to be kind right back. You started by marginalizing me. You didn't even talk to me, but to your son about me."

She fell silent, probably because she ran out of breath.

Aegir considered inserting himself between them, but Raene didn't appear to require his assistance. She was doing fine on her own. If she'd been steeped in Selkie culture, she'd never have stood up to Krise. He might no longer be the monarch, but he was the second most powerful Selkie in their pod. Some preferred going to him rather than Aegir, which suited him fine.

"What happened to the demon?" Krise demanded. "Is he coming with the pod?"

"The dragon killed him," Aegir retorted. "It really would be best for you to hear the tale in order."

"Humph. Maybe so." Krise set the liquor on a nearby table and sank to a pillow in front of the hearth.

"I'm going to make us something to eat," Aegir said. "We can talk over a meal."

Raene looked up, meeting his gaze with an unspoken question. He shook his head. "You rest. My turn to take care of you. Besides, Da will help."

"I will?" Krise didn't bother to mask his surprise at being asked to do anything that smacked of domesticity.

"Aye. Mosey outside and bring me two of the salted fish from the outdoor storage bin." Aegir held his breath. It was almost the first time he'd asked his da to do anything.

With a long-suffering grunt, Krise stood and walked from the cave.

Raene looked as if she wanted to say something, but she also looked exhausted. Dark circles rode beneath her eyes, and her shoulders slumped with fatigue.

"Sit," he told her. "Have some liquor. Doona fash about a thing."

"If I fall asleep, wake me to eat. I am hungry."

Aegir crossed to where she stood, swaying on her feet from weariness, and eased her to a group of cushions that formed a rough chair. "Rest, léannan. I will hide your skin next to mine." He added a smidge of compulsion to his words.

She didn't need to hear him rehash where they'd been and what they'd done once Krise returned.

Her eyes fluttered shut, and he straightened, returning to the kitchen end of the cavern, where he'd been planning a stir fry of fish and sea vegetables. He crouched to open the oven door. Some of Raene's cheese biscuits remained. Aegir smiled to himself. He remembered sticking them in the oven to keep them safe from marauding rodents. Clearly, Krise hadn't done a thorough search, or there'd be naught left but crumbs.

He closed the oven and grabbed a flat-bladed chopping knife.

Krise returned faster than Aegir expected, his hands full of fish fillets. He walked far more silently than a man his size had a right to and dropped the fish in the sink. A few pumps and he'd rinsed both it and his hands with seawater. "Is she asleep?" He kept his voice so low not even a magical creature could have heard.

"Aye." Aegir switched to telepathy to be on the safe side. *"She's exhausted."*

"Spends most of her time as human, eh?"

"Why wouldn't she? We turned her away."

"Nay, son. What ye mean to say is that I turned her away. Had I known how much spirit she had, her request would have met with a different outcome."

Aegir nodded and chopped fish into his vegetable pot. He added a bit of seasoning for flavor and a few drops of oil and directed a beam of magic to heat the mixture to boiling.

While their supper cooked, he sketched out an annotated

version of finding Raene in the sea, their trips to Arcadia, and Tarika's arrival. One thing he'd always appreciated about his da was that Krise was a good listener.

He asked the occasional question, but, mostly, he let Aegir talk until no more words came. He'd been stirring the fish mixture from time to time. It was ready to brown up in a frying pan. He grabbed the pot by its bale and motioned to Krise to follow him outside.

He could have used the hearth, but he didn't want to disturb Raene. She'd barely budged since he spelled her to sleep. His magic had prodded her in that direction, but he hadn't added anything to his initial enchantment. She slept on because she was worn-out. Magic could be a bitch when you used a whole lot in a short timeframe, especially if you weren't used to it.

The weather had done nothing but grow more hideous, rain giving way to a sleety snow. Wet rocks shone with an icy coating, making walking treacherous.

Krise drew magic about them as they huddled next to the outdoor cooking pit. His shielding deflected what fell from the sky but didn't do much to address the wind. Aegir encouraged the stones to heat in the same way as he'd done within. He poured the saucepan's contents into a large iron skillet. It wouldn't take much to finish their meal.

No need for telepathy out here. "Why'd ye summon me home?" he asked.

"Arcadia needs us. And not just one at a time. The Druids

paid me a visit—four of them, anyway—and what they said was unsettling."

"Go on." Aegir shot a pointed glance his father's way.

"The boundaries betwixt Earth and Hell have been weakening for hundreds of years—"

"I suspected as much, yet if that's so," Aegir broke in, "why have none of them told us? For that fact, the dragon dinna mention it, either."

"If anyone would know, 'twould be a First Born dragon," Krise agreed. "But they've always kept to themselves. No reason to bother with the rest of us. As to your other question, the Druids kept hoping things would reverse themselves. Their old ones have lived through many cycles where evil rose only to retreat."

"What made them decide this time was different?"

Krise nodded approvingly. "This is why ye're a better leader for our people than I ever was. Ye doona react but keep chewing a thing over until ye understand what drives it."

Aegir dialed back the magic searing their food. "Was that why ye insisted 'twas my turn at the helm?"

"Aye, that and other things. I am quite old, and I served our people well and faithfully—"

Aegir sliced a hand through the air. "Spare me the well-deserved rest speech. I've heard it afore. Ye dinna answer me about the Druids, though."

Krise blew out a noisy breath and shut his eyes for a moment. Aegir girded himself. It must be bad if his father was picking and choosing his words. Finally, Krise said, "No easy way to say this. Arcadia is dying. The Druids are its caretakers, and they feel the land's pain."

"But it's been here since before the dawn of time. It predates Earth," Aegir protested before he got hold of himself and shut up.

"Ye dinna ask the most important question. 'Tisn't like you."

Their supper was done, or breakfast or lunch if he was a stickler about what time of day it was. He cut the magic heating the mixture and hoped to hell it wouldn't grow stone cold before they got around to eating it.

"What happens if Arcadia falls? Will it be the end of magic?"

Krise nodded solemnly. "Aye, son. We will fade along with it. It willna be pretty because 'twill only be the demise of our magic—the good kind."

Breath whooshed from Aegir's lungs, and he swallowed hard. He'd assumed all magic—White, Black, and all types in between—were linked. To have only their magic die would leave the door wide open for Hell and its minions to overrun Earth. Other wicked creatures, the ones already here, would flourish too, embracing their freedom like a bunch of delinquents who'd been told school was out permanently.

"Dinna all magic spring from common roots?" he asked Krise.

The elder Selkie nodded. "It did, indeed. I doona ken how dark power could survive in the absence of its opposite, yet the Druids are convinced such is the case."

Aegir pinched the bridge of his nose between his thumb and forefinger, wishing he could roll the clock back to before he and Krise had this conversation. When he looked up, he asked, "Is there any hope?"

"We're still here, aren't we? Aye, until Arcadia falls, there is hope we may yet stem the tide. The Druids were apologetic as hell about not informing us earlier. Something about the battle they had against the Fae convinced them time was running out."

"Is it just us they've reached out to? Or are they circling the wagons?"

"I doona ken your meaning."

"Nay, ye wouldna. 'Tis a modern expression. Are they searching out everyone who works White Magic and requesting their aid?"

"I believe so. Why wouldn't they?"

"I have no idea. Ye're who they came to, not me. If we have a battle to plan, though, we must know who our allies are." He snapped up the frying pan and headed back inside.

Raene had moved from where she'd been sprawled across several pillows to standing at the pump. She was sluicing water over her face and hands. When she looked over at him, she didn't look quite so bleary eyed. "Thanks for taking care of supper." She offered a small smile.

"Sorry for assuming ye'd cook for us," Krise said from behind Aegir.

He almost dropped the frying pan. His da never apologized. Never.

Until now.

"I'm sorry too." She inclined her head. "I can get snappish. It's not one of my better traits. We had a few biscuits left, I think." She knelt in front of the oven and drew out the plate where Aegir had piled them the day before. "Feels like I made these a hundred years ago, so much had happened," she murmured and carried the plate near the hearth.

Aegir split the fish into three ceramic bowls. He handed them around, followed by forks. Raene rescued the spirits, which turned out to be mead, and poured some into three tumblers.

For a while, they ate and drank in silence.

When she lifted her attention from her plate, she said, "I heard the two of you talking outside."

"Sorry if we woke you, lass," Aegir said.

"You didn't. I was half awake, anyway. But I heard a little bit at the tail end of things just before you came inside. The part about magic dying, and us right behind it."

Words leapt to Aegir's lips. He wanted to reassure her things weren't as grim as they'd sounded, but he wouldn't lie. Especially not to her. His father's message almost couldn't have been any worse.

Setting his fork down, he said, "Aye, events have grown serious."

"But we knew that when we battled the Fae in Arcadia. The Druids were devastated war had breached their land. So were the trees." She pressed her lips together. "Do you know where to find the dragons?"

"Aye. 'Tisn't an easy journey, nor a short one, but we know where Fire Mountain is," Krise answered her.

"We helped Tarika and Britta. Would they help us?"

Krise reached across the low table and patted her hand. "'Tis a nice thought, lass, but dragons doona do aught for anyone who isna one of them."

"But if good magic dies, won't they die too?" Raene persisted.

It was a reasonable question, but not one Aegir had an answer for. He looked up and caught Krise's eye. His da turned his hands palms up.

"Fire Mountain exists in its own borderworld," Aegir said slowly. "I have no idea how—or if—'tis linked to Earth."

"We can ask them to aid us," Raene went on. "Worst thing that can happen is they'll refuse, but I don't believe they will."

"Why?" Krise fastened his clear green gaze on her.

"Tarika cried when she found her lost youngling. Cried and held him close. Anyone who does that won't allow all of us to fade away."

Aegir started to protest that Glaedr was another *dragon*. Dragons took care of their own. He didn't, though. Raene's blue-green eyes held hope. He couldn't stand to throw buckets of seawater on it.

"All right." He took another mouthful of his cooling dinner, chewing and swallowing. "When we're done, we'll visit Arcadia and the Druids and get as much information as we can. When we're done there, we'll travel to Fire Mountain."

"I suggest we split forces," Krise said. "I'll accompany you into Arcadia. Once we're done there, I'll rally our people, including the ones heading our way from Siberia. I'll light a fire under them and tell them to teleport."

"I thought you didn't want them here," Raene murmured.

"Seems I was wrong about that," Krise replied. "If we require an army, more Selkies will be welcome."

"'Tis a decent game plan," Aegir said. "I hope the dragons allow us entry. Once when I knocked at their gates, they sent me packing."

Krise frowned. "Was that when the sea serpents attacked our pod and three others?"

"Aye. I was seeking allies." Aegir shrugged. "I figure they knew I was there to request a boon, and the simplest course was to not hear me out at all."

"I always suspected dragons are related to sea serpents and dinna wish to raise claw, talon, or scale against their distant kin," Krise retorted.

"What happened?" Raene leaned forward.

"Och, lass, 'twas at least four hundred years back," Krise answered her. "We rustled up aid from the Druids and other Shifters. It turned out to be sufficient. Far more of us than sea serpents. After we killed half a dozen, the rest fled."

Grateful Raene and Krise had found common ground and were no longer sniping at one another, Aegir polished off the remains of his meal, washing it down with mead and a biscuit. Raene and Krise ate just as purposefully. They'd all need their strength, and none of them knew when—or where —their next meal would materialize.

He cast sidelong glances at Raene. He'd finally found the one woman he wanted for his mate, but anything personal would have to wait. If they botched the task that lay ahead, none of them would be alive long enough for something as frivolous as love to matter.

CHAPTER 12

Raene didn't let on how devastated she'd been by what she overheard. What was the point? Collapsing into a maudlin heap wouldn't change a thing, and it would deflect everyone's attention away from what they had to do.

Hers included.

Food and spirits helped. She was feeling more or less like herself by the time she'd finished her meal. The fish stew was simple fare. Well-seasoned and filling. A few more biscuits would have been nice, but she could always make more.

When would that be? A caustic inner voice spoke up.

In between crises, she retorted and got up to carry their dishes to the sink. Krise and Aegir had cooked. Cleaning up was the least she could do.

Aegir joined her at the pump. "Leave those. We need to go to Arcadia. Druids are an understated lot. If they just now came to Da with their problem, it tells me they should have kicked the door open years ago."

"Not so much understated as proud," Krise corrected his son.

Aegir faced his da. "Do ye remember Cathbad?"

"Of course. The Druidic seer. First one, and by far and away the strongest magically. His son's child was the one nourished by our pod."

"Aye. Jonathan. Angus came for him."

Krise narrowed his eyes. "I kent it. Ye doona approve?"

Aegir pushed his shoulders back. "Nay. The boy would have been better off with us."

"Ye only believe so because ye grew fond of him," Krise replied. "In the face of an all-out battle, the child is safer with Angus because the Celts will protect them both. Not that they care about the boy, but Angus is their pet seer-slash-lackey."

"Did Cathbad ever serve in such a role?" Aegir asked.

"Verra briefly and afore your time. He told the Celts to piss off. That was when he dropped backward in time to escape their tyranny, taking Angus with him."

"How'd this Angus fellow end up back here?" Raene asked. Myths had always fascinated her, particularly once she realized those in the stories were real people.

"I have no idea," Aegir replied and quirked a brow Krise's way.

"I'm not entirely certain, either. My best guess is Cathbad saw something in our time and sent Angus to check it out. While Angus was here, a couple of the Celts pounced on him, wiped his memories to cut off any retreat route, and put him to work. I'm sure they remembered Cathbad's exit and made certain Angus wouldna escape their yoke. Years passed, quite a lot of them, afore he got together with Arianrhod."

"That part of the tale, I kent," Aegir cut in. "The Celts assigned the two of them to deal with a problem. Dragons were vanishing from the Highlands, and they demanded assistance from the Celts—"

"I thought they kept to themselves," Raene interrupted.

"Normally, they do, lass, but this problem occurred on Earth. I suppose they assumed they needed some of us who were already here to address it. Regardless, Angus and Arianrhod met in Fire Mountain. Their attraction was instantaneous, and Jonathan was the result."

"Which would be why you said the virgin part of Arianrhod's claimed title was phony," Raene murmured.

Aegir nodded.

"Hmmm." Raene pushed her hair behind her shoulders, shaking it out of the way. It was mostly dry and had formed thick wedges of curls that hung in her eyes. "If those two could enter Fire Mountain, there's no reason we can't."

Krise pursed his mouth into an expression that didn't quite qualify as a grimace. "Arianrhod is a goddess, and Angus the spawn of the best-known seer in all the ages. Dragonkind respects such things. They probably dinna think twice when they barred their gates to my son. Selkies aren't all that high on the magical scale."

"But Tarika came to you for help." Raene looked at Aegir.

"Only because her problem was tangled up with other Selkies."

A thought slammed Raene between the eyes. She shouldn't say anything because then she'd reveal she'd scanned Aegir's mind, but she couldn't keep quiet, either. "That woman I saw when I, uh, helped myself to your memories. The one in a leather outfit with a bow. That was Arianrhod? She's the boy's mother? How could she walk away from him? I don't understand."

"I'm sure Johnathan wouldn't either. Magic already runs strong within him." Aegir's reply was edged with icy bitterness. "Angus will erase his memories just like the Celts did to him."

"You didn't answer me." Raene's fingers curled into fists all by themselves. "How could his *mother* walk away?"

"'Tis a long story, and we lack the luxury of time," Aegir said. "Briefly, as I ken things, the two of them hashed out a deal. Arianrhod spent the latter part of her pregnancy in the sea and gave birth with my Selkie pod in attendance. She and the boy remained with us for two years. Angus visited often."

"So, this whole thing was planned?" Raene cut in.

Aegir nodded and continued, "Arianrhod grew more and more worried. Her roles were incompatible. She couldna remain part of the Celtic pantheon as a virgin huntress and be a mother at the same time. Not the mother of a son conceived by normal means."

"She should have lied." Raene felt fiercely protective of the youngster she'd seen in Aegir's mind.

"It wouldna have worked," Krise said. "Her kin are gods and goddesses. They'd sniff out a lie, and they'd ken immediately who fathered the lad—once they got near enough to focus their attention on him."

"Never believe it dinna tear Arianrhod in two to leave her boy behind," Aegir said. "I was there. I saw her anguish. The simplest path for her would have been to not bear the child at all, yet she did."

"I've thought about that," Krise broke in. "She and Angus have information about the future. Perhaps Cathbad impacted their decision as well. Jonathan must have a crucial role to play, one momentous enough to convince her to birth him even though she understood she'd have no role in his upbringing."

Raene clamped her jaws together and stopped talking. The abandoned child, who hadn't truly been forsaken since his father had him, was none of her affair. Never mind he tugged at her heartstrings, reminding her of the children she'd never given up hoping for.

The crisis in Arcadia was far more pressing. They had the seeds of a plan, and they'd make it work. They had to. She was glad she lacked the history that was evidently weighing both Aegir and Krise down. They were certain the dragons wouldn't help, but at least they were humoring her by taking the time to travel to this Fire Mountain place to ask.

Not that dragons were everything, but they sat close to the top of her list of powerful potential allies. Amazing, since until yesterday, she hadn't truly believed they existed. But now that she knew, she had a hard time imagining any endeavor that had dragons on its side failing. Maybe she was engaging in wishful thinking. Maybe she'd journeyed so far out of her depth she was drowning in uncharted water.

None of it mattered. This wasn't a time to get mired in doubt.

"We've probably tarried far too long," she said, keeping her tone neutral.

"I'll punch through the barrier," Krise told them and led the way out of the cave.

Absent Aegir's magic, the hearth would cool. The dishes wouldn't do themselves, and leaving them went against her grain, but Aegir had been correct about them needing to hurry.

The storm that had sent the occasional blast of wind inside the cave had blown itself out. The sky was streaked with grays and silvers with a sliver of sunlight arrowing through them. The effect was surreal, ethereal. She took it as a good omen for them to depart in speckled sunlight rather than the midst of an ice storm.

She followed the men along the narrow path leading to the island's highest point. By the time she arrived, a portal edged with pale blue flickered. Aegir gestured her through, following once she'd stepped across the liminal boundary separating Earth from Arcadia.

This time, she came out in a part of the magical land she hadn't seen before. No convenient pile of clothing awaited, probably because she had no need for it. A castle rose before her, looking like it had medieval origins. Towers and turrets were scattered at intervals. The structure was built of rough-hewn logs and large stones with masonry between them. Its three floors were topped by a flat roof with parapets. The windows were on the smallish side, no doubt to help trap heat within.

She turned in a circle and saw a tall iron fence surrounding a cobblestoned courtyard. They'd come out within the castle grounds. Lush shrubbery, some festooned with flowers, lined the fence. A herd of ponies grazed off to one side. Outbuildings sprouted here and there.

Aegir touched her arm. "This way." He moved briskly toward a broad set of stone steps leading to what appeared to be the castle's primary entrance.

"What?" she teased. "No moat? No drawbridge?"

Aegir regarded her. "They're on the far side of the wall. Ye doona want to fall into the moat. Things swim deep within its waters that haven't darkened Earthen seas for many a long year."

"No more jokes," she agreed. "I'm nervous. It's how I cope."

He waited for her to catch up. Once she stood by his side, he wrapped a protective arm around her shoulders, and they started up the stairs. "This is the easy part," he told her. "Finding a way inside Fire Mountain will be much more difficult. We need as much information as the Druids are willing to part with. I'm hopeful if we build a strong enough argument, the dragons willna turn us down."

They walked through a generous central hall with rooms branching off on either side. Rush lights were placed at strategic intervals, and each room had a fireplace crackling merrily. Rich wall hangings depicted battle scenes and magical animals she'd read about but never seen. Unicorns. Griffons. The Minotaur. Birds with enormous wingspans and hungry-looking beaks.

"Everything is so beautiful," she murmured.

"Aye, Druids are quite the art connoisseurs," Aegir murmured back. "We're nearly to their meeting hall."

Double oaken doors at the far end of the corridor had been propped open. The hum of conversation rose and fell from within. Raene crossed beneath the lintel. A staunch blast of magic, probably containing something to dissuade those not pure of heart and spirit from entering, raked her from head to toe,.

A long trestle table filled part of the meeting hall. Made of scarred mahogany, it appeared to have been crafted long ago. Twenty Druids sat in chairs along its length, all looking the same direction. Krise perched in a chair facing the table and situated between it and the hearth. Two other chairs sat next to his. Aegir guided them around the table and to the waiting seats.

The chamber's walls were wainscoting topped by whitewashed timbers. Unlike the rest of the castle, nothing adorned them. The floor was made of flagstones fitted tight against one another.

Raene sat, folded her hands together, and waited. She was

the most unexceptional member here. She needed to remember that and speak only when spoken to. No blurting out opinions as she was wont to do. She remembered a few of the Druids from the battle with the Fae.

The Arch Druid rose from his spot in the center of the long table and bowed in their direction. His cowl had fallen aside, leaving his tonsured head bare. "Welcome and thank you for heeding our call so quickly."

"Thank you for trusting us with such sensitive information," Krise replied. Unlike the Druid, he remained seated. "We are, and shall always be, your allies."

Another of the Druids rose and filled silver goblets with a clear liquid that smelled like wildflowers in springtime. He set one in front of her, Aegir, and Krise.

"Afore we begin," the Arch Druid said, "I would have your blood oaths. Naught that passes within these walls will leave this room."

Raene looked at Krise and Aegir. Both were seated to her right. Aegir drew a small blade from within his jacket. "Ye have our word, but I have a question."

The Druid furled his brows. "Aye, and what would it be?"

"How will we gather allies if we canna tell them of the evil we face?"

"Of course ye may gather allies, but I will impart how the current predicament came to be. That is what must remain secret." He hesitated. "For it casts our brotherhood in an unfavorable light."

Aegir pricked the end of a finger and let a drop of blood

fall into his goblet. He passed the knife to Krise who did the same. When it was her turn, she watched the liquid in her tumbler turn from clear to blue when her blood joined with it.

Her vow to hold silent vanished, and she asked, "Do different types of magic wielders turn the drink other shades than blue?"

The Druid seated next to where the Arch Druid stood regarded her through narrowed eyes. "Ye're the one who sought healing from Arcadia not that long ago."

She nodded and mumbled, "Sorry. I promised myself I wouldn't ask questions, but it's tough not to."

"Ye have a keen mind," the seated Druid said. "Indeed, the blood test is for us as much as it is for you. It tells us, for example, that ye're truly a Selkie. Now if ye were a wolf Shifter, the drink would be red. Bird Shifters turn it amber, and so it goes."

Aegir and Krise lifted their tumblers and drank, so she copied their actions. The concoction was mildly alcoholic with rich overtones of the magic that had created it. Her discomfort dropped away, replaced by a dreamlike sensation. The sense of wandering through magical realms, two steps removed from reality, intensified as the Arch Druid began to chant.

He clasped his hands behind him and strode through the room. Wherever he walked, silver and gold netting followed him, draping its folds around all in attendance.

"There," he said at length. "We are ready." He'd stopped pacing and resumed his seat in the middle of the long table.

"I will be as succinct as I can," he went on, "for time grows short. Druids are Earth's guardians. We were here when Earth formed, and we have protected her from evil for the span of her existence. In the beginning, 'twas far simpler. Men were a primitive lot, and animals have always been wise enough not to damage their home. Our only foe in those days was dark power.

"It has always existed in one form or another, but as long as we could focus our efforts in a single spectrum, we managed to hold the tide and keep Earth safe. All that changed in the last hundred years. Men have grown progressively more wicked and self-centered. They no longer care for aught beyond what will profit them. We've tried. Goddess knows, we've tried. Back when we still had temples and a following, we sat with men and women and explained the likely consequences of their actions. No one listened. They all assumed the resources they squandered were limitless and they could make more. But how can ye replace breathable air and clean water?"

Aegir growled low in his throat. "The oceans are warming and dying. It willna happen overnight, but the coral is fading. Once it's naught but dried columns of porous bone, the rest of us sea dwellers will be in grave straits."

The Arch Druid held up a hand for silence and continued, "Wicked creatures like Fae and Black Witches and demons dinna go away. We had to split our meager forces with some of us continuing the ongoing battle against encroaching darkness and others begging humans to rethink their actions.

"Clearly, we tried to do too much with too little, and we failed on both fronts. Badly. Ever enterprising, the Fae and demons recognized our weakness and attack when and wherever suits them. A trend that's escalating beyond my worst fears."

A long, rattling sigh escaped him. Raene's heart hurt for what he'd suffered. Everything was interconnected. Her father's swan dive into Hell might not have happened if demonkind had remained firmly behind Hell's gates.

"And so," the Druid to the Arch Druid's right took up the tale, "here we are. The time of merely defending ourselves has come to an end. We must forge an effective offense, create a definitive victory that drives those who wield dark power back into their ratholes. It willna address the other problems, the ones created by human greed, but we could wipe enough humans to make a difference off the face of the planet with a thought."

His statement gave Raene pause. Perhaps humans weren't as essential as she'd always believed them to be.

"Where do ye envision this battle taking place?" Aegir asked.

"Aye," Krise spoke up. "What makes ye think they'll even show up?"

"The battle will be here," the Arch Druid replied. "On

Arcadia. The land suggested a strategy, and we believe it to be sound."

Raene leaned forward, listening. The dreamy sense of unreality had departed, leaving her intensely aware just how high the stakes were.

"The land is sentient," the Druid continued. "It will feign being far weaker than it is and will partially release the barriers keeping wickedness out. We are in agreement that Arcadia will present such a tempting target, a dark army will attack intent on claiming her rich magical well for themselves."

Raene fought the hot bite of tears. Her throat thickened with fear—and awe. Arcadia was making the ultimate sacrifice in hopes it would be enough. Courage was doing the right thing, even if it damaged you. That the magical land had offered itself told her how desperate things had become...

She shook her head to dispel her bleak mood. The others were talking, and she'd missed some of what they said.

"If Hell's spawn could divert Arcadia's riches," another Druid broke in, "they could establish themselves as masters of Earth and what remains of her bounty. They'd mow through the humans without a second thought."

"We may end up doing the same"—the Arch Druid's words were lined with weariness—"once we have demonkind on the run. Except we would take care not to kill them all."

It was the second time he'd suggested humans were irrelevant. Raene struggled to keep her mouth shut, managing by the thinnest of margins. She'd lived as a human, was friends with many. Most weren't greedy bastards stripping Earth of her resources. Maybe the Druids could start their carnage from the top down and leave everyone else alone.

"Raene?" Aegir elbowed her.

"Yes." She looked about. "Did I miss something?"

"I was sharing our plan to go to Fire Mountain. I dinna think ye were paying close attention, but ye might wish to hear this."

"I'll begin again," the Arch Druid said.

Raene winced and muttered, "Sorry." She stopped before blurting that the combination of magic, worry, and the drink had done something odd to her mind.

"If ye can secure aid from the dragons, we would be forever in your debt," the Druid went on. "Dragons are the oldest, most powerful magical beings on this world and others. 'Twill be difficult to convince them, though, since none of us carry dragon blood. Be sure to tell them that I, Brother Loran, will personally see to it that two Druids are permanently assigned to serve dragons, either in Fire Mountain or elsewhere. Forever."

Aegir stood. So did Krise and Raene. He nodded. "We will convey your message. It is a generous offer in exchange for their assistance. Is there aught else we need to know?"

The Arch Druid shook his head. "Whatever ye do, be quick about it. If we're forced into too many more conflagrations like the recent Fae battle, we shall be even weaker than we are now when the main event occurs."

"I will gather my people from every pod I can," Krise

promised. "What about other Shifters and Witches?"

"We have already put out the call," another Druid reassured him. "Today's meeting with you was but the first of many. We shall be as prepared as possible."

"I'll be in touch as soon as I have news," Aegir said. He gripped Raene's hand and strode from the room.

They left the castle and walked out into the opulent courtyard with its rich gardens. Krise called a portal; they stepped through. A small, cowardly part of Raene longed for her simple bakeshop, but she buried it deep. It would be a long time before she saw the village of Wick or her shop again. The hard truth was she might never return. Longing for the impossible was a waste of time and energy.

"Gentle seas, brisk wind, and plentiful fish," Krise called as he ran for the beach where he'd presumably left his skin.

"Same to you, Da," Aegir called after him. He turned to Raene. "Are ye ready for our journey to Fire Mountain?"

Not trusting what whiny excuse might slide past her resolve to be strong, she nodded and said, "No time like the present," a shade too brightly.

Aegir repositioned himself so he stood in front of her. "Ye'd be a fool not to be frightened, lass. If we annoy the dragons, they're more than capable of tossing us in one of Fire Mountain's volcanic pits."

"Well, let's be as diplomatic as we can." She managed half a smile and felt his power rise around them. Different from teleport magic, this spell would also draw them through time. At least she thought it would. According to fables, the dragons' home existed in a spot untouched by the normal time-space continuum.

A silvery gateway formed. Aegir motioned her through into a tubular structure with pearlescent walls glowing like wet oyster shells. He joined her and sank to a crouch, patting the spot next to him. "Settle in, lass. This will take a while. Doona touch the walls and avoid negative emotions. The guardian who manages the time portals will eject any who disturb his peace."

The gateway vanished, merging with the walls. She knelt next to Aegir, her thigh resting the length of his. The travel tube began to rock gently. "I thought the dragons' home wasn't linked to time."

"It's not. So we will travel to the very beginnings of everything afore we leave the tunnel."

She wanted to ask a thousand things, but maybe she should arrange them so they made better sense. One of her hands found its way into a pocket, and she curled her fingers around the gemstone she'd taken from the ocean floor. It quivered warmly in her palm almost as if it were laughing.

Did it understand it was returning to Dragon Central?

She chuckled.

"What's so funny?" Aegir asked, and she drew out the stone and showed him.

"This. I think it knows it's going home."

egir stared at the gem. Magic lit it from within, and he knew at once it had formed from a dragon's tear. Very few could touch them without losing a hand—or their lives. That Raene had filched it from the sea outside Gregor's castle and carried it all this way might bode well for their current mission. She'd never seen a dragon before, much less one shedding tears, so the ruby had to have come from their sojourn to the Kara Sea.

She turned it this way and that, and its light danced along the walls of the time travel tunnel. "It's so pretty. Almost like it's alive."

"It is alive, lass," he replied. "It holds a wee bit of dragon essence. Whatever possessed you to pick it up?"

"I'm not certain." She shifted positions until she faced him, taking care not to touch the walls. "I was amazed and delighted by how Tarika gathered the small dragon close and hugged it. I'd never have guessed her capable of tenderness. And I was even more nonplussed when I saw their tears turn to gemstones. I'd read about such miracles in the old tales, but I always figured stories like that were, well, just stories."

"That explains why ye took it, but not why ye werena struck dead or blind or maimed for stealing gems from a dragon," he said, keeping his tone as neutral as he could.

"What?" Her anxiety spiked, the shift in her mood quick and obvious.

He gripped one of her hands. "Calm yourself. Remember what I said about the guardian. He'll eject us from the tunnel and not allow us entry for whatever period of time he deems appropriate. Could be hours or days or weeks."

Raene nodded, and the wild look left her eyes. "You startled me. How could Tarika view me as a thief?"

"Ye've heard about dragons and their hoards?" At her nod, he went on. "Any gemstone in proximity to a dragon belongs to them, and it certainly includes gems they've manufactured. Dragon tears are a precious commodity. They used to bring incredible prices at underground marketplaces and were the best of bartering tools."

"Fascinating. I bet they'd still command a premium price," she noted. "But I didn't take it because I wanted to sell it."

"Good thing. The wrath of dragonkind fell on any man so foolish as to enrich himself from their gemstones."

Raene frowned. "So dragons used to be more common on Earth?"

"Aye, lass. Especially in the Highlands and other northern

climes where they flew freely, helping themselves to herds of cows, sheep, and oxen. Their scales are impervious to arrows, and by the time men switched to high-powered rifles, the dragons had mostly left. All but a few."

"I've never seen one."

"The last of them abandoned the Highlands about the time Angus and Arianrhod met. One particular dragon, Eletea, had been tricked by a lover who wished to rid himself of her. Once that problem was laid to rest, I believe she retreated to Fire Mountain."

"Yes but I'm more than two centuries old. I've wandered the Highlands for a long time and never seen a dragon."

"Were ye on the lookout for them?" He still held her hand. It felt good and right tucked within his grip.

"You're teasing me. Of course not. How could I be on the lookout for something I didn't believe existed?"

He nodded. "And there it is, lass. Ye dinna believe, so ye'd never have seen them." Aegir adopted a more serious tone. "When we arrive at Fire Mountain, assuming we're allowed past their gatekeeper, do not pick anything up. Not a rock. Not a gem. And certainly not the blocks and bars of gold and silver lying about. Be assured each item has been claimed by a dragon even if they haven't yet dragged it back to join the remainder of their hoard."

"Not even to look at?"

"Not even to stand near. Dragons are the most possessive creatures on all the worlds. They'll roast you with fire and ask questions afterward."

"I understand." She matched his somber tone. "I'll leave everything where it is. Should I offer the ruby back to Tarika?"

Aegir considered the question. Only two possibilities existed. Either Raene didn't mention it, and hopefully the dragon wouldn't notice it, which wasn't likely. Or she returned it, which would reveal she'd taken it in the first place.

"Guess I should have left it back on the island," Raene muttered after he'd been silent for a spell.

"If ye'd done that, it makes it appear ye truly did steal it. Nay, 'tis with us for a reason. We shall have to wait and see how things play out."

"I'm sorry." She tucked the ruby back within the folds of her jacket. "There are lots of rules, and I don't understand any of them. Hell, I'm not aware of their existence—until I've transgressed. Like when I tried to join your pod."

He tucked her other hand in with the first, holding tight to them both. "'Tis on account of living as human for most of your life. Ye'll learn about being a Selkie—"

"Not if I go back to my bakeshop," she countered.

He ran his free hand through his hair and gentled his tone. "The odds of you returning to Wick aren't predictable. If Arcadia has thrown her lot in with the Druids by creating an illusion sure to draw wickedness across her borders, we have moved into an endgame."

He took a measured breath, wanting to protect her but needing her to recognize how serious things were. "If we lose the battle, magic will fade. Surely, ye'll wish to spend what little time remains to us in the seas."

She closed her teeth over her lower lip, biting hard enough a drop of blood welled. "I'd figured out the part about Arcadia. I'm guessing such a thing has never happened before or it would be part of the old stories." Raene shut her eyes for a moment. When she opened them, she said, "I can't think about losing. It's not productive. Better for me to remain in the moment, fight what's in front of me."

He tightened his grip on her hands in silent support. He'd been so caught up in worry about his pod and what would happen to Earth once White Magic departed, he'd skirted the short-haul perspective.

They hadn't lost anything. Not yet. If the goddess blessed them, they'd succeed.

He twisted to glance at the rough time markers inscribed in the side of the tube. "Not much farther."

She pried her hands out from his and craned her neck to see what he'd just checked. "What language is this written in?"

"This far back, they're runes in ancient Minoan."

"No wonder I can't decipher them."

"Closer to modern time, the Guardian switched to Roman numerals. The marker we just passed suggests we've made it to about a thousand years before men started using Christ to mark the passage of time," he explained.

"Doesn't seem as if we've been in here for all that long."

"We haven't." Aegir suspected the guardian was privy to

the nature of their journey and had speeded things up. He'd never met the divine being who managed the time-travel portals.

"You're quiet," Raene observed.

"I've been thinking about the best way to approach the dragons and about the one who caretakes this portal through time. He and his brother, the Dream Guardian, wield enormous power."

"I may have met the Dream Guardian once," Raene said.

"Tell me about it," Aegir urged, fascinated because he'd never come face to face with either brother.

"Not sure if I can without tipping the negative emotion meter that's supposed to be the kiss of death." She smiled ruefully. "It happened after Rolf stole my pelt, when I was railing against my fate, but that will have to be enough for now."

"I ken well enough how devastating it must have been. Why do ye believe 'twas the Guardian?"

"Because his eyes matched what I've read of him. He never talked to me, but I looked into his eyes and a story unfolded. Turned out it was an accurate depiction of the next half century." She squinched her brows together. "I never imagined eyes could display a collage that held me riveted. It was like watching a movie."

"Later, I'd value hearing the whole story."

"If we have a later"—she smiled ruefully—"I'll tell it to you."

"Ye mention myths and stories a lot. I'm guessing ye like to read."

Her smile deepened. "I adore reading. It's pulled me through difficult times."

The rocking slowed and came to a halt.

"Ready yourself, lass. This next part happens fast." He stood and pulled her upright, holding her against him. The time-travel tunnel's walls faded, and a gateway formed, shimmering in shades of silver white. Aegir hustled them through it. Any hesitation at this point met with unpleasant consequences.

Once the guardian was done transporting someone, he was truly done. If you didn't move quickly enough, a blast of wind tossed you out of the tunnel onto your stomach.

The hot, dry, almost unbreathable air of Fire Mountain hit him like a wall and seared his nostrils. He imagined the small hairs within burning to a crisp. Raene gasped and shielded her eyes from the merciless twin suns beating down on them. Packed, dry red earth stretched in every direction, but it wasn't flat. Hummocks and boulders interrupted it at intervals. The glitter of gold and silver flickered invitingly from where the suns' rays bounced off assorted coins and bars of precious metals. Cliffs rose in the distance. Within them lay the dragons' council chamber and the single spring that provided water in this arid, volcanic land.

Aegir had been there before when the dragons had been more kindly disposed toward him than the occasion they'd sent him packing without so much as an audience.

"What happens next?" Raene kept her voice low, almost as if she were afraid of disturbing something she couldn't see.

"The dragons know we're here. One of them will show up soon."

"We didn't exactly come up with a plan," she ventured.

"Nay, lass. 'Twas wishful thinking on my part. No such thing as a plan when ye're dealing with dragons. They can sniff out partial untruths."

"So we lay our cards on the table?"

"Aye. If we get that far. 'Tis entirely possible—actually likely—the dragon who flies to meet us will refuse to hear us out. If that happens, he'll stand guard until we leave."

"Why not a she?" Raene tried to smile but ended up hiding her mouth in the crook of one arm. "Damn, breathing is a chore here," she mumbled.

Sweat dampened his forehead. He swiped a forearm across it, but not before some dripped in his eyes. The dragons could have settled anywhere, yet they'd bound themselves to this inhospitable borderworld. Supposedly, herds of wildebeests roamed, serving as both food and possibly entertainment when the males held their annual dominance displays. He had no idea what they grazed on unless the dragons planted grain in a distant part of Fire Mountain.

And he'd never actually seen anything living here other than dragons.

As they waited, he turned in a full circle. A string of volcanoes, some belching steam and smoke, circled the borderworld. Fire Mountain was the largest. He picked it out easily as it assumed a prominent position on the horizon. Anything that high should have snow, but not here.

Raene wiped her face with a corner of her jacket. She started to take it off, but then muttered something about the heat being worse without it. She sank to the sandy dirt. Before Aegir could correct her, haul her to her feet before some dragon decided she'd disrespected them by sitting, she jumped back up.

"Oh hell! That's hotter than the air, if it's even possible."

"They're watching us," he cautioned her, mouth right next to her ear. "I ken the heat is oppressive, but ye must remain standing."

"How long before our emissary of goodwill shows up?" Raene offered a lopsided smile. Sweat tracked down her face and dampened her hair, turning it a darker red.

"I doona ken."

He didn't bother to correct her, tell her it could just as easily be the hangman set to tighten a noose around their necks, as an emissary of anything positive. He rocked from foot to foot to mitigate heat burning the soles of his feet. He'd never had to wait this long. During his other trips to Fire Mountain, a dragon had descended from the skies moments after his arrival. He had no idea what the delay meant. Surely, Fire Mountain hadn't run out of dragons available to serve as a greeting party.

He sent magic zinging outward, checking. And withdrew

it fast. Dragons were here. Lots of them. Nothing to do but wait until one appeared.

Twin suns crossed the sky while they remained near where the tunnel had spit them out. Thirst became a constant, nagging companion. If he'd known how long they'd be here, he'd have brought water. He knew better than to cross to the opening he could barely see in the cliffs. Water lay within, but the pool was sacred to dragonkind. They'd kill anyone who drank from it without leave.

"Should we go?" Raene's voice sounded as cracked and dry as his throat.

He glanced at the sky for the umpteenth time. "If the suns reach the horizon and no one has come, then we shall, indeed, depart."

"Was this some kind of test? Leaving us here like this?"

He shook his head. He had no idea, and anyone who second-guessed a dragon was the worst kind of fool. He brushed a strand of Raene's hair back from her wet face. Much longer and both of them would run out of sweat. If that happened, they'd have to summon the time travel tunnel before the heat killed them.

The steady beat of huge wings carving through the still, windless air snapped his head up. Two dragons, one black and the other a coppery gold, winged toward them. The golden dragon was on the smallish side—for a dragon.

Aegir stood next to Raene, facing the approaching wyrms.

They landed amid a small shower of sand and rocks,

smelling of fire and sunbaked clay. Aegir bowed low. "Thank you for heeding our arrival."

"Pfft. We figured ye'd leave, but ye dinna," the black said. "My name is Keene." He nailed them with his whirling blue-green eyes.

"I told you they wouldna go without an audience," the gold said. "I am Eletea." Her whirling eyes were dark with copper centers.

"The dragon from the Highlands?" Aegir quirked a brow.

"We ask the questions." Keene punctuated his words with a blast of fire, turning his head at the last possible moment to miss immolating them.

Aegir batted back annoyance. The goddamned dragons were arrogant as fuck. "Fine. Ask away."

"We know why ye're here," Eletea intoned in a singsong voice that made him want to strangle her.

He started to inquire if keeping them waiting for hours was akin to refusing aid but didn't. Being chided once for trying to glean information was quite enough.

Raene squared her shoulders. "If you already know Arcadia is under attack, will you lend us your assistance?"

Aegir froze. While he believed in clear communication, he'd have traded a few pleasantries first, although the dragons were making that approach damned difficult.

"Ha!" Another blast of fire from Keene. "Ye havena been a Selkie for long." His nostrils flared and he leaned closer, snuffling like a pig hunting truffles. "How is it ye smell of Tarika?"

"They helped her, you cretin." Eletea smirked. "Ye never listen. Ye're too busy telling the rest of us how wonderful ye are."

Keene twisted his sinuous neck to look down at the other dragon. "Disrespect willna be tolerated, youngling."

Fire blasted from Eletea's mouth. It hit Keen square in the chest and bounced off harmlessly. Made sense their scales would be impervious to fire since they'd been forged in the stuff.

Eletea returned her attention to him and Raene. "The reason ye've been waiting for so long is we canna make up our minds about what to do. Some dragons council jumping into your war with demonkind. Others are less enthusiastic about setting such a precedent."

Aegir bowed low again. "I bring word from the Arch Druid. He promises two Druids will be assigned to do your bidding forever."

"With such an incentive, who could say nay?" Keene laughed uproariously at his own joke, puffing steam and smoke and ash.

"Speak for yourself," Eletea huffed. "I could find a use for my very own Druid."

"What makes ye believe one would be assigned to you?" Keen countered. "They're seers. Like as not, they'd help our two blind seers look into the future."

Aegir couldn't restrain himself. "Have you?"

"Have we, what?" Keene's eyes whirled faster, and Aegir looked away.

"Scryed the future of Earth?"

"Why would we do that?" Eletea demanded. "Humankind are no concern of ours."

"What happens to dragons if good magic fails?" Raene asked.

Keene replied, "Nothing."

In the same breath Eletea said, "We're not certain."

"Mmph. Which is it?" Raene persisted.

Keene puffed out his chest and crossed his taloned forelegs across shiny black scales. "There is no precedent, so we canna be certain."

"When your seers look in the pool or their glass or however they gather information," Aegir pressed, "what do they see?"

"That is for dragonkind to know." Keene's words held finality.

More wingbeats drew Aegir's attention, and he shielded his eyes with a hand. This time, a red dragon approached. As it drew nearer, he was certain it was Tarika. She landed in a flurry of heated air and displaced rocks.

Once again, Aegir bowed.

Raene walked to the red dragon. Reaching into a pocket, she held out the ruby. "When I took this, I had no idea I'd transgressed. Please. Allow me to return it to you."

Aegir wanted to throw his body between Raene and Tarika, but he held back. Sometimes, a pure heart and noble intentions went a long way toward righting wrongs. The dragon crouched and held out her forelegs. "Come close, little Selkie."

Raene scooted forward. Fear traded places with hope on her expressive features. She extended her hand holding the ruby and said, "Apologies, First Born. The stone was beautiful, and it sang to me."

Tarika lifted Raene easily, cradling her against her chest. "I appreciate your honesty. The reason it called to you is because I meant it to be yours, a gift from me to you for helping rescue Glaedr."

"How is he?" Raene asked.

"Thank you for inquiring. He will rise beyond his imprisonment, but we were not a moment too soon. The demon had already begun annihilating the protections around his mind. Were Glaedr older, he'd have had an easier time fighting back. As it was, he barely held on. He wanders in dark places, but our healers are confident he will find his way back to us."

"I'm so glad. Every story that has a happy ending is one more way for us to defeat evil."

"Indeed, little Selkie." Tarika bent forward and placed her gently on the ground. She turned to the other dragons. "Our leaders have spoken. We shall aid the Druids in their fight to preserve Arcadia."

"What?" Keene shouted. "It's preposterous. We have never bothered ourselves with human affairs."

"Check your facts. Arcadia isn't human," Eletea pointed out, her words dripping with derision.

"Ye need to learn respect," Keene sputtered.

"Oh, and I suppose ye're the one to teach me?" Eletea jeered. "Just like Cavet tried to do? Look what happened to him."

Aegir searched his memory. Cavet was the philandering dragon who'd tried to poison Eletea and lost his life for his crimes. Dragons didn't fuck around. Transgressions were met with death.

Fire flew from Keene's jaws. Before it finished burning, he'd vanished.

Tarika shook a talon at Eletea. "Ye really shouldna bait him."

"But 'tis so much fun."

"Our men are fragile." Tarika skewered the younger dragon with her golden eyes.

"Pfft." Eletea puffed smoke. "He bedded Arianrhod and then dumped her. What kind of man does it make him?"

Aegir swallowed surprise. Apparently, the virgin huntress was even less a virgin than he'd imagined. For some stupid reason, he'd assumed Angus was her only fall from grace and the stories about her having taken a dragon lover weren't true.

"Thank you so much for offering your aid," Aegir spoke up before the two female dragons wandered too far off track.

"How will we communicate with the dragons who will help us?" Raene asked.

"Ye willna need to," Tarika replied. "We shall sense your need and dispatch what assistance we deem necessary."

"But what if—?" Raene began.

Aegir cut her off with another round of thanks.

"Tell the Arch Druid we shall hold him to his word," Tarika said. "Our seers are anxious to mingle their brand of magic with Druid ability. Cathbad visits occasionally, and he is always a revered guest."

Aegir nodded pleasantly. Not only had they secured a promise of aid, but he'd learned many things on today's journey. "If ye've no further need of us, we'll return to Arcadia with welcome news."

Tarika bent once again. A slash from her talon marked Raene's forehead with a three-inch gash, and then she did the same to him. "Speed is critical, my friends and *allies*"—she stressed the last word—"so I am opening our travel portal to you this one time. 'Twas why I marked you, so the portal would accept you as one of dragonkind. Be sure to suck in a big breath. The trip will be short, but airless."

A glistening gouge opened in the arid ether, glowing red on every side. The baked-clay smell nearly choked him. Aegir gripped Raene's hand and jumped through into a far less commodious enclosure than the way they'd arrived. The walls of the oblong chamber were hot. Hotter than Fire Mountain had been. Breathing wasn't an option. He cradled Raene in his arms, hoping she'd find trapped air molecules in his clothing. Rather than a gentle rocking motion, the dragons' time-travel tunnel jostled them. He stumbled and ran up against a wall once. His clothing smoldered, and he didn't make that mistake again. Lungs burning from lack of air made his head spin.

Finally, when he was certain he was on the edge of lapsing into unconsciousness, the tunnel ejected them into damp and cold. He sank to wet ground, still holding Raene. Both of them were gasping and panting as they sucked oxygen into air-starved lungs.

"Christ!" Raene pulled out of his arms, still panting. "That was hideous. I thought dragons needed to breathe."

"Apparently, they can hold their breath a whole lot longer than we can." The grayed-out aspect had departed, and he could see again. Somehow, they'd ended up back on his island. It was raining, but he welcomed the chilly drops.

"I'll never complain about rain again," she murmured.

"Nothing like a wee bit of comparison to make ye appreciate what ye have." He got creakily to his feet and extended a hand to her. "Come on. We have to let the Druids know."

She lurched upright, clinging to his hand for support. "Thanks. I'm weak as a newborn colt."

He was too, but he'd be damned if he'd admit it. "Whatever possessed you to offer up the ruby? Ye scared the stuffing out of me when ye waltzed close to Tarika and held it out."

Raene shrugged. "I've always trusted my instincts. And the ruby wanted out. It has a way of communicating. I couldn't deny its request."

"Makes sense, lass. It understands Tarika is its maker, and it was seeking either a way home or permission to remain with you."

"That's as good an explanation as any other. Once we get through with the Druids, I'm starving. And thirsty. Standing around on Fire Mountain sapped everything in me."

He hurried to the locker outside his cave that held supplies and withdrew glass bottles that held seawater. A shot of magic turned it pure and drinkable. He handed her one and took the other for himself.

While he slaked his thirst, he called Krise with telepathy.

"Aye?" the elder Selkie answered immediately.

"The dragons are in."

After his whoops died down, Krise said, *"Good work. I chose well when I made you king."*

Aegir grinned. Praise from his da was rare enough, he'd welcome it no matter what form it took. It didn't matter that their laws were why he was king. The only thing Krise had control over was the timing of when the torch passed from father to son.

"What?" Raene asked and set her bottle down.

"Nothing. Arcadia awaits. How about if ye take charge of the spell this time?"

"Really?"

His smile broadened. "Really."

Raene was surprised how quickly her power rose when she called it. She'd assumed it would be sluggish since she was so tired. The stone vibrated against her side from its protective pocket. Power flashed and flared—so bright she squinted—and a gateway edged in violet formed. She stepped through, blinking away afterimages from the light, with Aegir right behind her.

He'd been amazing on their journey to Fire Mountain. Strong, confident, knowledgeable. And on the trip back, he'd done his damnedest to protect her, offering her what little air was trapped within the folds of his clothes. She yearned for his arms around her, longed for the feel of his body pressed against hers, but crises had a way of throwing people together.

And their life had been one continuing crisis ever since he'd spotted her in the seas beyond his island.

Maybe what she was feeling wasn't anything beyond longing for reassurance and comfort. If she'd had more experience with men, she might have an easier time sorting her confused swamp of emotions.

The gateway winked out, and she turned to face an unfamiliar part of Arcadia. "Which way?" she asked.

"Hold up a moment," Aegir replied. "The land will guide us."

She felt foolish. Not that she'd spent much time here, but the land had, indeed, provided for her. A path formed, leading through a thick forest. This time, the trees were just trees, not weapons; wind blew through their branches in a pleasant sighing. What a contrast to Fire Mountain with its furnace-like heat.

After twenty steps, the forest fell away, and they were back in front of the castle. Druids flowed out of its doors, down its steps, and through the iron gates that opened of their own accord. Accompanying them were animals. Bears. Wolves. Coyotes. Deer. Hawks and eagles soared overhead. It took her a moment before she felt their magic and understood these were all Shifters.

The Arch Druid came to a stop in front of them, and she felt the force of his magic scan her mind. It prickled unpleasantly but didn't last long. "Ye bring good news."

"We do," Aegir agreed. "The dragons accept your offer of two Druids to assist their resident seers, and they promised aid."

Howls, yips, barks, and shrieks rose from the birds and

animals ranged around them. The air developed a glistening aspect, brimming with magic as some reached for their human forms.

"How will we contact the dragons?" another Druid asked.

"We asked the same thing," Raene answered. "They said they'd know when we needed them and send what help they deem necessary."

"But then we canna plot battle strategy with them," the Druid who'd spoken before said unhappily.

The Arch Druid raised a cautionary hand. "Their offer is deeply appreciated, and it will have to be enough. In truth, 'tis far more than I expected. Dragons were warriors afore Earth emerged from the sun. They scarcely need our assistance with strategy. The reverse is more likely true, that we could benefit from theirs."

The other Druid bowed low. "Sorry, Master. I was not thinking."

Arcadia's healing energy rose through Raene's feet, leaving her with a refreshed, glowing sensation. She knelt and patted the wet earth. "Thank you. I needed that."

"Arcadia has become attuned to your energy," the Arch Druid observed. He angled his head as if listening. "Ye carry dragon essence. How can that be?"

She withdrew the ruby, holding it in the flat of her palm. "Tarika gave it to me for helping rescue her young dragon." The stone brightened, pulsing with clear light, almost as if it were urging her to say more. "Uh, actually, I took it from the ocean floor while in seal form. See, Tarika and the young dragon were both crying, and—"

"'Tis fine." The Arch Druid halted her flow of words. "Ye've a clear, pure spirit. And the ruby holds untapped power. 'Twill aid us in the battle to come, for I have seen such in my glass." He stopped for a moment, and then added, "Did ye have it when ye sat within the castle before?"

"Yes, I did."

A thoughtful expression creased his face. "Either the stone has become more closely linked to your magic, or it's growing stronger. Both are good. I couldna sense it when ye were here last."

"It might be a combination," Aegir volunteered.

"Indeed."

A burly naked man with unruly brown curls that hung to mid-chest and a full beard stepped forward. "So long as the Selkies are here, introductions are in order. The rest of us met during our meeting."

Aegir nodded. "Excellent idea. Apologies. I'm not as sharp as I could be. We stood for hours in Fire Mountain's heat waiting for the dragons to make up their mind."

"Understood." The brown-haired man stuck out a hand. "I am Gerald, leader of the bear Shifter clan."

Raene stood next to Aegir shaking hands with Shifter clan leaders. The names blurred, but she remembered Delia, a wolf, and Marko, the chief bird. Conversation flowed around her since Aegir was friends with some of the other Shifters. Someone shoved a glass of the same cordial she'd drunk before into her hand. This time it remained clear because she didn't add her blood to it.

When she started drinking, she didn't stop until the tumbler was empty. "Thank you." She handed it back to the Druid who'd brought it to her.

"No need for thanks. Between the drink and Arcadia, ye'll be good as new verra soon."

Aegir detached himself from a small group of Shifters he'd been chatting with and joined her, handing his own glass to the Druid. "Many thanks." He directed his next words at Raene. "Are ye ready to leave?"

She nodded. Worlds where everyone and everything were magical still didn't feel typical, and she'd been to two of them today. Odd. Wondrous. Incredible. But not comfortable by any stretch of her imagination.

The Arch Druid trotted to where they stood. "Return to your island. Rest as best ye're able."

"When would you like us to return?" Aegir asked.

"Arcadia is already releasing a portion of the barrier surrounding it—" the Druid began.

"So we shouldn't leave at all?" Worry poured through Raene. If the battle to determine the future of good magic was upon them, they had to remain.

"'Tis safe enough." The Druid patted her arm. "Arcadia is a big place. 'Twill take time for the barrier to weaken, particularly since it must appear natural and not a contrivance to entice our enemy. Once the lure is in place, 'twill take more time yet for Hellspawn to react to what they'll surely interpret as good fortune."

"I ken most of that," Aegir said. "In real time, what is your best estimate of when ye will require us here. I must let Da know, so the Selkies add their strength to our army."

"Anywhere between two and five days," another Druid said. "Ye'll know. Ye'll feel the disturbance in your link with Arcadia."

Aegir clasped hands with the Arch Druid. Raene did the same. Strength and magic flowed from his firm grip. In that moment, she caught a glimpse of how ancient he was. Older by far than any Selkie she'd ever met. Looking up, she captured his gaze and blurted, "You must know the dragons. You're as old as them."

A ghost of a smile formed. "Aye, lass. I know most all of them." He placed a finger over his mouth. "About my age, shall we keep that little morsel a secret?"

Two Druids standing nearby burst out laughing. One clapped his liege across the shoulder blades and said, "Sure and the lass keeping her mouth shut will stop that wee bit of knowledge from escaping."

The Arch Druid elbowed him and mocked his brogue. "Goddess preserve me from the Irish."

"And the Scots," rose in a chorus from several Druid throats.

It seemed as good a note as any to leave on. The next time they met, no one would be laughing or joking. Aegir must have intuited her thoughts because he latched a hand beneath her arm and guided her back down the short path they'd trod before.

This time, he summoned magic to return them to the island. Night had fallen, a velvety darkness that surrounded them. The rain had stopped, and a few stars twinkled overhead.

"Feel like a swim?" Aegir asked.

"Sounds wonderful." Once he mentioned it, she understood how much she yearned to splash through the sea in her seal form.

"Good. 'Twill accomplish two goals. Mayhap three. We can eat. I can talk with Da and not risk being overheard."

"What's the third?" she asked as she began stripping out of her clothes, sheltering the garments beneath rocks so they wouldn't blow away.

Aegir removed his boots, shirt, and trousers, tucking them in with her things. It was hard not to look at him. He had the most beautiful body with wide, muscled shoulders. Dark hairs scattered around deep copper nipples. His stomach was flat, displaying sculpted lines beneath. Long, graceful legs met in a triangle of spiky dark hair. His penis was as beautiful as the rest of him. Just starting to swell, it held promise so profound, she had a hard time swallowing.

"We'll see if there is a third." He snapped his fingers, and their skins materialized out of the ether.

She caught hers, wrapping herself in it. Shifting gave her something to do other than throwing herself into his arms and capturing his phallus in her hand. She wanted to explore his body so much it was a physical ache that left a hollow place beneath her breastbone. Hopefully, the need consuming her would abate once she'd lumbered into the sea.

The shift happened faster than she expected, like all her magic since she'd claimed the dragon's gemstone. Raene checked her cheek to see if it had come with her, but it must still be tucked away in her pocket. She used her flippers to move her across the rock-strewn shoreline and on into the restless sea.

Aegir was a few moments behind her, his gorgeous coal-black pelt developing shades of blue as he immersed himself in the ocean. For a time, they swam aimlessly, letting the currents play with them as they scooped fish and ate until they were sated. The silence between them felt companionable, not awkward.

She'd never had other Selkies to swim with, not for long, anyway, and his presence was comforting. She wouldn't have minded being alone in the sea, but having Aegir swimming by her side was better.

Much better.

Her desire for him hadn't actually lessened, but it was different, deeper, more of a full body tingling. She'd never mated as a seal, and although she had a fair idea of the mechanics, the possibility never held much appeal.

Until now.

Raene did her best to wrench her mind away from sex. Thinking about it intensified her need. She munched through more fish as a diversionary tactic and asked, *"Did you find Krise?"*

"Aye, I did. He's in the midst of gathering as many of us as he can. He feels the pull of Arcadia, much as I do, so he will know when to arrive."

She rose to the surface to breathe and flipped over onto her back.

"Ready to return, lass?"

She patted the water's surface with her flippers. She loved the sea. Loved being a part of all its moods. Donning her seal's body always thrilled her, just as leaving it hidden in the cave where she'd found her dying mother left bittersweet dregs in her soul.

"I'm never truly ready to leave the sea."

He swam close enough, his body touched hers. *"Tis on account of your dual nature. Some Shifters are more human than animal, but not us. That ye've managed to maintain your human side as well as ye have is surprising."*

"I had no choice."

Even she heard the bitterness beneath her words. She'd tried to join a pod and been rejected, so she'd assumed no pod would want her. Not that it would have mattered since she had no idea where to find other Selkies beyond her Scottish home.

"I'm sorry, Raene. Truly, I am."

"If you'd been king then, would my petition have had a different outcome?"

"Probably, but for all the wrong reasons."

"What does that mean?" she bristled.

"Och, lassie. Ye're so beautiful. All I've been able to do since we met is think about you, imagine making love with you. Ye'd asked what the third thing was. I was hoping ye'd accept me as your mate."

He lifted himself partially out of the water and looked at her, his seal eyes dark and intense and his long whiskers quivering. She longed for arms to draw him into, but maybe it was good she was a seal.

"But the war…" she began, not certain where she wanted to go with that.

"The war will happen. We may not survive. I would hold you in my arms, taste the wonders of your body before we're so lost in combat there's nothing around us but death and loss and suffering. We may not have another chance, Raene. I love you."

"You only think you do."

"Nay, lassie. I've lived long, and I've found in you what I've sought for centuries. Be my mate, Raene."

The caution that had been her constant companion all her life dribbled away like foam on the sea. So overcome with emotion, she could barely breathe, she said, *"I accept."*

The sea exploded as Aegir jumped high, clapped his flippers, and then did it again. She barked laughter at the spontaneous display of delight. One of his descents landed partially on top of her, and he rolled her belly down. *"Swim, darling. We could love one another as seals, but our first time should be as humans. I canna wait to reach shore."*

She couldn't either. *"Is there some rule about how mates come together?"*

"Nay, but I want my hands and my mouth, not just my cock. Have ye never had sex as a seal?"

"Nope. Too many unknowns."

"Excellent. I shall be honored to be the first. We will have many adventures, léannan."

She didn't mention the war again. Didn't want to think about it. Whatever small island of peace and love they could carve out during the next few hours would be their special place. One she would cherish if neither of them survived the struggle to maintain Arcadia as a repository of magic. If only one of them made it through unscathed, she hoped it wouldn't be her. To declare her love, only to have it ripped away, would be more than she could bear.

Don't. Her mind voice was stern.

Raene understood all too well. Her usual method of planning and second-guessing everything wouldn't work. Not here. And not with the man swimming by her side. If she wanted a prayer of returning to her nice, safe bakeshop, the time to have left would have been before she'd ridden a dragon. Before she'd gone to Fire Mountain, and certainly before she'd pledged her aid to the Druids.

Her belly scraped the shoreline. She called shift magic to become human and conceal her pelt. By the time her transformation was complete, Aegir's arms wrapped around her from behind. He turned her so she faced him. The setting moon provided plenty of illumination to study his beautiful face.

"Are ye certain, lass?" He cupped the side of her cheek in one long-fingered hand.

She nodded, too overcome by emotion to manage words. She was scared for them. For magic. For what would become of Earth if good magic failed, but she and Aegir only had now to love one another. She wouldn't ruin it by voicing her fears.

He smiled, lazily, as if they had all the time in this world and others, and draped wet hair behind her ears just before he closed his mouth on hers. He wrapped his arms around her, and she hugged him back, wanting to get as close as she could. This was nothing like how their last kiss had begun. His lips were demanding, almost rough as they claimed hers. It was the kiss of a man who knew exactly what he wanted. His tongue pushed inside her mouth, and she sparred with it. Teasing, biting, sucking, they moved from mouth kisses to stringing them along any vacant real estate they could find. He nipped her lips. She nipped back, licking saltwater off his skin as she followed the line of his cheeks and jaw with her tongue.

It was cold on the beach in the pre-dawn chill, but she scarcely noticed. Where her body molded to his, her nipples pebbled, sending sparks to her belly. His cock shot to attention, curving against her hipbone. She thought she'd die if she couldn't touch him, so she moved a hand from where she'd been gripping his high, tight ass and stuffed it between them.

He groaned when she closed her fingers around his erection, and she moved to the side a bit to give herself better access, but also to straddle one of his legs. She pressed the center of her heat and need against his damp thigh, hips thrusting with a will of their own.

Raene hadn't come in forever, and she was beyond the point of controlling her perpetually denied arousal. He raised his mouth from the hollow of her collarbone and lifted her easily, balancing her thighs atop his lower arms. She closed her legs around his waist, feeling the tip of him searching for her entry. She was so wet, a bit of slithering moved him into position.

He sank into her, stretching her, making her scream with heat and need as she clawed at his back. Once he was fully encased in her body, he stopped moving.

"Nooooo." She rocked against him, urging him to do something. She was so close, a stray breeze would push her over the edge into a long, rolling climax.

"Hush, léannan. Trust me," he crooned as magic cascaded around them. Tiny streamers brushed her nipples. Others moved lower, wrapping around her nub as he flexed his cock within her. He caught the back of her neck with one hand and kissed her again. The pressure of his mouth against hers coupled with her nipples rubbing his chest and the magical ribbons of light pulsing against her clit turned her entire body into heat and lust and desire. Climax pounded through her, followed almost immediately by an even stronger one.

Her breath came fast against his mouth, and she felt the quick beat of his heart in the magic surrounding her. She didn't realize she'd closed her eyes, until she pulled away from his kiss and opened them.

"Greedy wench. Will that hold you till we're inside and in a bed?"

She tightened her vault around him. "Damn. You feel amazing."

"So do you, darling. My darling. I hate to disturb you"—he twitched his cock—"but inside offers so many more options."

Raene laughed. "Like we get to lie down?" She hip-butted him. "And I get to taste you."

"Now there's incentive." He laughed too and lifted her off his cock. It jutted from his body huge, hot, and proud.

It was all she could do not to fall to her knees and take him into her mouth. "If you're dead set on inside, we'd best go now."

"What man could resist such an invitation?" He scooped her into his arms and ran lightly up the beach toward the cavern he called home when he wasn't in the sea.

CHAPTER 15

$\mathcal{A}$egir was grateful his control had held. When Raene had dissolved around him in a flood of heat and contractions—twice—he'd clung to the thinnest of margins. He wanted to make her come a hundred times. The expression on her face when ecstasy took her melted his heart. She'd trusted him, allowed his magic to titillate her. If he'd had to thrust to make her come, he'd have lost it. Not that he couldn't have recovered to come a second time, but this was better. It kept him riding a fine edge of lust and made him a more creative lover.

Her body fit in his arms as if they'd been made just for each other. The globes of her breasts pressed against him, and her skin was pure silk where he touched her. Soft, but with strength hidden beneath.

He carried her inside the cavern and sent a blast of magic at the hearthstones to warm the enclosure. It had grown chilly during their absence. Not surprising since they'd been gone a long time. Shouldering the curtain that stood between the main portion of the cave and the sleeping alcove aside, he sank to the low bed with her still in his embrace.

She'd threaded her arms around his neck, and was busy running kisses along his collarbone and up to his ear and back.

"Ye've a wicked tongue, lass."

She lifted her head and gazed at him. "I do, huh?"

"Aye." He rolled onto his back, still holding her, but she wriggled out of his grasp and knelt over him, tracing the lines of his body with both hands.

"You're so beautiful." She pinched a nipple on her way down to his hips.

Sensation ratcheted through him and he made a grab for her, intent on dragging one of her legs across his body so he could get back inside her, but she evaded him easily.

Raene traded her mouth for where her fingertips had been. Slow and intimate, she licked and tasted, making hungry little sounds as she moved from lips to cheeks and chin and on down his chest to his nipples and lower still. Sparks of exquisite lust speared him, the intensity so brutal it was all he could do not to grab her and impale himself in the mystery of her body. It had felt incredible the brief time he'd been within her, but he'd been so focused on not coming, he hadn't truly immersed himself in loving her.

Now he could.

After drawing her tongue across his stomach, moving side

to side to lick down each hipbone, she traveled lower and pushed his legs wide enough for her to kneel between them. Her long, wet hair fell across his loins as she let her lips hover over him. Hot breath puffed over the head of his cock, but she stopped shy of actually touching him.

He gripped the sides of her head, encouraging her to do more than breathe on him, but she was strong and resisted his urging. Suddenly a trail of unbelievable heat ran from the base of him to the tip. It took a moment before he realized she'd licked him.

And then, she did it again before curling a hand around his unruly appendage, an appendage screaming it was on the verge of release. He rode herd on himself as she swiped her tongue around the head of his penis. First one direction then the other before she finally, finally, sank her mouth over him.

He jackknifed his body around until the musk of her surrounded him. While she worked him with hands and mouth, he pushed a hand between her legs until he could tease her vault with his fingers. At the same time, he fastened his lips over her distended nub of flesh, nipping and running his tongue around and around the ridges of her clit. She writhed against him and worked him harder.

Aegir gave up a losing battle with control and became a slave to the sexual heat and need pouring through him. Raene was his. His. Her nectar coated his lips and tongue, and her vault tightened around his questing fingers before another climax raced through her. He felt her release in his bones, in his soul, and semen bubbled from his balls, jetting into her.

He came hard, but all she did was hold him tighter, stroking and sucking until their ecstasy played itself out. He untangled their bodies and lay next to her, holding her and crooning wordlessly in the Selkies' language. She clasped him to herself, clearly wanting to erase any distance between them.

The gesture warmed him and touched his heart. Raene had accepted him, wanted him with the same single-minded intensity he craved her. She'd been on her own for so long, he'd wondered if she could lower her walls and let him in.

"I love you, lassie."

"Love you too." She nuzzled his neck.

They might have dozed off. The next thing he was aware of was kissing her, tasting him on her lips and tongue. Desire spiked again, and he pulled one of her legs over his hip and entered her. Heat closed around him, and he rolled them until she straddled him, her hair trailing across his chest. Her pale skin was still blotchy with passion from their last round of loving, but the color deepened as he gripped her hips and rotated his cock deep within her.

"I wish we could be like this forever," she murmured, eyes brimming with emotion.

"We can, lassie."

"Promise?"

He started to say, "Aye, of course," but he wouldn't lie to her. He loved her too much for that. Instead he said, "I will move heaven, earth, and every borderworld imaginable to hold our love sacred. And create a place safe enough for you and our children. Ye do want children, lass?"

"Of course. I hope I'm not too old for them."

"Ye're not. As Selkies go, ye're on the youngish side." He tightened his grasp on her, running his fingertips over her back and shoulders. Her body was amazing, perfect with its high, full breasts, rounded hips, and flat stomach. Long legs and an ass that would drive any man crazy completed the picture. The images in his mind mingled with the reality in his arms, and he blessed the goddess who'd been watching over them the day he'd noticed Raene swimming in the seas.

A bittersweet smile curved the edges of her lips. "Thank you."

"For what?"

"Being honest. I know what we face." The wistful expression was replaced by fierce determination. "Today is ours. Ours. Nothing else will intrude."

Aegir wasn't as certain. He'd been expecting Krise to show up with a phalanx of Selkies at any moment, but he didn't know that would happen. Not really—and not right away. He pulled her so she lay on top of him and fastened his mouth on hers, savoring the incredible sweetness of the woman in his arms. His cock swelled with new urgency as he made love with her, knowing the magic they made together would only grow richer and sweeter as they became more familiar with one another's bodies.

Time passed. They made love, ate, and made love some

more. They were drowsing against one another when Aegir felt a swath of familiar magic moving toward them. He reached around Raene to drag a blanket across her body.

"What?" she asked sleepily.

"Da is leaving the sea. He'll be here soon with others."

Raene's blue-green eyes creased in the corners. "Will he be angry? I'm not a full-blooded Selkie like I imagine he wanted for a daughter-in-law. Plus, I'm scarcely on his favorite Selkie list. Not after how he and I carped at one another."

Aegir pushed to a sit and laughed long and loud.

"What's so funny?"

When he got grip on his mirth, he said, "Da will be overcome with joy. He's been nagging me to come up with a mate for several hundred years. In truth, he's been silent for the last fifty, but 'tis on account of him having given up."

"Oh. Well, that's good then, I guess." She grinned. "He likes my baked goods. I can just see the two of you sitting in my shop, eating it down to the bones."

Aegir bent and kissed her, short, hard, and sweet before getting to his feet. "I'll rescue our clothing. If we got verra lucky, it willna have rained since we tucked them beneath those rocks."

This time she laughed. "A day without rain? In Scotland? You're daft."

"Well, I did put mine on top of yours, so if anything got soaked, 'twill be my garments. Back verra soon."

"Thank you," floated after him.

He turned. "For what, léannan?"

"Taking a chance on me. I was such a bitch when we met."

"Och, I'm good at seeing through smokescreens people throw in my face when they're nervous."

"I was not nervous—" she began, but he ran to get their clothes and missed the rest of her teasing denial.

Night had become day, and the day shaded to twilight, while he and Raene had been lost in one another; the sky held a purplish cast to the west. Krise and a flood of Selkies were lumbering out of the water, shifting as soon as they could. Aegir gathered the pile of clothing he and Raene had left. Mercifully, the top layer was more-or-less dry, which meant it had sprinkled throughout the day, but not actually rained. He darted back to the cavern and tossed the clothes within.

"Here ye are. I'm just going to greet the others."

She'd walked beyond the curtain separating the sleeping alcove and stood near the hearth. Red curls fell past her waist. Nipples peeked through the curtain of hair, enticing, inviting. "Thanks." She winked and hurried to collect the garments she'd culled from the trunks in the northlands.

He turned to leave, but she called after him, "What about your things?"

"I'll get them soon, lass. A whole lot of naked Selkies are about to converge on this spot. More than will fit inside the cavern, truth be told."

"They must be on their way through to Arcadia."

He'd guessed much the same. The enchanted land would

provide both clothing and weapons for them, much as it had for Raene when she'd journeyed there on her own.

He hurried back the way he'd come and bowed to his father. "Da. 'Tis good to see you." He scanned the ranks of Selkies, recognizing some from Gregor's pod.

"Ye as well, son. We shan't remain long. Arcadia summoned me, and so I gathered all who were capable of fighting. The only Selkies left are the verra young and a few of the women to keep them safe."

"If fortune doesna fall to our side, nowhere will be safe."

"I ken as much." Krise nodded solemnly.

Raene walked from the cave and scooted to Aegir's side. She held out a hand to Krise, and he shook it. "I heard the part about Arcadia summoning you," she told him and then glanced at Aegir. "Did you sense the same mandate?"

He shook his head. "'Twill come soon enough, never fear."

"I didn't think we'd be left out," Raene replied. "I like to understand how things work, though."

Aegir raised his voice, projecting it through the rows of Selkies ranged between them and the shoreline. "There's little enough time now, and later there will be none at all. I have chosen a mate. Raene shall be my consort. We have sealed our commitment to one another."

Cheers rose along with catcalls and many, "It's about time," comments.

"Our people will take this as a good omen," Krise told her. "Superstition tells us an unmated liege tempts fate."

"How so?" Raene asked.

Krise smiled grimly. "It leaves him open to enticement from a host of female demon seductresses from succubae on down the line."

Aegir felt familiar magic and turned to see Gretta, his mum, striding purposely toward him. Joy at seeing her was tainted by concern. Her health hadn't been good, and she should have been one of the Selkies to remain beneath the waves.

Should have been.

Steel gray hair fell to her knees. Her face had a few lines, but her eyes were the same clear cobalt blue they'd always been. He opened his arms, but she swept by him and gathered Raene into a heartfelt embrace. "I am Aegir's mum. Ye've made me a verra happy woman today. I never thought my son would give up his footloose ways."

Raene laughed softly and hugged Gretta in return. "Someday, I'd love to hear tales of his bawdy youth."

Gretta took a step back. Water dripped down her naked body, mostly sheltered by her hair. "If the goddess blesses us, we shall have that *someday* to indulge in idle gossip. I'd like nothing better. A pleasure to meet you, daughter-in-law. My husband spoke well of you."

Raene inclined her head. "A pleasure to meet you as well. Krise and I didn't get off to a very good start. I'm relieved he's not holding my quick temper against me."

"He wouldna," Gretta said. "He has quite the temper too, though his is cloaked in sarcasm."

Aegir wandered through the assembled Selkies, greeting

his pod by name and finding out who the newcomers were. Everyone's mood was subdued; they all understood the gravity of what lay ahead. Some wouldn't return from Arcadia, but they went willingly.

If good magic flickered and died, none of them would survive.

Krise and Gretta flanked Raene, talking with her. Aegir smiled inwardly, hoping they weren't grilling her too much. Of course, they'd want to know all about her. Krise already knew Gregor had been her da. Aegir wondered who the Selkie half of her mum had been. He'd never asked her, and she might not know. Mating with humans was frowned on, so whichever parent had been a Selkie likely hadn't stuck around.

He gathered his people in a rough circle. Over a hundred Selkies stood proud. It was cold, but no one complained. He motioned to his parents and Raene, and they slid into place next to him.

Aegir raised his hands. "I will make this brief, for if Arcadia has summoned you, she'll expect your presence within her boundaries. I implore Poseidon and Amphitrite, king and queen of the seas, to bless our endeavor. To keep us safe and to strengthen our resolve in the face of the horror of demonkind."

He took a breath. "Ye will see things, hear things that will change you in days to come, yet never lose your sense of who ye are, or your connection to the seas. The oceans are ageless, timeless. They are our link to the infinite. And yes, I ken they're in trouble, but we can only address one problem at a time.

"Right now, that problem is Arcadia's need of us. She's never requested assistance before through her stewards, the Druids. We must not fail her."

Aegir scanned the assemblage. Cries of, "We shall not fail," were joined by closed fists punching the air.

"Goddess's blessings on each of you." He dropped his hands to his sides. There was no more to be said.

The Selkies filed past him one by one. He gripped each of their hands as they passed by him on their way to the island's high spot and its gateway to Arcadia. At last, he stood alone on the beach with Krise, Gretta, and Raene. Night had fallen, a dark night where clouds occluded both moon and stars.

He turned to his mum but before he could say anything, she held up a hand. "Doona tell me I should return to the sea. Ye're my liege and if ye order me to return, I'll have no choice." She pushed her shoulders back, rising to her full height, which still placed her a head shorter than him.

"She and I hashed this out," Krise said.

"Aye, and I told him if we lose this battle, all is lost anyway. If I dinna fight by his side, if I hid myself away beneath the waves and he died, I would never forgive myself. Even if we win and magic doesna fade, I doona wish to face a world without my mate by my side."

"Och, darling." Krise wove an arm around her waist.

"It's fine, Mum. I understand."

Breath swooshed from Gretta. She'd come fully prepared

to defy him—argue with him—and was relieved it hadn't come to that.

"We should go," Krise said.

"We'll join you presently," Aegir replied. "I suspect Arcadia can only absorb so many newcomers at a time. When she calls me, Raene and I will be there."

"When do ye expect the dragons?" Krise asked. His tone was casual, but Aegir heard the worry beneath. He understood because he wasn't totally comfortable with how he'd left things in Fire Mountain. Yet he'd had no choice. The dragons had promised their support and dismissed them. Remaining to hash out the fine points hadn't been an option.

"I wish I knew." Aegir exhaled sharply.

"If they promised," Gretta said, "they'll be there. A dragon's promise binds them."

Aegir arched a brow his mother's way. "And ye know this how?"

She smiled, except it was far more than an upward curve of her lips. Gretta offered one of those timeless female expressions that conveyed knowledge edged with superiority.

"I wasna always mated to your da. I had a long life afore that time. I may have run into a dragon or two."

Aegir waited, but it was clear his mum was done talking. He stepped close and hugged her. "Gentle seas, brisk wind, and plentiful fish."

"Same to you, son." Krise's voice had a catch to it. He had to be worried about his mate. Centuries older than him, her warrior days were long since behind her. But she'd been clear.

Aegir could order her back to the sea, but it would break her heart. And if Krise died, she'd never forgive Aegir for forcing them apart.

He gripped Raene's hand and watched his parents walk away from them.

"You're so fortunate," Raene said, her voice low. "To have parents who love and value you. Who aren't conflicted about who they are."

"Did your mum know both her parents?"

"Only her mother, the human half of her genetics. The Selkie didn't even stay long enough to see her born."

"'Tis probable he's still alive, your grandda."

She shrugged. "If seeking him out is anything like my experience with Gregor, why would I bother?"

Aegir picked his words carefully. "'Tis highly doubtful he sold his soul to demons. Gregor is the only Selkie I've ever heard of who did that. 'Tis far more likely he was taken with your grandmum and lured her to his bed. One of the ironies is that Selkie matings with humans usually create offspring—"

Raene shot him a shocked look. "Does that mean I'm pregnant?"

"Matings with humans, lassie, and only if the human wishes for a child. If we got verra lucky, you might be pregnant, but two Selkies are not nearly as fertile as a Selkie and a human."

She knitted her brows together. "So grandmum must have wanted a baby with her Selkie lover."

Aegir nodded. "Aye. Selkie men can be verra captivating. What woman wouldn't want a bairn from one of us?" He managed a deadpan delivery, and she punched him softly.

"You're amusing. Probably also freezing. Come inside and get dressed."

"Are ye tired of gazing on my nakedness already?" He waggled his hips at her.

"I'll never tire of looking at you, you captivating specimen, you." Her deadpan wasn't quite as good as his, and the last part of her words was lost in laughter.

Arms woven around each other, they covered the distance to the cave. It was warm from the hearth and their earlier lovemaking. He let go of her long enough to filch a bottle of mead from the spirit cabinet and crack the wax seal.

She picked up the glasses they'd used earlier and held them while he poured each of them a jot of the amber-colored liquor. "I'd like to propose a toast," she said.

"Funny," he replied. "'Twas exactly what I was about to suggest. Ye first."

"To victory. And to us."

"I'll drink to both of those, lass. Slainte." He clinked his glass against hers and drank deeply. His heart was so full, he was surprised it hadn't cracked wide open.

She linked an arm through his and tugged in the general direction of the bed they'd so recently vacated. He wrapped an arm around her and kissed her, as aroused as if they hadn't spent the entire previous night and all of today making love.

The kiss was developing a life of its own as their bodies

strained against one another when he felt Arcadia's summons deep in his stomach.

She pulled away from him, her eyes wide, worried. "I felt something. Kind of like a mule kicking me in the guts. It was Arcadia, right?"

He nodded. "Aye, lénnan. My léannan." He let go of her and began pulling his clothing on. "We mustn't tarry. Something about that call suggests trouble is already upon us."

Raene zipped her jacket to her chin and pulled up the hood. "I'm ready."

He wasn't, but he wouldn't tell her that the thought of maybe losing her cut his soul to bloody ribbons. He bent to lace his boots and turned to her. "Be careful, lassie. No heroics. Stay behind me, and—"

"I'll do what I have to," she cut in. "Let's get this behind us so we can figure out the rest of our lives."

He sensed her fear, but it wasn't holding her back. He killed the flow of power warming the hearth and clasped her hand. Together, they hurried to the spot where the barrier between Earth and Arcadia was thinnest. He'd just begun his incantation when a portal formed. It wasn't glowing as brightly as normal, which clinched his impression Arcadia was already under attack. Pushing his fears for Raene to a distant spot, he stepped past the boundary with his mate by his side. They'd do this together.

The goddess wouldn't be so cruel as to rob him of his fated love, not when he'd only just found her.

The portal snapped shut behind them as if Arcadia lacked the ability to hold it open. Raene twisted to face him. "I love you. No matter what happens, I love you."

He held her close for a long moment. "I love you too, lassie. And now, we must go."

Still holding her hand, he searched for a pathway, knowing Arcadia would direct them to where they were needed most. It formed off to their right, pale and luminous. The moment they set foot on it, the stench of blood and guts filled his nostrils. The clank and clash of battle rose along with the reek of expended magic.

"No armor for us this time," Raene observed.

"Arcadia is too weak to provide it," he told her and led them forward. The attack had come before the Druids thought it would, but it made sense. Arcadia powered their seers' visions with her enchantment. If the magical land had weakened sufficiently, everything dependent on its power would have deteriorated as well.

He summoned magic until it blazed around them. Raene wove hers in with his, adding to his ward. As ready as they were likely to be, they plunged through Arcadia's forests. Worry streamed from the trees, and Aegir moved faster. The trees knew everything. Interconnected by root and shared consciousness, their knowledge bit deep.

"Will the trees help?" Raene panted the question.

"As much as they can, lass. 'Tis their world too."

CHAPTER 16

*R*aene didn't understand how she was rushing through thick timber along a wavery path. She should have been too scared to move, but somehow the fear had shuffled aside, taking up residence in a spot that didn't immobilize her. So much was unfamiliar about fighting and battle strategy, she was intensely relieved she wouldn't be wrestling her own anxiety along with the enemy.

I did all right when we battled the Fae, she reminded herself. Then, the trees had bailed them out, though. She had no idea how much of their power came from their roots buried deep in Arcadia's soil. If they, too, drew their strength from the land, their ability to respond might be limited. She'd asked Aegir, but his answer had been equivocal, which meant he didn't know, either.

The path twisted around a giant tree bole and spit them out in a clearing. At its far side, a gaping black hole pulsed.

Suspended a meter or so in the air, it was edged with short, sharp protuberances that looked like fangs. Was the thing a giant mouth?

Aegir wasn't hindered by her uncertainty. Lightning flashed from his raised hands, mowing through a line of three-foot tall misshapen creatures with red eyes scattered across knobby foreheads. They carted clubs, so maybe they depended on force rather than magic to fight.

She took stock of the clearing and decided there had to be many battles raging across the land. This couldn't be the primary one since she didn't see any of the Selkies from the beach. Men and women pulsing with Shifter magic battled an assortment of ghouls, hobgoblins, and other oddities. Many of the Hellspawn had greenish ichor pooling from their mouths.

Poison. What else could it be with that rotten stench?

Raene jumped out of the way of a swinging cudgel. One of the little bastards had snuck around behind her and Aegir. Meant they weren't as dumb as they looked. She angled magic at its chest; it leered at her, unfazed by what should have killed it.

This one was taller with a hooked beak of a nose and patches of black hair strewn across a skull covered with suppurating sores. Something like a wave of darkness broke over it. When the coruscation cleared, it was a meter taller with skin splitting over places bone showed through.

Aegir was fully engaged killing a winged horde that had just emerged from the mouth-like thing at the other side of the clearing. She didn't want to distract his attention, so she eyed her adversary, trying to figure out what would at least slow it down. It raised its upper lip, displaying rotting teeth in black jaws.

"Awk. You're already dead." She drew back a pace. No wonder she couldn't kill the fucking thing.

One of the Shifters—maybe a bear from his broad-shouldered build—danced past and thrust a long blade her way. "Cut off its head. Only way. Then set fire to the remains."

Raene did a doubletake. She recognized him from their last trip to the Druids' castle. "Gerard?"

"Yup. It's me. You remembered."

Before she could ask more questions, like what incantation brought fire, he leapt sideways to avoid a ghoul dripping gray goop that reeked of death and rot. The thing half-landed on him, and another Shifter—this one female with tightly braided blonde hair—sliced a blade through the abomination.

It shrieked, high and thin and piercing, but it let go.

"Raene!"

Aegir's cry brought her spinning about, blade at the ready. The growing monster was taller still and centimeters away. She barely had space to swing the blade. The first time she tried, it bounced off. She stepped back, gritted her teeth, and swung the unwieldy sword once more.

This time, she put all her weight into it. The weapon was heavy, and she'd never had any training in fighting with blades—long or short. The monster ducked beneath the swinging steel. With nothing to stop its trajectory, the sword spun her in a worthless circle until she was able to dig in her feet and stop herself.

Before she got her bearings, sharp claws grabbed both her arms. The creature wasn't going to sit still and let her cleave it in two. No, it hefted her into the air until she was even with its hideous features. The smell was so atrocious, she'd have clapped a hand over her mouth and nose, but both still clutched the sword.

"Raene. Drop the blade. Do it now," Aegir yelled.

She let go and heard it clatter to the rocks and dirt. She saw a flash as Aegir raised it, but the creature that held her captive was so tall, he'd never be able to reach its neck. She writhed, trying to shake its hold on her, but she may as well have tried to move a boulder.

It was edging closer, laughing and spraying her with stinking spittle, as it prepared to take a bite out of her face or neck or whatever its not-so-feeble brain had hatched up.

Brain. Its brain had to be right behind its eyes.

Without stopping to think about touching the abomination, she lifted both hands and jabbed her extended index fingers right into his eyes. His howl of pain and outrage nearly deafened her, but he did let go.

She dropped to the ground like a stone, remembering at the last minute to curl into a ball to lessen the odds of breaking something. By the time she rolled to her feet, Aegir must have taken advantage of the monster bending over, probably to snatch her up again, and he'd beheaded it. Black blood geysered everywhere. A few jets spattered her before she scuttled out of the way.

The head was trying to roll back to the body, but Aegir gave it a stout kick. Magic bubbled from him, and the stinking, headless corpse first smoked, and then caught fire. The flames smelled almost as bad as the abomination had, but at least it was dead. Or dead again.

"What the hell was that?" she yelled.

"Hard to say. The undead take many forms beyond vampires."

She ran to his side and held out a hand for the long blade. He shook his head. "'Tis too big a weapon for you. It nearly got you killed."

She didn't bother arguing. Nor did she waste time thinking about her near brush with death. No point. She was still here. It was the most important thing.

Gerald, the bear Shifter who'd given her the blade, ran to them. His brown hair was gathered into a queue. Soot and blood streaked his face, but his brown eyes shone with sharp intelligence. "That." He pointed at the gash in the ether. "We have to shut it. Permanently. No matter how many Hellspawned atrocities we kill, more show up through that hole."

"What have ye tried?" Aegir asked.

"Damn near everything." The Shifter blew out a noisy breath. "The main battle is half a league distant. We have to get there, but we can't leave that hole open. If we do, it's like offering Arcadia to the enemy. You two were the last to show up in this spot. Arcadia led you here for a reason. Something about our combined magic will blow up that gateway."

"I hope ye're right." Aegir clapped the other man across the shoulders.

"Makes two of us," the Shifter retorted.

Raene twisted her head from side to side. For now, the flood of wickedness had at least slowed down. The Shifters, maybe thirty, all dressed similarly in brown hunting leathers, killed with a chilly precision and were making progress holding the clearing. It was as good an opportunity as they'd ever have to deal with the source of the fell creatures.

They might not get another chance. More things like the smoking ruin a few meters away might march through, and they were damned difficult to obliterate. A chill tripped down her spine. Done searching the clearing, she ignored the worry seeping through her. Bodies might be concealed in the woods, but, at least so far, the only dead were demonkind.

What had the brown-haired Shifter said? Something about the main battle being elsewhere. They had to get there, but first, they needed to address the portal that seemingly led right into Hell. As she watched, half a dozen spiderlike things popped through. Five times as big as the largest tarantula, they sidled forward and back on their insectoid legs. Unlike spiders, they had tails dribbling with orange venom.

She knew to stay away from their rear ends without being told.

"Oh for Christ fucking sake," Gerald muttered. He sent a swath of blinding red light. When it cleared, four of the spiders had exploded leaving noxious, sticky heaps of grisly protoplasm.

If she hadn't loved cutting up things in biology class, she might have vomited.

"I've got 'em." The blonde Shifter sent her own blast of magic at the remaining spiders. One was cleaved in half. The other scuttled for the woods, barely making it.

"Let it go," Gerald told her.

"Hurry," she urged. "If those fuckers keep us on the defensive, we'll never get out of here."

Aegir and Raene moved nearer the maw disgorging one threat after another. The two Shifters flanked them. "Careful," Gerald warned. "One of us tried to probe it with magic when we first got here. It sucked him inside, and he never returned."

"Good to know," Aegir growled. "If we canna test it, how can we determine what will defeat it?"

"Same problem we had," the blonde muttered. Something with wings and a long sharp beak swooped toward them. She dragged an arrow from the quiver she carried across one shoulder, notched it in her bow, and shot it out of the sky.

"You're a good shot," Raene observed and looked beyond the dirt streaking the woman's face, almost certain she was the same Shifter from the Druids' gathering. "Delia?"

"Yeah. It's me. Thanks. Arrows conserve my magic. It goes farther if I'm not using it constantly."

Raene noticed an empty spot off to the side of the gateway. She skirted closer, analyzing the border rather than the gateway itself for weaknesses. At first, she didn't see anything useful, but something wriggled at the edge of her visual field. She repositioned herself, stepping over and around creatures she didn't recognize. Once this was over, the first thing she'd do was locate a mystical library where she could read up on Wicked Monsters 101.

Assuming she survived.

She tilted her head a bit more. There. If she held a particular angle, she saw something like a snake—or maybe it wasn't anything other than fat black rope. Regardless, it had sewn the portal into something. It wound up and over and through the edge of the thing, extending all the way around the gash.

She'd never considered air having anything to grab onto, but this was Arcadia. Perhaps its atmosphere was different. "Come here," she called, hoping Aegir would hear her.

He came at a run, followed by Gerald. Aegir had crafted a rough scabbard, and the sword hung from his waist.

"What is it, lass?"

"Stand next to me," she instructed. "And examine the portal." She stopped there, not wanting to insert ideas in case she'd been hallucinating. It was possible she'd added a layer of wishful thinking to whatever lay in front of her. She wanted to obliterate the entry point from Hell as much as she'd ever wanted anything.

Aegir was taller than she was. He altered his vantage point twice before he said. "Aye. I see it."

"As do I." Gerald's tone was far less jubilant.

"Not a simple matter of snipping through it, eh?" Aegir asked.

"It's a demon shapeshifter," Gerald grunted. "Right now, it looks like a snake, but it can take infinite forms. It's difficult to see clearly, but there might be more than one."

Delia sidled close with her bow. "Damn it. Nope. Only one of the bastards. It's not a shapeshifter, but Uroborus. And here I was thinking we were making progress. How in the goddess's name do we kill it?"

"We don't," Gerald growled, sounding more like a wolf than a bear.

"Could the bunch of you hurry it up?" a black-haired Shifter called from where he stood in the center of a pile of dead demonspawn.

"Trying," Raene yelled back and culled through her brain for what she knew about the serpent who ate its own tail, thus forming a symbol of everlasting something-or-other.

"So long as it's connected, we'll never close the portal," she said. "How can we lure it to let go of its tail?"

"The bigger question is how did it end up one of Satan's minions?" Aegir gritted out. "Once Uroborus was a god in his own right. Or damned close to one."

"You might be onto something," Delia crowed and grabbed Raene's hand. "Come on. In the myths I read, the snake was partial to women."

"What are we going to do?" Raene asked.

"Fall on our knees."

"Not too close to that opening, I'm not."

Delia settled into a crouch far enough from the hole to appease Raene, who knelt next to her. Aegir and two more Shifters flanked them, keeping them clear of a batch of gnomes who had just marched through.

"We're going to pray to the wyrm," Delia murmured. "Appeal to his godlike nature. Urge him to break free of darkness, so his loyal followers can worship him again."

"Does he even have any followers left?" Raene was trying to piece things together.

"Not the point. We tell him he does. He believes it, and voila!"

It seemed like an incredible longshot, but she didn't have any better ideas, so she followed the wolf Shifter's lead. Deep within a pocket, the dragon-tear ruby vibrated, but she couldn't tell if it was approval or warning.

"Damn, I hope this works, Delia."

"Call me Dee for short. You're Raene."

"Good memory."

"Some days it's better than others. Ready? We have to make this believable."

"Ready."

Raene listened as Dee chanted an unfamiliar prayer in English interspersed with Gaelic. She urged the serpent to return to Earth, told him he was missed, loved. That the Gnostics had adopted him as a symbol of everlasting life and how thrilled they'd be to pay homage to him again.

Raene added to Dee's recitation at intervals, still on her knees, head bowed. She felt bad, like she wasn't holding up her part killing things as bodies plopped to the ground around where they knelt. Waves of sensation rolled from the ruby. Was it telling her to stop? To get back to killing things?

Dee fell silent. Maybe she'd run out of material.

"What now?" Raene asked softly.

"We wait."

"Did he hear us?"

Dee twisted to face her. "I'd love to say yes, but I have no idea."

The nearest trees burst into bloom and scattered flower petals in front of the portal. Raene swallowed shock and picked up where Dee left off, imploring the god to forsake evil and once again become the great deity he'd been in ancient Egypt and other places.

The trees were mostly evergreens with a few aspens mixed in. They did not have flowers. Not in the world she knew.

But white and pink and red petals kept on fluttering down until a pile half a meter deep created a swath between them and the shimmering portal. Nothing wicked had crossed its boundary in the last few minutes. Maybe, just maybe, Dee's idea was working.

If the god had been corrupted by Satan, it might take time for its thoughts to clear. She reached deeper, tried to actually believe their strange attempt would turn the tide in their favor. Hope pierced her, almost as painful as the monster's claws had been when it held her suspended in the air.

Done with tossing petals, the trees had taken to swaying,

except there was no wind. A keening roar filled the clearing, growing in intensity until her ears ached. She sent magic to protect them. It helped a little. The stone in her pocket pulsed harder still.

"Keep it up," Delia shouted. "I don't know what changed. Maybe it was the flower petals, but he heard us."

If Raene hadn't had her gaze fixed firmly on the portal, she'd have missed the transition. One moment, it was there. The next, it imploded in on itself. A cobra-sized serpent unfurled coil after coil and glided toward them.

"Thank you. Oh thank you." Raene bowed her head, and the snake slithered across her shoulders before doing the same to Dee. One of the trees bent forward, offering a branch. Uroborus reached up and glided onto the proffered bough. The tree straightened, and the serpent disappeared into its foliage. The ruby shifted from pulsating to something reminiscent of a satisfied cat's purr.

Raene got to her feet and offered Delia a hand up. "Brilliant. That was absolutely brilliant."

Delia looked pleased at the compliment. "Desperate times call for desperate solutions."

"We need to get moving," Gerald said.

"What do ye know?" Aegir asked.

"The primary battle isn't going well. I feel it whenever one of my pack dies, and I've lost fifteen so far."

"Aw crap. Gerald. You should have said something." Dee chided him.

"Why? Nothing we could have done about it."

"Are there many splinter battles like this one?" Aegir asked.

"I don't believe so," Gerald replied. "After all, there was only one serpent who could hold a gateway open. Only reason he could get a toehold here was he used to wield White Magic. Those who bonded to darkness from their inception couldn't have managed to open and maintain a portal in Arcadia."

"Not yet," Aegir muttered.

"Yeah, not yet," Gerald concurred, "but if Arcadia falls, all bets are off."

"Do ye know if the dragons have come?" Aegir asked.

Gerald shook his head. "Not from what I can gather."

"We'd heard from the Druids," Dee cut in, "that the dragons would be our allies." She shook her head. "If they're going to keep their promise, they'd better show up damned soon. While there's still something left to save."

"They'll be here," Aegir said. "I secured that commitment from them."

Raene hoped he was right about the dragons imminent arrival. They'd won a small battle here in this clearing. Emphasis on small. Gerald and Dee set off at a lope with the other Shifters behind them. She fell in at the end of the line with Aegir next to her.

"Rest while ye can, lass," he said. "Conserve your magic so it can replenish. What we face next will be far worse."

She didn't say anything. They'd live through this. They had to. And they'd save Arcadia. Magic couldn't die. She wouldn't let it. And then she felt like an idiot. Who was she? Only the smallest of magical cogs in an unimaginably huge wheel. What impact could she possibly have over the outcome of this war?

Almost as if it were trying to answer, the ruby rocked back and forth, scattering more of its magic. Raene closed a hand around the stone and found it warm to her touch.

Wish I understood you better.

She waited, but the stone didn't answer. Not in words, anyway.

The place Uroborus had touched her tingled. Power flowed into her from the arc across her back. Along with the ruby and the god's touch came hope and determination. The same optimism that had kindled while she knelt in front of the unnatural portal turned into an inferno.

"We'll come through this," she told Aegir.

"I hope so. I love you, lassie." He snaked an arm around her, and they kept right on running.

CHAPTER 17

The silence of the clearing yielded to grunts, groans, shrieks, and cries as they neared the primary battle site. Aegir sorted sounds, but the characteristic bugle of dragons was absent. Damn it. Had Keene and his faction prevailed after all? He couldn't see Tarika, a First Born, making a commitment and then welching on it, though.

Something had happened to Raene, a subtle transformation. Before, her fear was obvious, but now courage shone from her upright shoulders and defiant expression. He was glad for her but hoped her newfound valor didn't lead her straight into some demon's clutches. He'd been frantic when the undead creature dug its claws into her and picked her up, intent on absorbing her essence into its own.

If they got out of this, he'd insist on lessons in swordsmanship. And a crash course of study to teach her the various iterations of evil. His thoughts brought him up short. Was he expecting one battle after the next, forever? According to the Druids, a win now would beat darkness back for years.

Aye, but not forever.

He came to a halt, forcing her to stop next to him. "Hold up, lass."

"Why are we stopping?"

"So we can assess what we face. And so I can try to reach Tarika with telepathy."

"What if she's not close enough? What if she's not one of the delegation they sent?"

"We shall discover answers to both your questions soon enough."

"Do you think the ruby might help?" She rooted through a pocket and held it out to him. The gem gleamed invitingly.

Aegir considered it. The dragon tear had been a gift to Raene, not to him, which meant it was matched to her energy. He closed her hand around the stone. "Thank you, but it will perform best if ye wield it."

She nodded and dropped her hand back into a pocket. "I'll try to raise her too, then."

He held them behind the last row of trees, sensing their outrage and unrest. Plant energy was normally peaceful, soothing, but these trees were angry at the desecration of Arcadia, their land. An enormous plain spread before them. So large, he couldn't see its far side. Hundreds of Shifters were engaged in fighting the same types of demonspawn they'd left behind.

No dead Selkies. Not yet. Much like Gerald, he'd have felt it if any from his pod had died. He wasn't so certain if the magical bonds had stretched to include the newcomers from Gregor's group, though.

"It's overwhelming," Raene said close to his ear. "So many dark creatures. Where do we even begin? There's not a gateway here—not one I can see. How are all the bad things getting through?"

"'Tis the place Arcadia lowered its barriers," he explained. "Demonkind doona require a portal in this spot. They can waltz in."

He switched to telepathy. *"Tarika. Are ye close?"* He waited through the space of twenty breaths and tried again.

Raene drew her brows into a thick, worried line. "She can't hear you. I tried too, but with the same result. Nothing. I figure she's too far away."

"That is one explanation. I can think of others." He was trying to remain hopeful. They couldn't tarry much longer on the sidelines. It didn't take a seasoned general to understand things were going badly, and not just because he'd finally felt the life flicker and die in a Selkie from his pod.

"None of it matters. Let's go." She tugged at his arm. "They need us out there." She jerked her chin at the battle. The dirt ran with blood. Red, black, and other muddy colors from dead Hellspawn.

Just as he'd sensed the trees' unrest, he also felt Arcadia groaning beneath his boots. The land was fighting back, but it was weakening. A whispery sound caught the edges of his attention, and he turned to see Uroborus drop from a nearby branch to Raene's shoulders where the serpent curved around her before gliding to the ground.

She crouched and extended a hand to the snake-god. "Did you travel all this way in the treetops?"

"Aye, little sister," it replied in Gaelic, forked tongue flashing in and out of its mouth. "My kin will arrive verra soon."

Aegir knelt next to Raene intent on asking who Uroborus's kin were. His memory of the snake-god was he traveled alone. "Thank you for—"

"No time, Selkie king. Stand tall and fight." In a flash of light, the snake vanished, only to reappear in the midst of the nearest conflagration. Shifters, Witches, and Druids fought two Harpies. Soul stealers. If they got close enough, they extracted your soul through your mouth and claimed your humanity, turning you into their slaves.

Still crouched next to Raene, he kissed her gently. "Uroborus is right. It's time."

Together they rose and started forward. He draped wards about them, but they were temporary. He'd have to divert power from the wards, or he wouldn't be worth a damn fighting.

"What's that?" Raene tilted her head up. "The ruby is jumping about like a mad thing."

He focused beyond the crash and din of the fight and the screams of the dying and heard bugling. Or thought he did. It was very faint, and he might be imagining it because he wanted to hear it.

"Do you hear it?" Raene demanded when he didn't answer.

"Aye. It sounds like dragons, but it makes no sense. They'd use one of their time-travel tunnels, and it would spit them out here."

"They must have chosen a different exit point. I'm far from an expert on the ruby, but it's so excited, the dragons must nearly be here." Her voice rang with confidence. It was contagious, and he stopped running all the reasons it wasn't dragons through his head and glommed onto the reasons it was.

Uroborus had raised his sinuous coils a meter above the field. He was larger than he'd been before, and a ululating cry broke from his triangular mouth. Arcadia's skies split above them, and dragons poured through the silvery veil separating the bastion of White Magic from the rest of the universe.

Fire shot from the dragons' mouths, along with ash and smoke. He felt the heat of their anger at having to be here in the first place and at the damage Arcadia had already sustained. Keene and Eletea had given contradictory answers about whether Arcadia was linked to dragon magic. That so many dragons had shown up meant it had to be, or they wouldn't have bothered. They'd have sent a dragon or two and called it even.

Cheers rose all along the length and breadth of the killing field, but they didn't last long. Dragon presence didn't eradicate the thousands of dark warriors who were still out for blood. Many Selkie allies would die today, but when the groups nearest Aegir turned back to face their adversaries, he sensed renewed vigor in their attack.

He counted fifty dragons before he stopped tallying arrivals, and they were still coming. A large, gold male swooped low. The snake-god leapt into his outstretched talons and wound himself around the dragon's thick neck. Power gleamed around the snake as he jumped from dragon to dragon, growing more substantial with each leap.

"The dragons are his kin?" Raene asked.

"It appears so, but I had no idea. Hurry, lass. The Selkies need us." Aegir ran into the depths of the fray with Raene right next to him. He used magic to locate his pod, ducking attacks launched at them as they skirted several spots where the fighting was intense.

The Selkies had taken up a position better than halfway down the field. They fought griffons, three Furies, and a Harpy along with assorted smaller goblins and ghouls. Someone—probably Krise—had sorted them into groups, and each group targeted a particular segment of enemies. The air, already tough to breathe, grew far worse amid dragons belching smoke, fire, and ash.

Gretta stood next to her mate. Lines of strain carved deep into her face, and she swayed on her feet. He wanted to go to her, but she wouldn't appreciate him noticing her weakness. A dragon bugled merrily overhead and spewed a ribbon of fire in front of the Furies. Jumping back, they shook their fists at the sky. Power sheeted from them, but it wouldn't reach so high. Intent on destruction, they took to the skies. The dragon, clearly enjoying itself, added more flames to those already blazing on the ground and cut a fiery path through the air that knocked one Fury ass over teakettle.

They were immortal, along with the Harpies. If the dragons made them miserable enough, perhaps they'd retreat to wherever they'd been before the specter of an easy victory and Arcadia's rich magical trove had lured them here.

Raene had taken on two hobgoblins. After her fumbling efforts with the undead, she'd developed grace and a certain style. Plus, her magic was stronger. The ugly little Faeries chivied her from both sides. She leapt sideways, twisting midair with power shooting from her hands. One of the hearth Faerys clutched his chest, moaning piteously.

The other flopped atop his fallen companion, shielding him. Raene advanced on them both, grim determination stamped into her face. It turned her beauty into something harsh and threatening. "You want me to spare you? Go back to where you came from."

"Can't," the hobgoblin on top wailed. "Satan will cast us into the pit."

"Then go somewhere else," Aegir told him.

Words in a language Aegir had never heard shot from one hobgoblin to the other. Weak power built around them, and he readied his own magic to finish them off.

"They're leaving," Raene told him. "Look quick! Behind you."

He twirled in time to avoid a mace aimed at his head. A troll was advancing, but not fast. They were built from stone, and it made them clumsy. Other trolls lumbered behind it. Where had they come from? They hadn't been here a moment before.

A quick glance unnerved him. The numbers they faced had at least doubled since the dragons arrived. As if Satan—or whoever was orchestrating this—had troops they'd held in abeyance.

Overhead, dragons bugled and trumpeted as they banked, dove, and regained lost altitude to do it all again. They seemed to be enjoying themselves, but being virtually indestructible was quite an advantage. Dragon scales were impervious to damn near everything.

Aegir assessed their corner of the field. Where they'd been holding their own, now they were badly outnumbered. He used magic to project his voice and rearranged their ranks to more effectively deal with the flood of wicked creatures. Some were truly evil. Others, like the hobgoblins, had been co-opted by darkness. Once upon a time, they'd been hearth Faeries, neither good nor bad.

He created lines, pairing weaker Selkies with stronger ones. Raene stayed near him after the troll had nearly cracked his skull open. Dark magic, some in the form of lightning bolts, some in sheets, some in darts, attacked them from all sides. Sectors of the fell host who didn't have magic used brute force along with maces, cudgels, and batons.

Two more Selkies fell, one dead and one so near death,

Aegir hastened his passing to end his misery. Trees shambled into the fray, helping groups positioned nearer where they'd been rooted.

The dragons had stopped playing and flew in tight formations, maximizing their fire and its destructiveness. Some things, like the trolls, weren't vulnerable to fire. Stone didn't burn, but even the trolls' dimly lit brains would drive them back into darkness if the field turned against them.

The Furies were back, shooting their own brand of magic, red bolts coated with fire that exploded on contact. Aegir barely avoided one. He was tiring but sucked air into smoke-seared lungs and kept on slugging. When he tapped power from Arcadia, she gave what he needed, but not an iota more. A shriek from Gretta dropped him back through the lines to where she and Krise had been fighting.

Krise had fallen to his knees. A black-feathered arrow pierced his shoulder. Everything the enemy used was saturated with poison, so the arrow had to be as well.

"Da. Doona let the poison spread."

"Trying." He jerked weakly at the arrow.

"Stop. I'll get it out." Aegir had to hand it to Krise. The man was nothing if not stoic. He assessed the wicked-looking shaft. It would have to be sawed through on both ends before he could extract it. Lacking tools, he told Gretta, "Make certain he doesna move."

"Aye." Tight-lipped, she hunkered low enough to drape a protective arm around her mate. She followed with ropes of silver Selkie magic to hold Krise steady.

Half a dozen Selkies formed a defensive circle around them. It wasn't foolproof, but it was all Aegir had. Focusing his magic into a thin beam, he sliced through the front end of the arrow, and then the back. As soon as he was able, he pulled it out, casting it aside. The wood burned his palm; he could only imagine what it had done to the inside of Krise's body. Brown ichor shot from both sides of the hole that went all the way through his da's shoulder.

"I'll take it from here," Gretta said.

"Ye should teleport home with him."

"Nay. We shall remain. He'd never forgive me if he missed seeing our victory."

"Go on. I'll be fine now." Krise sounded marginally stronger.

Aegir didn't have the energy to argue with either parent. He stood and worked his way beyond the circle of Selkies.

"Look!" One of them directed his attention to the skies.

"Aye," another chimed in. "That just happened."

Aegir stared, fascinated and thunderstruck. Raene rode a red dragon that had to be Tarika. Uroborus was draped around her and the dragon, and a clear, white light shimmered around the snake-god and Raene.

Tarika trumpeted. "Clear everyone off the field and into the trees." The dragon's voice echoed in his head.

"Do the trees know?"

"Of course." Tarika didn't bother to mask her irritation. "Do it. Now. This will go much faster if we doona have to worry about our aim."

"Take care of my mate."

"Uroborus has adopted her. And she has the ruby. She'll be safer here than down there. Move! I willna ask again."

Aegir wondered what the hell adopting Raene meant. If the snake-god had taken a shine to his mate—soon to be his wife—he wanted to know all the ramifications.

Later. He'd sort it out later.

He told the Selkies nearest him to clear the field, and then he ran from group to group sending delegates to make certain everyone knew. A wave of Shifters and Selkies and Witches and Druids fought their way into the protective cover of the woods.

"Last call!" A gold dragon shouted from the skies.

Aegir ran his gaze across the field. It looked as if everyone from their side had followed the dragons' instructions. He dialed in his third eye and probed with magic. And then he looked again. Damn it! A group of Witches was still in the field, hidden behind an invisibility illusion.

They were on the far side of the clearing, but he'd take his chances. At least a dozen were still in harm's way. Dragon fire rained down, annihilating everything it contacted. The dragons weren't taking any chances and were running with their power dialed to maximum.

With all his senses—magical and physical—on full alert, he threaded his way between geysers of fire, smoke, and steam. Gasping, panting, choking, he battered his way through the Witches' wards, slicing through them easily.

"Why are ye all still here?" he demanded.

"Our sister is hurt. We can't move her," a Witch with silver-and-black hair replied. She was wrapped in a black robe with runic embroidery; rings circled most of her fingers.

"Does it take twelve of you to nursemaid her?" His tone was harsh, and the women looked away. He knelt next to a Witch with blonde hair lying on her side on the ground. Still alive, but not for much longer from the looks of things.

"What happened?"

"Fire from the Furies surrounded her," the first Witch said. "She didn't burn, but it entered her mouth and nose. She fought the magic, but it overtook her. We'd have been too slow if we tried to carry her, so we build as strong a ward as we could. She's pregnant. We're dying out. We need every young Witch—"

"Drop your wards." Aegir cut off her flow of words.

"But then we'll all die," another Witch protested.

"Nay. I'll summon a dragon to take her." He looked at the blonde Witch. "Once she's safely away, the rest of you will follow me to the safety of the trees.

"We'll take our chances within our wards." The silver-and-black-haired Witch said firmly.

"Nay. Not a choice for ye to make. Drop your wards, or I shall dismantle them for you. Except if I do it, 'twill take longer and then we truly will all be in danger."

Amid grumbling and hooked finger curses, the wards fell. While the women worked, Aegir aimed words at Tarika. *"We need a dragon to transport a gravely injured Witch."*

"Where?"

"Find me, and ye'll have it."

A blue-scaled dragon with whirling dark eyes dove out of the sky moments afterward and gathered the prostrate Witch in its forelegs.

"Where will our sister be?" a Witch asked.

The dragon snorted steam. "With one of our healers, and not a moment too soon. Foolish humans."

"We are not human," another Witch countered.

"Ye may as well be." The dragon beat its huge wings and gained elevation fast.

"Make a single file line behind me," Aegir instructed. "Keep your eyes sharp. Use magic too. We're headed for the distant tree line." He extended an arm toward it.

"Why not the nearer one?" one of the Witches asked.

"Because my people are where I pointed."

The Witch with the black-and-silver hair gripped his arm. "We'll be all right, and we will go to the closest safe haven. Thank you so very much for rescuing Auriel." She motioned to the other Witches and they took off, ducking and weaving, for the protection of the forest.

He watched them for a moment. Once he was confident they'd make it to the relative safety of the trees, he hustled back the way he'd come, picking his way as he jumped dead bodies and skirted fires cropping up and spreading across the clearing. The only fodder for the flames was the dead, but plenty of them littered the field.

The air was filled with smoke and the noxious stench of burning fur and flesh and spilled entrails. He all but dove past the forest perimeter, sucking air like a fish trapped out of water. What he inhaled was cleaner here. Not much, but some. Shielding his eyes with a hand, he scanned the skies. Through a rising layer of smoke, he found Tarika and Raene. Fire blasted from the dragon's mouth as she obliterated a row of misshapen creatures with animal heads and humanlike bodies.

Next to Tarika, a formation of four dragons focused fire on a sector of the field. Working from the outside in they kept at it until naught remained but flames. A quick glance told him most of the other dragons had created similar configurations, splitting the field and methodically burning their way through it.

Once they were done, he had no doubt nothing would be left alive. Beneath him, Arcadia's power swelled. The land was singing, rejoicing. It knew it would triumph.

Aegir grinned. Nothing for him to do here. The dragons were more than capable of finishing this fight. He hurried through substantial tree boles looking for Krise. His da was leaning against a tree with Gretta by his side. The elder Selkies looked far better than they had when Aegir left them.

Before he could get any words out, Krise shook his head. "Doona waste time on me. I'm fine. Thanks to quick thinking on your part, the poison dinna have a chance to spread. We lost four Selkies this day from our pod and three from Gregor's. Their bodies are behind me."

Aegir understood. "I will commit them to magefire and consecrate their passing." He motioned to a few other Selkies, and between them they carried the bodies beyond the trees to a spot untouched by darkness. Silently, his pod and Gregor's gathered in a ragged circle.

Aegir kept his prayer short. "We offer our fallen companions to Poseidon and Amphitrite that they may swim forever in gentle seas."

"Gentle seas," rose from the Selkies ranged around him, and Aegir doused the bodies in magefire. It crackled to life, fast and furious. The dead would burn quick and clean, leaving only ashes. As the fire burned itself out, the Selkies talked quietly among themselves, trading stories of the fallen.

Aegir left them to their mourning. Selkies hadn't been the only casualties today, but Arcadia was safe. So long as she existed, their magic would prevail over evil.

He walked past Krise and Gretta and out onto the battlefield. Dragonfire had moved from actively blazing to smoldering piles. They'd run down soon enough. He picked his way through ashy heaps and stood tall, waiting.

Tarika circled to land along with several other dragons. It appeared everyone else had returned to Fire Mountain, or wherever they lived. Not all dragons chose the dragons' ancient home for their residence.

As soon as the red dragon was on the ground, she bent and helped Raene down. She ran to Aegir and into his open arms. "We did it," she cried.

He held her tight and stroked her hair. "Aye, lass. That we did." He didn't mention the dead. That part could wait. The dragon bathed them with steam. Aegir laughed and let go of Raene.

"I can take a hint," he told Tarika and turned to face her.

The dragon's jaws were parted in what might have been a smile. Uroborus slithered down from her bulk. The snake was enormous, ten times the size he'd been while he held the gateway for evil. His body shimmered and glistened, fading in and out of view as he shifted through forms.

A shiny black dragon with golden eyes and golden scales decorating his dark hide stepped from the multitude of transformations. Aegir's eyes widened. "Oberon's balls! Ye're a dragon?"

Tarika blew more steam. "Aye. He is one of our First Born who was lost to us for eons. Ye have our undying gratitude for returning our brother to the fold."

Raene's smile was so broad, it spread from ear to ear. "No wonder the ruby was so excited it damn near jumped out of my pocket."

"Did ye know?" Aegir asked her.

"Only at the very end. But isn't it wonderful?"

Uroborus puffed steam until a cloud surrounded all of them.

"Gather the leaders from all the factions who fought this day," Tarika instructed. "We must talk."

"Where?" Aegir asked.

"The Druids' castle has a big courtyard," Tarika replied. "Be there in half an hour." She bugled and rose into the air, followed by all the remaining dragons including Uroborus.

At least it explained why the snake's cry had split Arcadia's ether, and pulled the dragons through.

Aegir raised his mind voice and boosted it with magic to reach the farthest corners of the forest surrounding the battleground. *"Pack and coven leaders are meeting at the Druid's castle in half an hour. Honor your dead. Send your people home. See you verra soon."*

Hand in hand with Raene, he backtracked to join Krise and Gretta. Together, they'd open their hearts to Arcadia and follow the path she showed them. A path sure to lead to the castle.

"We lost some of our people today, didn't we?" Raene asked.

"Aye, darling. That we did."

"I'd like to pay my respects before we leave."

"Of course." His heart swelled with gratitude and love. "Ye're such a treasure." He circled deep into the trees and led her to where he'd incinerated the Selkies. Most of his pod and Gregor's had already left.

Raene bowed her head and stood for long moments over the ashes. Once she looked up, she offered a wan smile. "We can go now. I'm sorry I never got to know the Selkies who died today." She took a measured breath. "Let's hope you still feel like I'm a treasure after I get through picking your brain for all the things I should have learned growing up."

"We've time, lassie. All the time we'll need. I'm curious what Tarika has to say that requires all of us. Do ye know?"

She shook her head. "We'll find out together."

They reached his parents. Krise nodded crisply. "I've released everyone to return home."

"I figured as much." Aegir nodded back. "Shall we?"

"I already called up a pathway for us," Gretta said and pointed at a sector of dirt that had taken on a definite glow. She sent a penetrating look at her son, and Aegir muffled a snort. It was her way of reminding him she'd been right about remaining by Krise's side through the battle.

"I'm thankful ye were here to alert me about Da."

"What happened?" Raene's smile faded. "Are you hurt?" She turned to Krise.

"Nay, lassie. A flesh wound. We have to get moving." Taking Gretta's hand, he trotted briskly along the shining path.

Aegir draped an arm around Raene's waist before following after them. "What really happened?" she whispered.

"I'll tell you later."

"He looks like he's none the worse for wear."

Aegir chuckled. "He's a tough old bastard."

"That's no way to talk about your father." She tried for serious, but giggled, ruining the effect.

"I'm grateful so many of us survived today," he murmured.

"I was a hell of a lot safer than you and your parents, but I'm glad too. I told Tarika we had to keep an eye on you and run interference if anything bad happened."

Surprise rolled through him. "Och, lass. Ye were watching out for me the whole time?"

"Of course. It's what lovers do, isn't it?" She cast a sidelong glance his way, and he stopped long enough to close his mouth over hers, cherishing the feel of her lips beneath his. If it made them a wee bit late, who would complain about it?

Everyone was drunk on victory. Surely, it would have a mellowing effect on the dragons and the Druids, both sticklers for following orders and being on time.

CHAPTER 18

Raene fell headlong into Aegir's kiss. Time dripped past while their lips were glued together, tongues sparring. Desire was so near the surface, it was all she could do not to rip their clothing off, but then they'd be even later than they already were.

The ruby pulsed, quietly at first, but it was definitely upping the ante on what felt like nagging. Finally, reluctantly, she pulled away. "I don't want to, but we—"

He placed two fingers across her mouth. "I ken, lassie. I dinna mean for things to wander quite so far afield, but ye're quite the fetching one. And now, we must hurry."

She trotted beside him. The stone had quieted as soon as she got moving. "You're pretty damned fetching yourself, Selkie king."

He laughed. "Doona say I dinna warn you. About how we Selkie men can get under your skin."

"Ha! And other places too."

The shining trail took a hard right, followed by a left around ancient tree trunks. The buzz of conversation told Raene they didn't have far to go.

"There they are!" Tarika punctuated her words with trumpeting so loud it hurt Raene's ears.

She and Aegir hustled into the courtyard in front of the Druids' castle. Dee and Gerald were there, along with the Arch Druid, flanked by two Druids she'd seen before. Aegir nodded at a Witch with long silver-and-black hair. Must be one of the ones he'd chivied off the field after the dragons had ordered it cleared. Other Shifters she didn't recognize stood at their ease. Everyone's relief was palpable. No matter what came next, they'd saved Arcadia—and their own magic.

"We can begin now," Uroborus said. "Each of you will step forward and state your name and affiliation. I will begin. I am Uroborus, First Born Dragon and the symbol that life on Earth shall never fail."

"Why did you leave Fire Mountain?" Raene asked.

Tarika huffed smoke her way, but Uroborus said, "I choose to answer her. The others here need to know as well." He straightened amid the clanking of scales. "Dragons are a rather, ahem, insular lot." He angled a pointed look at Tarika from beneath hooded lids.

She made shooing motions with her forelegs. "Och. Ye always did have a taste for the dramatic. If ye'd wait a moment, I would hear who stands with us in this courtyard, and then ye can continue. I am Tarika, First Born Dragon, I am also bonded to Britta Kilkerran, dragon shifter and Countess of Cumbria."

Four dragons ranged between her and Uroborus—a gold, a blue, and two greens—rattled off what were probably their names in something that sounded like Gaelic, but it might have been a language unique to dragons. Regardless, Raene would have been hard-pressed to repeat their names since they all ran together in a mellifluous blend of sound.

Dee stepped forward. "Delia, leader of the wolf Shifters." She shook blonde braids behind her shoulders.

"Gerald, head of the bear Shifters and Delia's mate."

A tall, rangy man with gray hair and keen dark eyes stepped forward. "Marko, leader of all varieties of bird Shifter."

"Susannah, head Witch in the British Isles," the woman with long black-and-silver hair murmured.

"Aegir, Selkie king, and this is my mate, Raene."

"Krise, retired Selkie king and my mate, Gretta."

The Arch Druid stepped forward. "I am Brother Loran, and these monks are Stephen and Richard. They are who shall return to Fire Mountain per my promise to dragonkind to provide two Druids in exchange for today's assistance saving Arcadia."

He took another step toward Tarika and fell to one knee. "Thank ye, First Born. From the bottom of my heart, I am so grateful, I doona have adequate words."

"Get up," Tarika said briskly. "No one with magic bows to me. Besides, once we stopped playing at war and settled in, no enemy could have withstood us. Dragon fury is a force of nature. Had Satan and his princes been on the field, we'd have chased them back to Hell in the midst of the carnage." She scanned the group. "Ye three." She puffed steam toward the back of the assemblage. "Come forward and name yourselves."

A white-haired man and two younger women, one blonde and one red-haired walked closer to Tarika, stopping a respectful distance away. Like the Shifters, they wore formfitting leather clothing. Bows hung from their shoulders along with quivers full of arrows. The man inclined his head. "We are White Fae. We are few, but loyal to Arcadia and White Magic. We fought alongside you this day and sustained losses."

He stopped to draw a breath. "We considered leaving, not attending this council, yet we decided not to let our dark cousins taint what we are."

The Arch Druid raised a hand. Magic shot from it and traveled lazily, examining the Fae from head to toe. "Humph. Ye speak true."

"Not much point in lying. Not in the midst of a group such as this," the man retorted.

The White Fae stood their ground. They seemed edgy, but no one made a move to teleport out of the courtyard.

"We welcome you into our midst. Any who fight dark magic are our allies," Tarika said and glanced at Uroborus. "Make it snappy. I have information I wish to impart."

The black-and-gold dragon inclined his head. "I shall do my best long-lost sister."

Tarika rolled her golden eyes. "Reminders willna buy you additional time."

"Such a taskmistress." The dragon's golden eyes danced with mischief that didn't match his words. "As I was saying, dragons are a bit on the stuffy side. Millennia ago, I set off to explore the world beyond Fire Mountain. Earth was verra young then, and men dwelt mostly in caves. I spent long years in many different forms, culling through the world of men. They lacked purpose, meaning. Many were cruel, others merely pathetic.

"A verra long time afore Christ's birth—and wasna it intriguing how he went from man to god for no apparent reason?—I discovered that my snake's body inspired both fear and hope. Religious groups accepted me as a symbol of the divine, and their adulation augmented my power.

"Years passed. My desire to return to Fire Mountain first grew smaller and finally frittered to naught. Dragons no longer sought me out. I assumed my brethren had forgotten all about me, and I was comfortable with that outcome."

"We never forgot about you," Tarika cut in dryly. "Generations of young dragons turned you into a legend."

Uroborus tilted his head back and blew a gout of flames high into the skies. "I am not proud of what happened next, but one day Azazael and Beelzebub paid me a visit. They brought rich gifts and sat and chatted for hours. It had been such a long while since I'd spent time in the company of magic, I rather enjoyed the attention and the companionship."

More flames blasted skyward. "My seduction at the hands of evil dinna happen quickly. I venture as much as three or four centuries passed afore my first trip to Satan's halls. The lord of Hell planned well. He set traps, snares. Once I was within his kingdom, my mind and my will werena truly mine again. I wandered in darkness, living on crumbs from Satan and his princes, until earlier today when these two women"—he pointed at Raene and Dee with a foreleg—"reminded me who and what I am."

Even though Raene had known he was one of the First Born, she'd had no inkling of his fall from wisdom and grace. She squared her shoulders. "I am honored to have played a role in returning you to your rightful heritage."

"As am I," Dee chimed in. She shook her head. "I was playing long odds. I had no idea they'd yield such rich fruit."

Tarika leveled her spinning gaze on Uroborus. "Ye are returning to Fire Mountain?"

"Aye, sister. Epiphany may have been a long time coming, but I'll not stray again."

Tarika raked her eyes over the other dragons. "Ye heard him."

"Aye, we did," they replied almost in unison. "And we shall hold him to his word."

"That was unnecessary." Uroborus managed to sound hurt and angry at the same time.

"Ah, but in my estimation 'twas," Tarika replied.

The black-and-gold dragon opened his mouth, but shut it with a *clack* Raene felt in the pit of her stomach. Dragons had a mouthful of teeth. Maybe hundreds from the sound of things.

Tarika huffed smoke and steam. "One thing out of the way." She glanced at Brother Loran. "Do your monks agree to abide by all of our laws and customs in Fire Mountain?"

Stephan and Richard bowed their heads and murmured. "Aye, of course."

"Will ye release them at intervals to return to Arcadia?" the Arch Druid asked.

"So long as they serve well and faithfully, they will be released after six years. At that point, we will expect two more of your order to replace them."

"Agreed," Brother Loran said.

"Two things down," Tarika muttered and folded her wings more firmly across her back. "Listen well, all of you. We did strong work today. We dealt a significant blow against evil, but we are not done. Ye canna let your guard down. Not today. Not tomorrow. Not ever. The battle against darkness willna go away. It is something that will always be with us, lurking in shadows and ready to crop up if we relax our vigilance.

"I willna lie to you. Dragonkind were quite contentious regarding our part in today's victory. Many counseled we should stay out of anything that dinna directly impact Fire Mountain. They needed reminding, in clear and absolute terms, that if Arcadia fails, Fire Mountain will be at grave risk."

Tarika balanced from one large hind leg to the other and back again as she pushed her curved spine straighter amid cracking bones and rustling scales. She extended her forelegs and made a circle with her curved talons. The sphere is our magic. Everything is interconnected."

She moved one foreleg until her talons were offset by ninety degrees. "This"—she waggled one forefoot —"represents dark magic. Like ours, yet not. All power sprang from the same roots. Magic can trace its beginnings to before Earth formed from the sun. Long afore Fire Mountain was more than a gleam in some dragon's eye, magic was brewing. Rich and heady and pure. How good and evil magic split from one another isna important. The vital part is ye never forget our power has common elements with that which we fight."

"It's bound to make things harder," Aegir muttered.

"Aye, and 'tis how Uroborus was snared by Hell's minions."

The black dragon looked away, his earlier defiance absent. He might have been embarrassed. Raene couldn't tell.

"What are ye proposing, Madame Dragon?" Brother Loran asked.

"'Tisn't a proposal so much as a stipulation," Tarika retorted. "Many dragons willna approve, but from today forth, we shall work together. If ye—any of ye—are threatened by dark magic, we would know about it. And we will do likewise. I hope battles such as today's willna become frequent, but today cemented our commitment as associates. As allies."

The dragon folded her forelegs across her scaled chest. "I

would have your oath afore ye leave." Rather creakily, she settled to the ground.

"Oath as in olden times where ye take our blood?" Krise asked.

Tarika nodded. "Exactly, Selkie. Will ye be the first?"

"I would be honored." Krise walked to where the dragon towered above him, despite her sitting on the ground. He reached an arm upward. Tarika slashed a fingertip with her razor-sharp talons and bent her head to lick the drops of blood onto her tongue.

One by one, everyone in the courtyard mirrored Krise's actions. When it was Raene's turn, Tarika smiled at her. "Little Selkie, who is now my little dragon-rider. Come visit Britta and me anytime."

"Aegir and I would be delighted to return to Fire Mountain." Raene smiled. "Next time, I'll make sure not to wear winter clothing."

"Next time, ye'll be our guests inside our caves. They're quite a bit cooler than where ye waited while we argued how to proceed."

Night was falling, the sky streaked with purples and pinks, when the last of them offered blood to the dragon. She sighed and pushed her bulk out of the dirt. "Only one last item, and then my dragons and I shall go home."

Raene waited, wondering what it might be. She was weary but filled with wonder at Arcadia's power pulsing beneath her feet. The magical land had done nothing but grow stronger the longer they remained in the Druids' courtyard.

Tarika shuffled until she stood in front of Raene and Aegir. "Ye are mated, but not officially wed." She puffed steam around them, warm and soothing. "Your nuptials will take place in Fire Mountain one month from today." Tarika turned in a full circle. "Everyone here shall attend."

"We may not have enough magic to trip the time travel tunnel," the White Fae male said.

"It will work for you," Tarika reassured him. "I shall have a discussion with the Guardian. He owes me a favor or two—or ten." She laughed, puffing smoke and turned back to Raene and Aegir, quirking a scaly brow. "Well?"

"We are honored," Aegir said.

"And touched," Raene added. "Thank you so much for offering to host our wedding."

"It's not entirely altruistic, little Selkie. I wish to be there, and this is the easiest way."

"I want to be there too." Uroborus jumped into the conversation. "Which makes Fire Mountain a perfect location. Hell, I wanted to marry her myself. Would have if she weren't taken." His whirling gaze sought Dee out of the group. "Guess ye're mated too?"

Laughing, she stepped forward. "Yup. That I am, but I appreciate the offer. It's quite a compliment."

The black-and-gold dragon puffed smoke. "I owe both of you—everything. And I shall never forget. It ye ever need aught, ye've only to call on me."

Tarika's golden eyes whirled faster. "'Tis quite a commitment...brother."

"I mean every word."

She nodded slowly. "I believe ye do. Come, dragons. Time for us to be gone."

Amid a flurry of magic and brilliance, all six dragons vanished, leaving fiery contrails and residual smoke.

Raene stared after them. "Even after everything, it's still hard to believe they're real."

"It is, isn't it?" Dee walked closer and held out her arms. Raene hugged her. "Thanks for trusting me on short notice."

"It wasn't as if we had a whole lot of options," Raene said. She stepped out of Dee's embrace. "The hard truth is I've spent most of my life as a human. I don't know how to take full advantage of my magic, so I have to trust others who do."

"Hard to argue with success." Gerald joined them. "Congratulations on your upcoming nuptials." He smiled and extended a hand.

Raene shook it; so did Aegir.

Krise and Gretta moved closer. "It would be my pleasure to give the bride away," he told Raene. "I knew your da afore evil took him. He wasna such a bad sort. Verra old school and strict in his younger years."

"Aye, and I shall be your matron of honor," Gretta said. Smiles wreathed her face. "Never thought I'd see my son married. I have to be close enough to make certain he doesna change his mind."

"Thanks for the vote of confidence, Mum." Aegir looked askance at her.

"The best predictor of future actions—"

"Is past performance," Aegir finished for her, adding, "I'm scarcely a lad in short pants anymore. I adore Raene. All will be well."

Gretta gave him a quick hug. "I'm certain it will, but I want to be close by just the same."

"That's very kind of both of you," Raene said and cast a pointed look Aegir's way.

"What? First Mum and now you. Did I do something wrong?" He gazed fondly at her.

She grinned. "It appears we have a wedding to plan, but I don't recall you asking me to marry you."

Aegir broke out laughing. When his mirth had subsided to chuckles, he said, "Och, for a moment there, ye had me worried. All my talk about loving you and wanting you for my mate doesna count?"

She shook her head. "A girl likes to be courted."

"What are you waiting for?" Gerald asked Aegir.

"Aye, mate. Down on one knee," Marko urged, followed by a squawk that gave him away as some type of raptor.

Aegir took Raene's hand and sank to one knee before her. "Léannan. Darling. Love of my life. Will ye have me for your husband?"

She'd been teasing him about proposing. When he actually spoke the words—words she'd longed to hear—her throat thickened with emotion. Hot tears pricked the backs of her eyelids. She tried to say yes, but nothing came out, so she nodded.

He flowed to his feet and took her into his arms, the hand

he still held sandwiched between. "Are ye all right, lassie?" he said low against her ear.

She nodded again and managed, "It's time to go home."

"Which home?"

Still feeling overcome with the enormity of everything—the battle, the wedding, suddenly having a family when she'd been alone forever—she had to think a moment to determine what he meant. She'd assumed they'd retreat to the Selkies' cave on the unnamed island in the Orkney chain.

Gretta patted her on the shoulder. "We'll be on our way, dear, while the two of you sort things out."

"Us too," Dee said.

"See you at Fire Mountain in a month," Gerald added and winked broadly.

Raene extricated herself from Aegir's arms and turned to bid everyone farewell. Once the Shifters, Witch, and White Fae had left, the Druids retreated inside their castle, leaving her and Aegir alone in the courtyard.

"We can go wherever ye wish," he said. "The cave or your shop in Wick as humans. Or the Selkies' castle as seals."

"We could do all three," she said. "Obviously, not all at once, but we could go back to the cave until we've recovered a bit from today. I'd love to show you my shop, even if it's the last time I'm ever there."

"Why would that be?"

She swallowed hard and looked away. "Well, it's not much. Just a little bakery. You're king of the Selkies. Surely, you've better things to do than hang around while I whip up scones and biscuits and pasties."

He cradled one side of her face in a large hand. "Marriage is about us, lass. Not just about me. If ye want to spend a few months a year whipping up goodies, we'll figure out how to make it work."

She smiled shyly, but couldn't look away since he held her in place. "I'm a lucky woman."

"Funny, I feel the same way. If ye substitute man at the end of things."

"Let's never lose sight of where we are right now." She wrapped an arm around his back, holding him close.

"We won't, darling. I shall cherish you always. Let me take us home."

His familiar magic, full of the scent of the sea, rose around them. She inhaled deeply and lost herself in his power. When it cleared, they stood at the crest of the small island midway up the Orkney chain.

Hand in hand, they walked the path leading to the cave. Her skin's magic thrummed softly from where she'd concealed it. "I'm happy," she murmured. "So happy it's spilling out everywhere."

"I am too, Raene. My Raene. Hurry, my love. I canna wait to bed you."

"Is it only bedding me?" she teased, borrowing his brogue.

"Nay. I shall watch over you as ye sleep and catch us fish from the sea. I'll talk with the Dream Guardian, and we'll plan a tryst in his magical lands."

"Now, that sounds intriguing." The cave came to life around them, hearth kindling and lanterns casting a soft glow. Raene let go of his hand. "But the bedding idea came first, and here we are." She began unfastening his jacket, heart beating faster in anticipation of what lay ahead.

"Aye, lassie. Here we are, but this way is faster."

Magic flared around them, rich with the salty tang of the sea. When it cleared, both of them were naked. The clothing they'd worn was strewn across the floor. He swept her against him and crushed his mouth over hers.

She kissed him back with a fervor to match his. Aegir was her man. Her mate. Soon to be her husband, and she was the luckiest woman in the universe. She'd have told him, but her mouth was busy.

Sensation flared hot and urgent. Thoughts departed, and she immersed herself in the magic the two of them spun together.

One month later

Fire Mountain

Aegir lay on his side watching Raene slumber in a chamber the dragons had prepared for them deep underground. The month between the battle and now had flown by. He hadn't expected to fall in love with Raene's cozy bakeshop with its small apartment above, but he had. He'd spent long, lazy hours in the kitchen with her, handing her ingredients and putting trays in the ovens. The locals hadn't expected her back for months, and they'd mobbed the place demanding she make their favorite treats.

Her customers had teased her mercilessly about holding out on them and not giving away that she had a secret beau. But news of their upcoming wedding also provided an excuse for them not to linger long.

After ten days at the shop, they'd snuck away one night.

The closed sign didn't specify a reopening date, but he was certain they'd return. Wick was a delightful hamlet, so Scottish, he expected bagpipes to burst into song at every corner, piping in time with the clop of horses' hooves when farmers brought produce to the weekly outdoor market the old-fashioned way.

They'd spent a week in the sea. It had given Raene time to meet the other Selkies, and them an opportunity to get to know her. The rest of the time, what little there'd been, they'd returned to the cave where they chatted, cooked together, and made love in every imaginable position. Not that they hadn't taken full advantage of the bed above her shop too.

They had.

The more time he spent with her, the more he appreciated her. She had a bright, inquisitive mind, absorbing Selkie lore as fast as he provided it. Beyond that, she possessed a soft, compassionate side. Losing her mum after a long period where the two were estranged had cut deep. He hoped the loving group of Selkies would provide a sense of family and belonging for his mate.

She stirred, her lovely blue-green eyes fluttering open. "How long have you been awake?"

He shrugged. "A while."

"How much time do we have before the ceremony?"

"Enough. Ye doona have to rush."

"Good." She reached for him, her intent crystal clear, but he shook his head.

"Not that much time, lassie."

Raene laughed, silvery and joyful. "We do get wrapped up in each other."

"Do I hear a complaint?"

"Oh my goodness, no." She pushed to a sit and grinned at him. "Lucky for us, the dragons don't insist on that old custom of separating the bride and groom for days before the wedding."

"I believe that custom was to ensure the couple dinna jump the proverbial gun."

"Ha! For us, the barn door is open, and that cow long gone."

Aegir laughed. "We're quite a pair, ye and me."

"How so?"

"We've lived so long, we mix metaphors, but it doesna matter. I always ken your meaning."

Raene pushed the blanket aside and walked to a raised table holding an ewer and a basin. She bent and rinsed her hands and face, drying them with a towel.

"Ye've the most beautiful body." He'd been focused on the perfect globes of her high, round ass and the way her long legs traveled to meet them.

She hung the towel back on its hook and turned to face him. "Why thank you."

"'Tis the truth. Any man would find you stunning."

"None of them were falling all over themselves to claim me," she pointed out.

"Because ye were saving yourself for me." He laughed and

got out of bed. "We should dress. I'd be surprised if our guests haven't begun arriving."

Raene crossed the room to a carved wooden chest and cracked the lid open. "I don't understand." She knelt before the chest and drew out a white leather skirt painted with gold runes. "This isn't what I brought to wear. It's lovely, but—"

He knelt next to her and sifted through the chest's contents pulling out matching white leather breeks, a richly embroidered cream-colored tunic woven of silk, and a leather vest sized to fit him. For Raene, he laid out a sky-blue tunic decorated with what might be dragon flames woven in with ocean waves. Her vest was made of snow-white fur. At the bottom of the chest were two pairs of ankle-high boots made of buff leather with blue and red laces.

"A gift from the dragons, if I'm not mistaken," he said and ran a finger over the wave-and-flame pattern on her tunic. "This might be Tarika's way of branding you as a dragon-rider."

Raene rocked back on her heels. "I never thought to ask, but is it unusual?"

"Aye. Verra. Dragons doona often suffer anyone on their backs. They've never seen themselves as horses or beasts of burden." He cleared his throat. "How could they when they believe they stand at the verra top of every food chain."

"Intriguing." She stood and stepped into the skirt, tying its leather lacing so the fabric snugged against her hips. Next, she pulled the tunic over her head and snapped up a hairbrush.

He dressed as well, never taking his eyes from her loveliness.

"Are you certain I shouldn't put my hair up?" she asked. Freshly brushed, her red locks spilled down her back in a cascade worthy of any dragon's fire.

"It's beautiful just as it is." He slid the vest into place over his tunic and bent to slip into the boots. Soft and supple, they hugged his feet.

The door to their chamber swooshed open. Britta waltzed inside. "Tarika is too big to fit in this portion of the dragons' cave system. Convenient we can trade bodies when we need to." She was dressed in a simple emerald-green gown, and her red hair, more coppery than Raene's, hung down her back in a riot of curls.

"Must be time to go," Aegir said.

"Aye." She pinned him with her golden eyes, eyes almost exactly like Tarika's without their spinning aspect. "How do ye feel about riding Uroborus?"

His jaw fell open. Of all the questions he might have anticipated, this one hadn't occurred to him. "I would be delighted. Honored." He stammered a bit, but got the words out.

"Excellent." Britta opened her mouth and puffed steam. "Tarika thought it would be perfect if each of you arrived on a dragon, this being Fire Mountain and all."

Raene clapped her hands. "I get to ride Tarika again?"

Warm laughter burbled from Britta's throat. "She's as eager as you. I swear, if she and I ever figure out a way to still be bonded but hang onto our own bodies at the same time, one of my dreams is riding the dragon I'm bonded to."

"I hope you'll be able to," Raene said. "It's a thrill like no other."

"Except mayhap bedding your mate," Aegir tossed in *soto voce.*

Britta laughed. Raene did too. "Men." She rolled her eyes.

"Aye, yet they're truly incredible creatures." Britta was still laughing when she led the way out of their chamber and along numerous branching corridors.

"Good thing ye're here," Aegir said. "I'd have had to resort to magic to find my way out."

"Och aye. These tunnels are never the same twice running. For any of us. Tarika is directing me, else I'd be lost as well," Britta replied.

The red, dry light of Fire Mountain fell across the passageway. It had grown much warmer as they traveled upward. Quite a contrast to Earth where things got hotter the closer you came to Hell's gates.

Britta ran ahead, shedding clothing as she went. By the time they exited the cave system, she was Tarika again, steam puffing from her open jaws. Uroborus stood next to her rocking from one hindfoot to the next. Aegir glanced around. The knobby, cracked red dirt stretched in all directions with Fire Mountain belching smoke in the distance.

"Where is everyone?" he asked, wondering about their guests.

"They're here, but we've hidden them," Uroborus answered.

"Aye, how else can ye make a grand entrance?" Tarika chimed in. "This was my idea, and we shall create a spectacle the likes of which has never been seen on Fire Mountain."

Aegir inclined his head. It wasn't wise to point out that he and Raene had to be the first non-dragon couple to wed in the dragons' special world. He strode to Uroborus and focused magic to settle himself on the dragon's back. Raene walked to Tarika who bent to gather her carefully and set her into place.

"Probably not the time to tell you"—Uroborus huffed smoke—"but I've never had anyone atop me."

"We'll figure it out." Heat from the dragon's hide warmed the leather of his breeks, but it wasn't unpleasant.

"Here we go!" The black-and-gold dragon took off running and leapt skyward, wings flapping hard. Wind buffeted Aegir as they climbed. It was cooler up here, probably because he'd escaped the heat radiating from the borderworld's surface.

Uroborus banked first to one side, then to the other. "How are ye doing?"

"Never been better. This is amazing. Incredible. Thank you so verra much for volunteering. I've always loved riding, and I ken how much dragons hate having anyone on your backs."

The dragon huffed smoke-tinged laugher. "True enough. But Tarika is a hard woman to say no to. She wouldn't have stopped nagging until one of us gave in. 'Twas a small enough favor, and I gave my word to your bride that I would honor any request."

"I remember, yet Raene dinna ask this boon."

"Close enough, Selkie. Close enough. When ye live as long as I have, ye learn not to split hairs." He carved a figure eight, seemingly waiting for something. Tarika bugled two high notes, and Uroborus said. "That's our cue."

When Aegir glanced toward the ground, craning his neck around the dragon's to do so, he saw their guests ranged near the entrance to the dragons' cave system. Everyone's eyes were focused on the skies.

Tarika flew toward them, banking right at the last moment. Uroborus banked in the opposite direction. Flying half a circle, they repeated the maneuver three more times. Aegir suspected they were honoring the four directions, an element in traditional Celtic weddings.

"Hang on," Uroborus instructed. "Almost there, but this will be tricky."

The dragon flew straight up, his long neck extended. Tarika did as well. Both dragons spewed fire, which blended into red and golden ropes with a bluish cast to them, not unlike the decoration on Raene's tunic. One of the ropes wound around him and his dragon; another around Raene and Tarika.

Dragon magic built around Aegir; the air heated from all the dragonfire. As he watched, the individual fiery ropes joined and formed a circle around all of them, dragons and riders alike. It burned merrily for a few moments before breaking apart and spinning off into the ether.

"That was unbelievable," Aegir crowed.

"I thought ye'd like it." The dragon sounded immensely pleased. "'Tis my symbol. The circle. I dinna think Tarika would agree, but she loved the concept."

Aegir patted the dragon's scaly hide. "I do too. I'm verra glad ye broke free from the dark lord's hold."

"Not a day goes by I doona bless Raene and Delia for what they did." Uroborus's words held a somber note as he skidded in for a landing.

Aegir hopped down and turned to face the dragon. He bowed low. "I am so honored to have ridden you."

"'Tis an open offer, Selkie. Return as ye can to my lands."

Cheers rose from their guests along with cries of "Bravo" and "I want to ride too."

Tarika touched down amid the adulation. Raene jumped off and ran lightly to Aegir's side. "We're ready."

"I ken as much, but what happens next?" Unlike the weddings he was familiar with, he hadn't been offered a script.

"Come along with me." Gretta had left the group of guests and stood by his side. "We shall make our way to the dragons' meeting chamber within and await your bride."

Aegir hooked a hand beneath his mother's arm. "Lead out. Ye still doona trust I willna bolt?"

Gretta snorted. "I admit, 'twould be a wee bit difficult.

Even if I wasna here, Tarika would hunt you down and ensure ye honored your vows."

"Och, ye mean the ones I haven't yet uttered?" He was baiting his mother, but he couldn't resist.

"Just like your da. Always a joker," she muttered and drew them forward. Apparently, she knew where they were going. Good thing because he didn't.

"I love you, Mum."

She twisted her head and cast a fond glance his way. "I ken it. 'Tis a happy day for me, but I bet ye're euphoric. That dragon display was something. I couldna tear my gaze from the skies."

"Wish I could have watched and ridden too, but given a choice, I'd pick dragon riding any day."

"Means I raised you right." Gretta beamed at him.

The oppressive heat lessened as they moved deeper into the cave system. Gretta guided them down a short side corridor and into an enormous cavern. A long raised area at the far end of the room held three lit tapers.

A tall man with amber eyes stood behind the candles. Long dark hair framed his sharp-boned face, hanging loose in front, but the back portion was braided close against his skull. Dozens of braids trailed down his back. Leather garments embellished with red-and-blue dye clung to his frame, and boots laced to just below his knees. A war axe swung from a sheath by his side, and a broadsword was attached to his back by a scabbard with thongs that wrapped around his body. Still more weapons draped from cunningly crafted bits of rawhide.

His face held the same ageless quality that marked all magic wielders.

Aegir sprang forward, covering the distance to the dais in a few strides. "Cathbad? 'Tis been years, but it must be you. No one else carries that war axe and broadsword."

The man nodded. "Aye, it's me, and I shall officiate at your wedding today. Tarika, one of the younger Druids, and I all have roles to play. First, though, ye must hear something from me."

Aegir gathered himself, unsure what the ancient Druidic seer would want with him.

Cathbad faced him squarely and draped a spell around them to shield his words. "Ye gave my grandson a solid beginning. Ye loved him, nurtured him. Doona harbor ill will toward my son. He had no choice but to ease Jonathan's way by ensuring he doesna remember Arianrhod. He will recall her when the time is right, but that willna occur for many decades."

Cathbad gripped Aegir's arm. "Also, doona think badly of Arianrhod. Ye've no idea what she has suffered for her choices. I am who told her she must keep Jonathan when he was little more than a thought within her body." He paused, perhaps for emphasis, before going on. "'Twas a difficult, nay an impossible, path laid at her feet, yet she rose to it with grace and her usual unbending will. Ye should respect her."

The seer's words held both sadness and conviction. Aegir nodded his understanding. "Will I see Jonathan again?" The words ripped from a place deep within him that hadn't yet healed.

Cathbad smiled, the expression out of place on his craggy face. "Aye. Ye will meet him again once he is grown. He will turn out to be a man we can all be proud of—a man on whom the fate of the world rests—and your part in that willna be forgotten."

Aegir opened his mouth to ask more, but Cathbad shook his head. "'Tis all I shall reveal, and I'd not have said as much as I did if I dinna ken your pain." A wave of his hand undid his privacy spell. "Turn around. Your bride is about to walk to you. She is lovely."

Aegir turned away from Cathbad. While they'd talked, the chamber had filled with dragons and their guests. Krise and Raene stood at the upper end of the chamber. Tarika and a Druid hurried down the aisle and took up spots on either side of Cathbad.

Druids had always joined Selkies in marriage. To have one at his wedding here in Fire Mountain touched Aegir. He and Raene had been honored in so many ways today. Their wedding would become part of Selkie lore, told and retold to generations of young Selkies. He wondered idly if dragon younglings would hear about the Selkie wedding held on Fire Mountain. It seemed remote, but he hoped so.

As if drawn by his thoughts about young dragons, a small, golden dragon pattered down the aisle clutching a cushion with two shiny golden rings balanced atop it. Each was set with two stones, a blood-red ruby and a deep-blue sapphire.

"Not yet." Uroborus made a move to snag Glaedr, but Aegir waved him back and trotted toward the dragon who'd been conscripted as ring-bearer. He might be young, but he was of a height with Aegir.

"I am so grateful ye've recovered," Aegir told him. "Your abduction was a stain on Selkie honor."

The youngling aimed its whirling eyes right at Aegir. "'Twas my own fault." His voice was high, musical. "Had I not modeled myself after Uroborus, fancied myself a great explorer, I'd never have been captured."

"Enough!" Tarika clapped her taloned forelegs together. "We have a wedding to perform. Doona lose sight of those rings," she warned Glaedr.

He bobbed his head. "I shall guard them with fire and life."

"No dragon could ask for more." Tarika might have been smiling.

Music swelled from off to one side. Three dragons played instruments. A lute, a lyre, and a harp from the looks of them.

Krise started down the aisle with Raene by his side. His da looked proud, and Raene was glowing with happiness.

As she joined him, tucking her hand beneath his arm, his heart cracked wide open, bursting with love for the woman by his side. He turned them to face the three who would marry them and let the words of the ancient bonding ceremony wash over and through him, searing his soul.

Magical marriages were forever, but he wouldn't have it any other way. After the ring ceremony came the part at the end when their blood mingled. Instead of flowing into pale linen, Tarika sealed their wounds with her tongue.

"Ye've been blessed by dragon essence," she told them. "Ye will be together forever more, through this life and all lives to come. I, Tarika, First Born of Dragons, have spoken."

The music, which had grown softer, swelled to fullness once more. Cheers and hoots and dragon bugling filled the cavern in a joyous cacophony of sound. He looked straight at Cathbad. "Thank you for what ye told me."

"Ye're welcome. Now take your bride to the chamber next door. The dragons have made dinner for you, and I'm hungry. Takes a lot of magic to travel through time. I need sustenance afore I can return."

"Fooooddddd," Glaedr crowed and raced up the aisle and out the door.

Tarika laughed indulgently. "Go ahead, you two. Kiss so we all can eat. If we doona hurry, Glaedr will have eaten the plates down to bedrock."

Aegir didn't need encouragement. He took his bride, the woman he was bound to throughout time, and lowered his mouth to hers.

You've reached the end of *Dragon Fury*, a spinoff from my Dragon Lore series. I do hope you've enjoyed it. There are four more books in the Dragon Lore series. They can all be read as stand-alones, but they're better read in order. Curious about how Angus and Arianrhod met and fell in love? Read *Highland Secrets*. Fascinated by dragon shifters? Take a peek at *To Love a Highland Dragon*, a story chockfull of Witches and time travel. Do you want to know more about Jonathan after he's grown up? Take a look at *Dragon Maid* and *Dragon's Dare*. You'll meet Britta again, the woman Jonathan falls in love with. Her mouthy blood-red dragon, Tarika, is part of all these stories too, as is Cathbad, immortal Druidic Seer.

Keep on reading for a sample of *Highland Secrets*. But before you do that, please leave a review for *Dragon Fury*. It only takes a moment. Doesn't have to be fancy, but reviews mean so much to authors. Be sure to let other readers know what you loved about this book.

ABOUT THE AUTHOR

Ann Gimpel is a USA Today bestselling author. A lifelong aficionado of the unusual, she began writing speculative fiction a few years ago. Since then her short fiction has appeared in many webzines and anthologies. Her longer books run the gamut from urban fantasy to paranormal romance. Once upon a time, she nurtured clients. Now she nurtures dark, gritty fantasy stories that push hard against reality. When she's not writing, she's in the backcountry getting down and dirty with her camera. She's published over 70 books to date, with several more planned for 2019 and beyond. A husband, grown children, grandchildren, and wolf hybrids round out her family.

Keep up with her at www.anngimpel.com or http://anngimpel.blogspot.com

If you enjoyed what you read, get in line for special offers and pre-release special reads. Newsletter Signup!

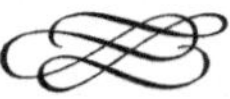

Angus Shea stroked beneath icy waters off the northern tip of Ireland, blending his energy with a pod of Selkies. The sea creatures cut through choppy waves in front, behind, and above him. He'd rather dive and play in the deeps with them—and if it were any other day, he would have—but he needed to keep an eye on the skies, so he edged toward the surface, pushing his head free.

Celene, a coal-black Selkie he'd done more than swim with, edged close enough her lush pelt stroked his skin. He draped an arm around her, and she nuzzled his neck with her snout.

"Where have you been?" She spoke deep into his mind. Accommodating vocal chords were part of her human form, not her seal, and he'd never learned the Selkies' lyrical language.

"I spent a little time at my home in Scotland, but mostly I've ranged far from the Irish Sea."

"That tells me less than nothing." She nipped playfully at his shoulder with her squared-off teeth.

"Prying ears are everywhere." He leaned into her warmth, enjoying a respite from the cold water.

"We could go where no one would hear."

He was tempted, so tempted he toyed with saying yes and taking a break from watching for the dragon he expected. Dragons interpreted time in their own way, and the damned thing might not show up today or tomorrow or even this week. If it showed at all.

How much could he tell the Selkie?

An answer crowded on the heels of his question.

Nothing.

Angus shuttered his mind, so the creature swimming by his side couldn't read it. Much as he yearned to talk with someone, anyone, about the impossibilities the gods tasked him with, prudence won out. Not that this assignment was worse than any of the others, but he'd finally figured out they'd never end.

I could say no. Tell them I'm done.

He cut off the bitter laugh that wanted out. Whoever had the balls to refuse the Celts risked swift and certain punishment. He could hear Gwydion, master enchanter, or Ceridwen, goddess of the world, laughing their heads off— before they cut out his tongue or killed him on the spot.

"You don't have to say a word." Celene went on, almost as if

she'd peeked into his thoughts before he took care to protect them. Selkie laughter buffeted him, spraying him with a warm, rich melody mixed with salty water. *"I have to admit I'm curious, but I miss your body."*

He missed hers too. She'd been his only break from solitude for more years than he wanted to admit. He cast another glance skyward. Though he tried to be subtle, he heard a smug murmur near his ear and knew he hadn't fooled the Selkie.

"You wait for an Ancient One." The tenor of her mind speech shifted as she shielded it from nearby Selkies. Without stopping for him to corroborate, she forged ahead. *"We can take up the banner and watch for you. My kin will let us know."*

Angus picked his way carefully, as if he walked through a field of unexploded ordnance. "I appreciate the thought, but no one can know of my comings or goings, lass."

"We know more than you think." Celene batted him with a flipper. *"In truth, very little escapes us, but here isn't the place to share what I heard about your latest mission."*

Concern rippled through him. If the Selkies knew, who else might? Hell, he didn't know much beyond his assigned meeting place with the dragon, and that they'd be heading into danger.

What else was new? Danger was so second nature, his adrenaline pumps barely flinched at anything these days.

"Come with me." Either Celene was oblivious to the turmoil rumbling through him, or she ignored it. She swam from beneath his arm and herded him toward shore. *"There's*

a secluded glade deep in marsh grass. No one will find us, and my kin will keep watch for the dragon. I already asked."

The Selkies would do their best—and maybe today it would be enough—but they were no match for evil that had sunk its roots deep into the fabric of the Old Country and the rest of this world. It was why the gods stooped to using him—half-mortal, half-divine, or whatever the hell he was—to do their dirty work. Arawn, god of the dead, revenge, and terror, caught him skulking in the time-travel tunnels when he wasn't much more than a boy and trapped him, cutting off any possibility of return. To make certain Angus remained, the god altered his memories, so he had no idea where he came from.

Now almost twenty-five years later, Arawn and the others still came up with enough for him to do that a life to call his own was out of the question. The carrot they dangled was the truth about his birth, but they never came close to telling him. The stick was his fear of what they'd do, if he told them he was done.

Over time, he'd stopped asking about his origins. He cared, but it wasn't worth the energy to run up against their stony faces and cunningly-crafted half-truths that told him exactly nothing. Despite his reservations about a quick dalliance with Celene—and maybe missing his rendezvous with the dragon—he was sick of his self-imposed isolation.

She chivied him into shallow water. Once she was certain he'd follow, she drew ahead easily. As if the other Selkies understood, the pod dispersed. When he peered through gray-green water for their multi-colored pelts, they weren't there.

By the time he clambered onto the rocky shore, Celene had shucked her skin. In human form, she opened her arms to welcome him. Long black hair shrouded her almost to her feet. Violet eyes gleamed in welcome. Her generous breasts peeked through the curtain of hair, their copper-colored nipples already pebbled with wanting him.

Angus had tucked his clothes beneath a rock before joining the Selkie pod. Because he swam nude, no clothes were in the way as he plunged into Celene's offered embrace. God, how he'd missed the touch of another against him, skin to skin. Celene's body felt warm against his chilled one. She closed her arms around him and ran her hands down his back, lingering over the curve of his butt.

He hugged her in return. The scent of her, salt and mint, flooded his mind with images of their lovemaking, and his cock hardened between their bodies. He trailed his fingertips down her smooth skin, marveling at how different she felt from a human woman. Velvety and charged with electricity. Some Selkies walked among humans, even took permanent partners. Angus didn't understand how they eluded discovery.

Celene closed her mouth over the junction between his neck and shoulder, licking, sucking, biting. He moved a hand from her back to cup the side of her face and lowered his lips over hers. The moment he touched her, desire engulfed him.

Hot, urgent, desperate, he sank his tongue into her waiting mouth.

She grappled with his ass, pulling his body hard against hers as her hips writhed and breath hitched in her throat. Tearing her mouth from his, she gasped. "Too long. It's been too long."

Liquid heat trailed the path of her mouth as she licked her way down his chest, stopping to tease his nipples. He kissed the top of her head and wove his fingers into her long hair. Every nerve came alive with wanting her, but it ran deeper than that. Touch was such a basic need, and he'd denied that essential part of his humanity—along with every other comfort.

For what?

No matter how much he gave the Celts, they took every shred—and him—for granted. He wanted to get a job, blend in with humans. Something mundane like driving a cab, or flipping burgers in a grill, but his requests were denied. The Celts provided for him. So long as they housed and fed him, why would he need to clutter his time with anything as humdrum as earning a living? What if they needed him, and he was in the middle of washing dishes in some nameless restaurant? He could almost hear Gwydion's voice. See the master enchanter with a long-suffering look on his face—

He wiped his Celtic masters from his mind. This time was for him and Celene. No one else belonged in his head. Just because he'd chosen a semimonastic existence was no reason he couldn't give her everything she needed. Months had passed since they'd last been together, maybe as much as a year. He moved back enough to fill his hands with her breasts, rubbing her erect nipples before he bent to suck on them, remembering the little biting motions she loved.

A low guttural moan escaped her, and she threaded her fingers through his hair, holding him against her breasts. She began to sing as he loved her. A series of low, sweet notes rose in cadence and intensity as she lost herself in his touch. He'd asked her about the music once, and she told him it was how sea people vocalized their joy. The music filled him with unbearable hunger, poignant, mind-bending need for another person's touch.

Although he'd never done it before, he raised his voice and joined her song. The change was instantaneous. In that moment, he sensed her loneliness and isolation, twin to his own, and he knew both of them needed more kisses, more touches—even more than they needed sex.

"Lay on your belly." His voice rasped with wanting her. He tore tufts of marsh grass and arranged them to make her a bed on a sandy stretch between rocks.

She lay down, continuing to sing. Angus sang too, as he straddled her and ran his hands down her back rubbing tension from her muscles. He followed his hands with his mouth and strung kisses across her shoulder blades and down the line of vertebrae from her neck to the curves of her ass. Between their song, the feel of her skin beneath his fingertips, and his cock getting stiffer by the moment, waiting became almost painful, yet he held back, not quite sure why.

The rhythm and cadence of her song shifted as he alternated his mouth and hands across the sculpted planes of her back. The intense pressure in his balls receded almost as if he'd reached a peak, though he hadn't come. Maybe she sensed his need for warmth, contact, much as he'd sensed hers.

"Move off me so I can look at you." Celene flipped over to face him, kneeling above her. Rose and gold splotched her pale skin, and a broad smile split her exotic, high-cheekboned face. "Today was different. You sang with me. You've never done that before."

He shrugged, suddenly self-conscious. "It felt right. Even though I wasn't inside you, what happened between us felt right."

She cocked her head to one side and trained her gaze on him. "Are you sure you don't have sea blood?"

A flicker of annoyance at the Celts' staunch refusal to disclose anything about his birth narrowed his eyes. "I have no idea what I am." He ticked what he did know off on his fingers. "I'm not immortal, but I'll live a thousand years. My magic is closer to seer and witch than anything else, yet I'm neither of those. The covens acknowledge me as one of their own, but only because the local witches are too kind to tell me to go away. The time-travel portals accept me." He shrugged again. "I don't suppose knowing more would make a hell of a lot of difference."

"You're not from Scotland, even though you live there." She stated it baldly, as fact.

He frowned. "Why would you say that?"

"Your speech. There's something about the lilt of Scotland that's impossible to rid yourself of. You don't sound Irish or British, either, at least not from the time we live in." Her nostrils flared. "Maybe that's it."

"Maybe what's it?"

"You could be from the past, and not just a few years back, but perhaps hundreds—or more. I'm not old enough to recall what human speech sounded like then, but some Selkies are."

"Fine." Frustration tightened his chest, like it always did when the mystery of his origins became a point of discussion. "My first memories are when the god of the dead dragged me out of a time-travel portal when I was fifteen."

"I'm sorry." She draped a hand over his hip, cradling it. "I've upset you."

He started to protest, but she silenced him with a look. "Don't insult me with a lie, Angus, but you don't have to talk about it, either. Such a pretty man." She stroked hair back from his face. "With your deep brown hair and amber eyes. Did you know they shade to dark gold when you're angry?"

She was trying to divert him with flattery, but he wasn't buying it. "You have no idea what it's like not knowing—" He shook his head, and the rest of his words died unspoken. It didn't matter what she knew or didn't know about him. She'd never be more than an occasional lover, and both of them knew it.

"It could be more," she said softly, obviously having been in his mind.

Angus took her hands in his and gazed at her. "You get more of me than anyone, and you see how pathetically little that is. There's nothing more to give."

"There could be," she persisted. "You could refuse next time they send you on—"

He bent toward her and laid a hand over her mouth. "I'm not free. Not now. Not ever."

"I don't understand." She pushed his hand away and closed very white teeth over her full lower lip.

He smiled crookedly. "Not sure I do, either. Every man has a life's work. No matter how I feel about it, maybe this is mine."

Even though it wasn't wise, he started to ask what she knew about his current assignment, but a flash of unusual energy drew his gaze skyward. He leapt to his feet. A copper-colored dragon circled to land not far from him. Maybe the Ancient One had seen him with Celene and decided to be considerate.

Not very fucking likely. Dragons were a force unto themselves.

"I have to go," he said. "Let me walk you to your skin, so I know you're safely on your way home."

A sad expression crossed her face, creasing the skin around her eyes into a network of fine lines. "It's right here." She scrambled to her feet and gripped both his upper arms, forcing him to look at her. "Thank you."

"For what?"

"Being you." She brushed her lips over his and moved to a

marsh grass thicket. In moments, she'd dragged her pelt over her human body. Transformed into a seal, she waded into the surf.

Before it engulfed her, she turned to gaze at him. *"Be careful, and think on what I said."*

He didn't answer, just watched her head bob in the waves before turning toward his clothing. It wasn't far from the place Celene had led them. His body felt vibrant, alive, and he still tingled from her touch. He longed for a woman of his own, children, a home, before he stuffed the impossible so deep under wraps he couldn't mourn the loss.

Angus moved the large rock he'd placed over his clothes to protect them from the wind. He pulled a ragged dark blue fisherman's knit sweater over his head and stepped into thick, black woolen trousers. Settling on a log, he pulled on socks and laced up stout leather boots. Though the breeze was raw, he'd worn neither hat nor gloves.

Ready as he figured he'd ever be, he covered the fifty yards to where the dragon had settled up the beach. He didn't recognize this one, but he'd only met a bare handful of the hundreds living in Fire Mountain and on other worlds as well. When he drew near, he bowed his head respectfully and waited.

"I don't like this any better than you do," the dragon muttered. "Come close enough I don't have to broadcast our business to the world."

Angus walked closer. He could've suggested the dragon use telepathy since all the Ancient Ones were conversant in the technique, but he kept his mouth shut. The dragon was smaller than many he'd seen. Copper scales shaded to burnished gold on its chest, and dark eyes with golden centers whirled so fast they held a hypnotic quality. Lethal, six-inch-long red claws tipped its stubby forelegs. The dragon stood upright on hind legs tipped with the same sharp claws and kept its gaze averted, not saying anything.

What the hell? Every other dragon he'd met was proud, imperious, and quick to remind Angus of his inferiority. This one seemed young, but was it? After another long few minutes, Angus tossed respect—and caution—to the winds.

"What's your name? And what are we supposed to be doing? All Ceridwen told me was to meet you here."

The dragon opened its mouth, and a gout of flame landed scant inches from Angus's boots.

He frowned and drew his brows together. "If we're going to work together, I need to know what to call you." He sent a speculative gaze across the air between them. "If you annihilate me, they'll just assign you a new partner, and I'm a hell of a lot easier to get along with than any of the Celts."

"Tell me something I don't know," the dragon rumbled and belched smoke.

Frustration in its voice struck a note in Angus's soul, and he gestured with both hands. "You may as well tell me who you are and what we're supposed to do together." He infused his words with subtle persuasion. If the dragon didn't care for the Celts, either, they'd likely get along well enough.

"Why? What I should do is leave." The dragon sounded sulky—and scared.

"If you could, you'd already be gone." Angus was as certain of that as he was of anything. The dragon needed him for something, and whatever it was, the Ancient One wasn't particularly proud of it. "What happened? Am I some sort of punishment for you?" Tension settled like a steel bar across his shoulders, and he curled his hands into fists before he realized what he'd done.

"Oh I'd be gone, would I?"

The dragon ignored Angus's questions, and it mimicked his tone with eerie precision. It furled its wings and flapped them a time or two. Dirt swirled; small pebbles slapped Angus in the face. The creature belched steam and looked so distraught, he felt sorry for it.

"My life's not exactly a picnic, either," he ventured, on a hunt for common ground. "I'm a permanent mercenary, with no time off and no possibility of parole."

That got the dragon's attention, and it focused its whirling gaze on him. The golden centers of its eyes deepened with fiery motes that looked like little shooting stars. "Why would you want a respite from being a warrior?"

Good question.

"Because I'm tired. I'd like what most men have."

"What's that?" The dragon raised its brows, and its scales clanked against each other in a dissonant tinkling.

He shook his head. "It doesn't matter. The sooner you spit out whatever you need to say, the easier it'll be. The worst part about holding something you're ashamed of inside is it eats at you until you're nothing but a hollow shell."

Wings flapped, and those intense, whirling eyes shifted to the rocky beach. "I've been banished. Ceridwen said if I worked with you—and we were successful—I might be able to return."

Angus kept surprise out of his voice. "Banished from Fire Mountain?"

Steam puffed from the dragon's open mouth. "No. Idiot. I could live with that. They've banished me from the Highlands. My home."

"What happened?"

"It doesn't matter." The dragon threw his words back at him. "We have to go to Fire Mountain, where I'm to find one of the First Born. Once we have him—or her—"

"One of the six First Born dragons?" Angus broke in, scarcely believing the dragon's words. "They'll never show themselves—unless it's in their best interest."

Another wing flap and a defiant head toss. "There are actually ten. One of them was my father."

"When's the last time you saw him?" The words slipped out before he could stop them. Dragon males frequently didn't hang about once mating was over with, but the trembling mass of scales in front of him likely didn't need to be reminded.

"Never. Mother said he was too immersed in battles on another world to return for our hatching."

He unclenched his fists and hunted for something

soothing to say that wasn't an outright lie. Dragon energy poked past his wards and into his mind. He tried to block it, but couldn't.

"You believe locating a First Born is hopeless." The dragon sounded resigned. "I may as well throw myself into a crater on Fire Mountain. I'll never see the Highlands again—or my mate." More wing rustling and the dragon rose a few feet off the ground, clearly intent on leaving.

"Hold on." Angus loped forward until he was right beneath the dragon. "I didn't say that—or think it, either. I don't know enough to make any sort of judgment. How about if you start at the beginning? If we're going to work together, I deserve that much."

The dragon circled a few times, indecision stamped in its erratic flight pattern.

"I know what it is to be alone." He kept his voice gentle. "And to not have anyone who cares if I live or die."

Maybe it wasn't totally true. Celene might shed a tear or two, but she'd be the only one. He kept his gaze trained on the sky, relieved the dragon wasn't putting distance between them. Something about the creature's pain tugged at his heart and made it feel like a kindred spirit.

The copper dragon folded its wings and settled heavily to earth a few feet from where Angus stood. It straightened its shoulders and tipped its chin defiantly.

"My name is Eletea," the dragon announced, revealing its gender.

"Angus Shea, though you likely know that."

"I killed a mage, who fancied herself a dragon shifter." Eletea's eyes whirled faster, as if she dared Angus to say something.

He crinkled his forehead as he dredged up what he knew about dragon shifters. "Don't mages take their chances when they show up seeking a dragon to pair with?"

She nodded once, sharply. "The mage seduced one of us into believing her. I saved him by killing her, but he turned on me. Reported me to the dragons' council, and they roped the Celts into deciding my fate, since the one I killed had Celtic blood." Eletea's scales rippled in the dragon equivalent of a shrug. "I don't understand why they're bothering. It's not like I went after one of the gods. They're immortal. The one all the fuss is over barely qualified as a Celt."

Angus kept his expression neutral. "Celtic blood aside, I thought mages only bonded with same sex dragons."

"That was another problem," Eletea said, sounding vindicated. "No one saw it but me, though."

Sensing the worst was out on the table, Angus settled on a nearby rock and invited, "Start at the beginning. We have time."

"No, we don't," Eletea protested. "We should have been at Fire Mountain yesterday." She hung her head. "I didn't know what I wanted to do, so I flew and flew and flew. I almost didn't land this afternoon."

Angus did his best to project optimism. "Let's open a time-travel portal and be on our way to Fire Mountain." At the dragon's reluctant nod, he went on. "I understand you have your own ways of returning home, but if you travel with me, you can fill me in as we go."

What he didn't say was it probably wouldn't matter when they arrived at the dragons' home world. First Borns wouldn't give them the time of day, whether they showed up early, late, or right on time. He held many concerns, such as what would a First Born do, assuming they could locate one? But he held those cares inside for now.

He could have dreamed the future. Instead, he summoned a spell to take them to a time-traveling portal. Once the undulating gray-pink tube admitted them, he gradually paid out questions.

Reticent and quiet at first, Eletea finally began to talk.

HIGHLAND SECRETS, CHAPTER TWO

*A*rianrhod slumped lower in her chair, wishing she could find a graceful way to leave. The Celtic gods' council hall had been in Inverlochy Castle in the Scottish Highlands for centuries. To human eyes, the place lay in ruins, but magic could resurrect most anything. The afternoon's discussion had dragged on for hours, and she wanted nothing more than to slip out a side door and go hunting.

Or pour herself a stiff drink.

Or send a bolt of magic to silence the Morrigan permanently—if that were even possible.

She scanned the opulent room and tried to find something to focus on aside from the Battle Crow's ongoing rant. Twelve-foot-high oaken doors carved with runic symbols decorated one end of the room. Crystals and natural stone in every hue of the rainbow made a prism of sunlight flaring through leaded glass panes. Rich carpets covered the stone floors, thick wool woven with depictions of Celtic glory. A fire burned in an enormous hearth situated across from the entry doors.

Ceridwen sat in her usual place before the blaze, cauldron before her. From time to time, she stirred the bubbling mix with an enormous wooden staff. When she cleared her throat in a muttery growl, a handful of Celts looked up from where they'd scattered themselves about the room, no one too close to anyone else. If Arianrhod read their expressions correctly, they were as sick of the Morrigan's pontificating as she was.

Arianrhod straightened in her chair and came to her feet. Before she could open her mouth, the Battle Crow morphed into one of her other guises. Instead of a huge avian presence, she looked like a medieval noblewoman with long dark hair coaxed into intricate braids. Dark eyes regarded Arianrhod, and the Morrigan bent so her breasts almost spilled from her tightly cut maroon gown with long, daggéd sleeves.

With an eye roll, Arianrhod snapped, "Save it for the men. I've heard more than enough about your fourteenth cousin five times removed, who was killed by the young dragon. And about the dragon your kinswoman planned to bond with, demanding the other dragon's life. How many times can ye tell that tale, anyway? And why is this cousin so bleeding important?"

"Do ye want dragon shifters to die out entirely?" the Morrigan demanded.

Arianrhod shrugged. "Not certain I've given it much

thought, but I canna see where it would make much difference. Magic wielders come and go."

"How can ye say such a thing?" the Morrigan screeched.

Ceridwen vaulted to her better than six-foot height. Long black hair streaked with silver fell to her knees, and her dark eyes mirrored an ever-changing collage of images. Body-hugging tan leather breeches and a hip-length tunic woven with green and golden thread covered her lithe frame. Knee-high leather boots wound up both legs. She extended an arm, index finger pointed at the Morrigan's chest.

"I, too, weary of this. Ye havena said aught new in the past turn of the glass. I declare this topic closed." She crossed her arms beneath her breasts and eyed the Morrigan, apparently expecting an argument. When she didn't get one, Ceridwen added, "I've taken care of the problem."

The Morrigan narrowed her dark eyes. "Really? How?"

"I sent the dragon in question, a young female named Eletea, to Fire Mountain to seek a First Born. They can read her intent and proclaim her guilty or innocent of malicious intent."

"Pfft." The Morrigan waved a dismissive hand. "How do ye know this Eletea will do your bidding?"

"Because I forbade her from returning to the Highlands, and I'm sending Angus with her." An arrogant smile crossed Ceridwen's ageless face. "Even if they doona find a First Born —and they may not—he can dream the truth."

A flicker of something between annoyance and fear crossed the Morrigan's features, turning them grim and threatening. Before Arianrhod could drill into what that expression meant, the Battle Crow morphed back into her avian form. Shrieking her displeasure, she flew out an open window.

"Would that it were always so easy to rid ourselves of that one," Andraste muttered. The goddess of victory, dressed in her usual tan battle leathers, rose to her feet, stretched her arms over her head, and glanced at the assemblage. "I'm leaving, if 'tis all the same to you." She tossed heavy blonde hair over her shoulders and swept her shrewd green eyes about the room in a clear challenge—should anyone question her right to go.

"Wait." Arianrhod faced the other woman. "We havena addressed the rumors of dragon shifters running amok along with their dragons. In truth, I doona think of it often, but the Morrigan's words—"

"Eletea will take that up with the dragons in Fire Mountain. 'Tis at the core of her rationale for murdering the dark mage," Ceridwen cut in and shifted her unsettling gaze to Arianrhod. "Since ye expressed interest, mayhap ye could meet them there."

"Them?" Arianrhod quirked a brow.

"Angus and the dragon." Ceridwen eyed her oddly. "Ye werena paying attention. I just said that."

"Sorry." Arianrhod didn't want to get into an argument. Easier to apologize and have done with it. "I'll go. No problem."

"Come closer."

Arianrhod walked until she stood nose to nose with Ceridwen, staring at the images marching across her eyes. What she saw made her heart beat faster. Blood ran in rivers around dying dragons, with a huge crow feasting on one of them. The goddess of the world was warning her to watch out for the Morrigan. And to take the renegade dragon shifter problem seriously.

Arianrhod opened her mouth, but Ceridwen shook her head and switched from imagery to deeply shielded mind speech. *"Lachlan and his dragon havena been seen for hundreds of years. They vanished without a trace. Britta and her dragon retreated to an earlier time. We must know if foul energy has infiltrated the dragon shifter bond. If incentives to tempt even the staunchest mage to dark power exist, I would know of them."*

A smile split Arianrhod's face, and she showed Ceridwen a mouthful of teeth. This was better than hunting game. Evil was the finest challenge of all. She inclined her head. "I welcome the assignment."

Ceridwen tossed her head back and laughed. "I dinna doubt you would, not for a moment."

"Would ye care for company, sister?"

Gwydion, master enchanter and magician warrior, strode to where the women stood. He'd obviously been listening in on her private conversation with Ceridwen— or trying his damnedest to—which annoyed the hell out of Arianrhod. His long blond hair was done up in the Celtic warrior pattern of multiple small braids layered over each other, and his blue gaze augured into

Arianrhod, no doubt seeking why she'd volunteered so readily. Gwydion favored robes. Today he wore black silk, sashed in red. The staff that never left his hand shone with a pale, white light. The inner glow illuminated its eldritch carvings in bas-relief.

Arianrhod wrenched her gaze away from the staff. It was as hypnotic as a cobra; she'd been trapped more than once trying to make out the runes running up and down its polished sides. She turned to face her brother squarely. "I can be far more unobtrusive if 'tis just me."

He drew his brows together into a thick, disapproving line. "Aye, but two can accomplish twice what one can." He waved his staff at Ceridwen. "Tell her she must allow me to accompany her."

"I'll do no such thing," the goddess of the world replied. "If she wishes your company, 'tis for her to request it."

"I'll call for you if I have need of reinforcements." Arianrhod forced a much cheerier smile than she felt and made her eyes guileless. Gwydion had only offered to come along because he was bored. He didn't care a twit about helping her. Never had. They'd been at each other's throats since they were children.

Gwydion took a step back and mock bowed. "See ye do that...sister." With a sweep of his robe, he vanished.

"Good call." Ceridwen spoke into her ear. "The less anyone knows about why ye've decided to pay a visit to Fire Mountain, the better. Had two of us shown up, we'd need a stated reason. One the dragons would believe."

"That's the kicker, eh?" Arianrhod whispered back. "Not the most trusting race, dragons."

"Understatement, my dear. Now get moving and take care that brother of yours doesna follow your tracks."

"What about Angus?"

Ceridwen sent a wry smile skittering her way. "Och, the dragons adore seers, plus he isna one of the gods."

Arianrhod frowned. "Aye, I've never met him afore. What exactly is he?"

"Does it matter?" Ceridwen responded to her question with another, which meant she didn't plan to answer. "He's helpful, which is all ye need to know."

Arianrhod cloaked herself in magic and summoned a traveling spell, aiming for her castle in the Scottish Highlands. She'd swathed the medieval structure in so many layers of invisibility, no one would ever be able to catch her by surprise. She was fairly certain Gwydion had no idea where she lived, and she aimed to keep it that way. Whitewashed stone walls formed around her, and she blew out a tightly held breath. Before she relaxed entirely, she sent power spinning in a wide arc to make certain she was alone.

Good.

No one had breached her home's defenses since she left. She stared around the great room, appreciating its simplicity. She'd never gone for the opulent wall hangings or rich carpets the other Celts preferred. Her home boasted broad, gray flagstone floors with the occasional throw rug to give chilled toes a break. Fireplaces graced every room, and she used them for heat rather than installing more modern central heating because she preferred the crackle of wood to the *whoosh* of a forced air fan. Her manor house could have housed a hundred. There were rooms she hadn't laid eyes on in centuries. Mostly, she shuttled between the great room, the kitchens, her bedroom, and the room where she kept her bows and knifes. Guns had come into fashion, but she didn't care for them. Too noisy and bulky for her taste.

One concession to modern life was a green-veined marble bathroom off her bedroom with a hot-water-on-demand system. Nothing quite like drawing a bath without having to heat the water with magic. Another place she'd caved was installing a large, clunky computer, complete with access to a fledgling Internet. She didn't totally understand the Advanced Research Projects Agency NETwork, but it was useful for research—far easier than digging through tomes and scrolls in her enormous library.

Despite nagging from her Celtic kin, she'd drawn the line at a mobile phone—or any phone, for that fact. She could reach anyone she wanted telepathically, so she didn't need an electronic sidekick.

Whistling a wordless Gaelic folk song, she trotted into the armaments room and slid golden arrows into a quiver that she tossed over her shoulder. Next came a knife she tucked inside a thigh sheath. She picked a powerful crossbow, decided she didn't need anything further, and chanted to open a time-traveling portal. For years she'd transported herself to one of the entry points that would move her where she instructed. During a trip back from a depressing future where mankind had mostly annihilated Earth's resources, she'd accidentally ended up in the sub-basement of her manor house.

That was how she knew her dwelling housed an entrance, and she'd used it shamelessly ever since. Why squander power if she didn't have to? A pearlescent, tubular structure formed before her. She walked through a portal and settled herself inside. Its walls were grayish and warm as if the conduit were alive. She chanted a different incantation to seal herself into the time shaft. Her magic held a pungent scent for this particular casting, like motor oil mixed with salt water.

Fire Mountain existed beyond time on a borderworld that shared a frequency with Earth. If it didn't, she suspected no one but dragons would be able to access it. The shaft vibrated as Arianrhod moved backward in time to the ancient dragon stronghold. She hunkered into a squat for the long journey, taking care not to touch the pulsing walls. No point in being jettisoned because she pissed off whatever—or whomever— infused life into the channel. That had happened more than once, and it took variable amounts of time before the guardian allowed her access again. Being stuck with dinosaurs—which had happened before—wasn't high on her list.

Excitement thrummed through her, and she considered how to proceed once she arrived at Fire Mountain. Mayhap she could pretend she was interested in pairing with a dragon. She narrowed her eyes and chewed thoughtfully on her lower lip. Should she join with Angus and the dragon, Eletea? Or pretend she knew nothing about them? If she chose to masquerade as a wannabe dragon shifter, would the Ancient Ones believe her?

"Why would they?" she muttered. "I haven't shown the slightest interest in anything dragon-related since the dawn of time." Perhaps she could tell them she was bored, that her life lacked meaning, purpose. All true. Immortality held a big downside, particularly since somewhere along the line, she'd fashioned herself as the virgin huntress.

Arianrhod rolled her mental eyes. Why the hell had she thought that was a good idea when Danu suggested it? At the time, she'd hoped to escape Bran's attentions, but she hadn't planned on a millennia tossing and turning in an empty bed. The god of prophecy—Bran—was as big a pain in the ass as he'd always been, but at least he had a cock...

She winced. It had taken stealth and cunning to maintain her artfully crafted persona and still have a sex life. Nothing frequent enough to draw attention, but she'd lain with an amazing coal black dragon. He'd worried his kin would shun him if their affair were discovered, but it hadn't made a dent in his hunger for her.

Nothing quite like the forbidden to fan those flames.

Truth smacked her between the eyes. Loneliness and lust were why she'd volunteered so readily to make the trek to Fire Mountain. And why she'd sidestepped Gwydion. The last thing she needed was a witness if she stumbled onto Keene— or another likely candidate. Dragons lived forever. Perhaps

Keene might be interested in another fling—for old time's sake if nothing else.

Usually she stopped herself from thinking about her past and what she wished she'd done differently, but she couldn't shut off her thoughts. If she'd had children, real children, it would've made such a difference.

The two sons she'd conceived magically were odd. But how could they have been aught else? She'd been forced to jump over a magical rod to prove she was a virgin, and twin sons were the result. Dylan sank into obscurity, retreating to the seas when the strain of day-to-day life without enough power to light a candle became too much to bear. Lleu would've left as well, but Gwydion subverted every single one of Lleu's escape plans as he grew to manhood. Lleu blamed her for Gwydion's meddling, and she hadn't laid eyes on him for a very long time. She suspected Gwydion hadn't, either.

Her empty life mocked her, but she was damned if she could figure out what to do to change it. It wasn't as if she could march up to Ceridwen and the others, clear her throat, and say, "Sorry, but I'm sick of being a Celtic god. Think I'll be a mortal for a while. And hey, if that doesn't please you, I'll take to my owl form and be done with the lot of you."

"Oberon's balls!" She crashed one fist into an open hand, taking care not to jostle the traveling portal. "I have to pull my head out of my ass. Ceridwen handed me a fascinating problem. I need to focus on it. No dragon fucking. No diversions. Go in. Put my head down. Get the job done."

Nice lecture, but can I do it?

Arianrhod stroked the shiny bow draped over her shoulder. It was a work of art. She'd made it herself from yew wood, not cutting any corners, so it took months for the wood to shape and cure. She twisted her mouth into a wry smile. The huntress part of her title was fine. It fit, and she enjoyed the cunning, planning, and forethought it took to outsmart prey. If she was sick of the pretend-to-be-a-virgin part, who could blame her?

The rhythm of her traveling tube shifted. Arianrhod glanced at a node to check her location and understood her journey would be over soon. She rotated her shoulders to relax and ready herself, thought about her virgin huntress title once more, and laughed.

"The virgin part may grate, but I adore being a huntress. Fifty percent isn't bad," she told the gray-pink walls as they shuddered to a stop. "Most people don't even get that."

Keep right on reading! https://www.anngimpel.com/?portfolio=highland-secrets